Itto Warner Weiner
Feb. 75.

A
TRIUMPH!

"This is one of those rare books in which a
soul is revealed. I think we dare not fail to read
Elie Wiesel. The soul he reveals may well
be that of the reader!"
St. Louis Post-Dispatch

"A truly powerful novel."
Library Journal

"In his personal, poetic style he continues
to be the most eloquent spokesman, not only
for the Jews of silence but for the
whole human race."
Chicago Tribune

Other Books by
Elie Wiesel

Had the peoples and the nations
known how much harm they brought upon
themselves by destroying the
Temple of Jerusalem, they would
have wept more than the children
of Israel.

THE TALMUD

order to discourage the local squire who pursued her with his infatuation.

Finally, we come across Kolvillàg in the writings of the great poet Shmuel ben Yoseph Halevi, whose litanies form part of certain liturgical services for the High Holy Days. This is what he tells us: "On the fifth day of the month Heshvan in the year 5206, a frenzied mob ransacked the holy community of Virgirsk. All the children of Israel, beginning with the three judges, were lined up in the marketplace, facing the church. There, under the eyes of an amused populace, they chose to die rather than renounce their faith. By nightfall three hundred and twenty corpses lay strewn across the marketplace stained with blood—and there was nobody to bury them."

These are the scant bits of information I succeeded in uncovering about this ill-starred town. And so I shall know it only through the voice of its last survivor. His name is Aziel and he is mad.

No, said the old man, I will not tell the story. Kolvillàg cannot be told. Let's talk of other things. Men and their joys, children and their sorrows—let's talk about them, shall we? And God. Let's talk about God: so alone, so irreducible, judging without truly understanding. Let's talk about everything, except . . .

I had met him one autumn afternoon. I remember, I shall always remember. The sun was setting, red and violent. I thought: This is the last time—and the thought made me sad. Then I said to myself: No, not so. It will rise again, as always, perhaps forever—and that thought too made me sad.

Where do I come from? You are a curious young man. Do I ask where you are from? Oh well, today's youth respects nothing and nobody; and worse, even boasts about it. In my day old age conferred certain privileges. The closer man came to death, the more consideration he received. The oldest man was the most privileged; people would rise as he passed, solicit his advice and listen in silence. Thus he would feel alive and useful, a part of the community of man. Today things are different. You consider old men embarrassing, cumbersome, fit only for the old-age home or the graveyard. Any means of disposing of them is acceptable. They are a nuisance, those old people. You find their presence an unbearable burden. It is the Bible in reverse: you are prepared to sacrifice your parents. In my day, in my country, men were less cruel.

Oh, yes, I am old—four times your age—but fortunately I have nobody in the whole world, which means that nobody wishes me dead . . .

Yes, I come from far away. From the other side of oceans. From the other side, period. Driven from my small town, somewhere between the Dniepr and the Carpathians, a town whose name will mean nothing to you.

A small town, like so many others, a small town unlike any other: a handful of ashes under a glowing red sky, its name is Kolvillàg and Kolvillàg does not exist, not any more. I am Kolvillàg and I am going mad. I feel it, maybe I already am. There is, deep inside me, a madman claiming to be me. Kolvillàg is what drove him mad.

Don't ask me how it happened, I have no right to divulge that. I promised, I took an oath. With the others, like the others. Bound by oath as much as they. True, I was the youngest, but age is irrelevant. I was present at the conspiracy, I participated in it. And now it is too late: I shall not go back on my word. It ties me to a destiny that is not mine; it belongs to that part of me that yearns to remain faithful unto death, unto madness, faithful to

14

the madness which consists in declaring over and over: It is too late, too late.

Yes, one cannot push back night as one cannot contain the waves of a raging sea. The clock will tick off the hours even while the dwelling is engulfed by flames. Am I that dwelling? wonders the madman. Or the clock? You are the fire, answers the old man.

Anyway, what does it matter who I am. What I have seen, nobody will see, what I am keeping back, you will never hear; that is what matters. I am the last, do you understand? The last to have breathed the fiery, stifling air of Kolvillàg. The last to witness its ultimate convulsions before the beast withdrew, satiated but unappeased, monstrously immense yet weightless, almost graceful, like the morning breeze, like the flame that caresses the body before consuming it. The beast did not see me—do you understand?—that was my good fortune, my salvation. But I saw it. I saw it at work. Alternately savage and attentive, radiant and hideous, sovereign and cunning, it won with ease, reducing to shreds whoever saw it at close range, inside the bewitched and cursed circle. It turned the town into a desecrated, pillaged cemetery. Crushing all its inhabitants into a single one, it twisted and tortured him until in the end he had a hundred eyes and a thousand mouths, and all were spitting terror.

Scenes of apocalypse, nightmares begotten by sleeping corpses—I wish I could describe them, I wish I could tell all there is to tell. I shall not. I am sworn to silence. They made me take an oath. To break it means excommunication. Such a vow is sacred. One's commitments to God can be undone by a simple incantation. One's commitment to man, and certainly to the dead, cannot. Your contracts with the dead, the dead take with them, too late to cancel or modify their terms. They leave you no way out. Formiable players, the dead; they hold you and you are helpless.

That is why you will not succeed in making me talk. I
will circle around the story, I will not plunge into it. I'll
beat around the bush. I'll say everything but the essential.
For you see, I am not free. My voice is a prisoner. And
though at times words bend to my will, silence no longer
obeys me: it has become my master. More powerful than
the word, it draws its strength and secret from a savagely
demented universe doomed by its wretched and deadly
past.

*And so it is to him I owe my experience of Kolvillàg.
And much more. Mysterious messenger from an imagi-
nary city, he showed it to me from afar, one autumn night,
when the only call I could perceive came from the other
side.*

You want to die? How can one blame you. This rotten
world is not worth lingering in, I know something about
it: I covered it from one end to the other. To repudiate it,
you have chosen suicide? Why not, it's a solution like any
other, neither better nor worse. I myself have explored all
the possibilities. Action, inaction. Penitence, escape. I
turned friendship into a cult and the word into an adventure. I alternately preached faith, blasphemy and forgiveness. I made people cry, I made them dream. Vain
attempts: the game is rigged since death wins in the end.
I even made them laugh. The cripples, the unfortunate, the
condemned, I made them laugh. Only to have death laugh
louder still. I understand your invoking it. I followed all
other avenues, ended up in every hell. I lived in cities, in
forests, with men and away from them. I survived more
than one war, took part in more than one mourning. I
tried oblivion and solitude, more than once was I ready
to abdicate—but I did not: my life does not belong to me,

neither does my death. All I can call my own is a forbidden city I must rebuild each day, only to watch it end in horror each night. You don't understand? Don't try. This invisible city exists only for me and subsists only in me. I cannot tell you more; to speak of it is to betray it.

And yet, the old man will speak. He doesn't know it now, but before the tale reaches its conclusion, before the two strangers part ways, they will have traded their secrets. Each driven by his despair, his helplessness. In the final stage of every equation, of every encounter, the key is responsibility. Whoever says "I" creates the "you." Such is the trap of every conscience. The "I" signifies both solitude and rejection of solitude. Words name things and then replace them. Whoever says tomorrow, denies it. Tomorrow exists only for him who does not seek it. And yesterday? Yesterday is Kolvillàg: a name to forget, a word already forgotten.

So you have had enough, the old man is thinking as he scrutinizes the young man's profile. You prepare yourself to die and I inevitably become judge or witness. Except that I am tired, too tired to play destiny.

Above them, the streets and alleys have sprung alive with workers on their way home. Lovers are walking hand in hand, laughing and embracing. Below, the river succumbs to dusk. The reddish sky turns gray; soon it is dark. A chilly breeze blows through the barren trees. The buildings across the street seem dark and threatening. Here and there a window lights up, mysterious and reassuring. And you, you are waiting for night, the old man muses. You wait so as to follow it. Never mind, don't deny it, I see through you. Despair that sticks to the skin. Disgust that drives away curiosity. Thoughts that are heavy, opaque.

17

And then this weight crushing your chest, this pasty tongue cluttering your mouth. Don't deny it. I know those things. You are only waiting for night to come and swallow you. And it is up to me to hold you back. Why me? Because I am here. Because I have eyes to see, a mouth to protest. I could have been elsewhere, I could have been looking the other way.

In the distance, near the city hall square, there is bedlam. People milling about, shouting insults at one another. The electoral campaign is in full swing. Vote for this, vote for that. Vote for this one because he personifies promise. No, vote for that one because *he* personifies promise. Orators harangue the crowds. Applause, whistles. Trust me: I who this, I who that. There is no end to candidates. And each says the same thing. Each sacrifices his interests for those of the people: it should consider itself fortunate, the people, to have such defenders, such devoted friends. But the friends of the people are not each other's friends. Provocations, fights, pandemonium. Accusations fly back and forth. Exhortations: Let us change society, let us change man. In the name of mutations, one does away with systems. Down with the Establishment, long live the Revolution. Disorders, riots. Coups d'état. Down with government, long live imagination. Down with life, long live death. I have heard these slogans before, in another place. Barcelona, Berlin. Men change, their cry remains. I am too old to let myself be taken in. These battles no longer concern me. Yet your particular choice does. Here I am, responsible for your next step. As though you were my son. As though I had a son.

The old man recalls Prague in the twenties, Berlin in the thirties. The tragic gaiety of some, the sham devil-may-care attitude of others. For Azriel, death is an old acquaintance; he knows how to track it down, how to unmask it, fight it. To men in the throes of despair, he would say: "To face death lucidly is one thing, to surrender out of weakness or inadvertence is another. I don't ask you to go back on your decision; I only tell you to act freely." Freedom: the big word. Supreme temptation. In the name of freedom, I put you in prison. In the name of the future, I condemn you to capital punishment. Do people still kill themselves out of despair? How is one to know.

Here is twilight trailing its heavy, silvery shadows. And here are the first stars playing with the waves and reflections of another somber and silent world. You usually come here for walks with your girl, right? You speak to her, you tell her things, all sorts of things, right? Not tonight. Tonight you are alone as only a rejected lover can be. Foolish, but your heart is heavy. Foolish, but you don't believe in love. Life? A huge joke you might as well be rid of. Your reasons? You have many, I wager. They never vary. One either loves too much or not enough. One either suffers or makes others suffer. One engages the whole world in battle; not easy to fight the whole world. It's all foolish, so why cling to a barren existence? God committed an injustice by giving Himself a toy made of His own scale, and man must set it right, erase it by erasing himself, is that it?

The old man and the young man stare at each other for a moment, their eyes locked, unblinking, uncompromising.

"Who are you?"

The old man does not answer. Who am I? Azriel? Who am I? Moshe? Question of questions. When he opened his eyes, Adam did not ask God: Who are *you?* He asked: Who am *I?*

"What do you want of me? I don't know you, I have never seen you before."

He thinks I am mad, the old man muses. With reason. One must be mad to want to speak to a stranger, to hope

19

to save him. One must be mad to hope. Do I frighten him? Madness frightens him more than death . . .

Sky and river become one and suddenly Azriel understands that one may want to drown in darkness where all is beckoning and mystery.

"You must not," says the old man. "You must not commit the irrevocable. You must not oppose despair to despair. Or fire to fire. One evil can add to another but not diminish it. If you kill yourself, you commit one more injustice. What will you have proven? I advise you rather to stay. And face night."

"And life too?"

"Yes. Life too."

"And death too?"

"Yes. Death too."

And lowering his voice, the old man continues: "But you will never see Kolvillàg. So you have nothing to fear. You have been spared the worst." And in an even lower voice, almost a whisper: "I am not telling you not to despair of man, I only ask you not to offer death one more victim, one more victory. It does not deserve it, believe me. The most beautiful of deaths is hardly that; there is no beautiful death. Nor is there a just death. Every death is absurd. Useless. And ugly. Is that your wish? To add to the ugliness of the world? I am telling you to resist. Whether life has a meaning or not, what matters is not to make a gift of it to death. All you will get in return is a corpse. And corpses stink—I know something about that. Stay, I tell you. Stay on the threshold. Like myself. And like myself you will avenge Kolvillàg . . .

"Kolvillag: you don't know what it is. A melodious, enticing name, don't you think? You wouldn't think of a slaughterhouse. And yet, and yet. But I must stop. Don't worry, my dead friends: I shall not repudiate you, I shall not allow a stranger to desecrate your sanctuary. I shall be careful. The event shall remain whole. I shall tell neither cause nor effect. I shall not reveal the enormity of the secret, I shall only indicate its existence. I shall show only the spark. One glimmer will be enough. If afterwards you still want to die, my young friend, you will at least know why.

"What I saw in Kolvillàg, not only during its last night, was the eruption of total violence, the rule of madness in the absolute sense, as though the absolute had become unhinged. As though the Creator, in a fit of joyous and destructive rage, had granted full freedom to His creatures, crazed by their burden of divinity, driven to madness and nothingness, suddenly resembled one another in their passionate hatred and vengefulness.

"Caught in the turmoil, adolescents and parents, beggars and rich men, wise men and fools uttered the same unheeded cry. Slayers and victims foundered in the same well, condemned to the same anonymity. Good and evil fought over the same role, the same privileges. At one point, had I dared, I should have cried out: 'Woe to us, God is not God! Woe to man, the Master of the Universe has gone mad!' But I dared not. And then, there was my promise, my pledge. I tightened my lips, bit them till they bled; I did not shout. Sheltered by the woods, high above the valley, I watched the conflagration spreading, approaching by huge leaps. I didn't run, I didn't panic; I didn't even move. I thought: What for? And also: Let him come, the avenger, I am expecting him, I'll relinquish this tree, this forest of trees to him, I shall give them to him as an offering, I shall gladly yield to him both the mountain and the valley. And the rest with it."

Suddenly the old man shivers. "And you, aren't you cold?"

"No."

A foolish question, but the old man is always cold. Old age? Lack of sleep? Even in summer he wears two shirts.

"Are you hungry?"

21

"No."

"Thirsty?"

"No."

Speak, the old man thinks. The best way. Make him speak. Speak to him. As long as we keep speaking, he is in my power. One does not commit suicide in the middle of a sentence. One does not commit suicide while speaking or listening. Nor in the middle of a meal. Make him eat, drink, get drunk. But nothing interests him. And yet, and yet. He should be roused, shaken. Go on speaking? How long? On whose behalf, on behalf of what? On behalf of the dead. What business is it of mine? And yet, and yet. One must act, do something, anything, invoke a certainty, any certainty. To hell with principles, vows. The true contest must take place on the level of the individual. It is here, in the present, that the Temple is reclaimed or demolished. It is not by legitimizing suffering—and what is death if not the paroxysm of suffering—that one can disarm it. The mystery of the universe resides not in the universe but in man; perfection can be attained only by the individual.

So you hope to defeat evil? Fine. Begin by helping your fellow-man. Triumph over death? Excellent. Begin by saving your brother. Make him understand that escape into death is more senseless than escape into life. A man who does not fear death is a fool who wants to die. Fear is a healthy thing, it implies a rejection of death. Proof: Kolvillàg was crumbling under fear. No connection? Wrong. If you are tired of living, young man, it is because in Kolvillàg death was victorious. The abyss inside you was opened there. In your own way, you are a ghost. A survivor. Except that you have no story to relate. You wish to take your life in order to give yourself a story. You'd like that of Kolvillàg, eh? And then you'll live, eh? No blackmail, please.

I cannot give you that which is not mine. I don't have

22

the right. Don't push me, I won't relent. Others have tried with no success. A word of advice: chain your gaze, rein in your thoughts; they must not venture too far, beyond the accepted bounds. You risk stumbling over a people engulfed in silence and protected by it, and you would lose your mind.

There followed feverish days, filled with excitement. My involvement with Kolvillàg became deeper, more intense, turned into obsession. I ate little, slept poorly. How can I explain its hold on me? I couldn't explain it to myself. Could I have seen in Azriel a personification of the prophet Elijah, the one the disinherited, the down-trodden dream about? Or of my grandfather, who died over there in the tempest? I couldn't say. Did he help me to escape? Accept myself? Fulfill myself? Possibly. It hardly matters. Psychoanalysis is not my strong point. Azriel knocked down the walls I had erected around myself. Something important and genuine happened to me while I discovered the city that lived inside him. By allowing me to enter his life, he gave meaning to mine. I lived on two levels, dwelt in two places, claimed more than one role as my own.

In one night he had me adopted by his entire community. So much so that I could find my way in his town. The streets, the gardens, the public buildings. Every chimney, every lamppost. The asylum with its dried-out wooden roof, where wanderers found shelter and food.

Across the street, the big general store. The police station, the church. The House of Study with its crumbling walls, the old synagogue with its impressive entrance. The Jewish school where on Saturday afternoons Shaike and his exalted friends prepared the revolution, the victory of the oppressed in a world where poverty would be a virtue envied and bought by the rich. The rabbi who, it was said, slapped impertinent merchants but later had himself secretly whipped by an anonymous servant. The priest with his sanctimonious airs of pious martyrdom. They notables, the president. Moshe the Madman and his overly drunkenness. The beggars, amateur actors all, who on Purim eve succeeded in eliciting applause; as long as the festivities lasted, they were the unchallenged masters of the town. Leizer the Fat, Yeddel the Cripple, One-Eyed Simha, Awrom the Wise, Adam the Grave-digger; I watched them live, I was present at their discussions. I laughed at their intrigues, shared in their sorrows. The alliances, jealousies, complicities, daily adventures and secular traditions which together create the climate and the pulse of a town, well, Azriel had communicated them to me as a gift.

As for the storyteller, he intrigued and fascinated me. Who was he? A saint? A madman? A Just Man disguised as vagabond? He lived alone in a wretched little garret. His neighbors avoided him, the janitor trembled as he spoke of him. After he disappeared, none of his personal belongings could be found. I would have given much to lay my hands on his Book; but he had taken it with him, of course.

Through constant pursuit of the character, I succeeded in uncovering his tracks. Thus I learned that he was regularly received in some of the most elegant salons as well as in the Marxist student house. He patronized the North African Jewish restaurant and the Home for Aged

Anarchists. He, whom nobody succeeded in knowing, knew many people. He was equally at ease quoting from the Talmud or Mao Tse-tung; he mastered seven ancient tongues and a dozen living ones. Haughty with the powerful, humble with the deprived. To professional philosophers he taught philosophy; to tycoons, the stock market. Young people loved him: he listened, teased, appeased. He made them understand what was happening to them; it was always more serious or simpler than they had imagined. They came to him, each with his problem, his small personal tragedy. He arbitrated their quarrels, ideological and other, and imposed sentence. The boys told him of their emotions, the girls discussed politics: a world upside down. Even when he scoffed at them, he was forgiven. Too old to envy success, too alien to this generation to judge it. His words were deeds; he had no ulterior motives.

I approached, questioned many who had spoken with him. Unfortunately, they were of no help. Yes, all remembered him, but not in the same way; their portraits did not coincide. Some spoke of his round, puffy face while others described it as angular and expressive. They recalled his massive head, out of proportion to the rest of the body. And his eyes? Light and gentle, according to some; somber and penetrating, according to others. I would ask: What about his hands? For I myself still see them, see them drawing patterns in the air, accentuating this sentence, denigrating that thought. But they looked puzzled. What was so extraordinary about his hands? And what about his voice? I asked. Do you remember his voice? On that point, they all agreed: his had been a deep, resonant, often raucous voice.

I discovered the small synagogue, deep inside the Jewish quarter, where he had taught Talmud in Yiddish to an audience made up of Polish and Hungarian immigrants. A first thought, crazy, absurd, made my heart jump. What if they all came from over there, from Kolvillàg? No, impossible. They were born elsewhere. Slobodke, Wizhnitz, Satmàr. Still, just in case, I did ask: Kolvillàg, does that name mean anything to you? Shaking their heads, they answered no. Kolvillàg? Don't know, don't know. Your teacher Azriel came from Kolvillàg, I would say. They opened their eyes wide. What, his name was Azriel? They had known him by another name: Katriel. Some smiled as they recalled him, others cried. But, in all honesty, they may have cried because of me. Or over me.

The most striking fact about Azriel was furnished me by a youngish man with a delicate, moving face: "We had just finished the Tractate on Shabbat. As is the custom, the reader recited the Kaddish d'rabbanan; *and our Master's inflection was so singular, so heartbreaking that none among us answered amen, and yet we felt that all of creation was answering amen."*

"I remember," says the old man:

Sitting on a stool next to the door, a woman dressed in black cries and cries in silence. On the table a candle consumes itself.

"Why a candle in midday?" I asked my mother.

"It's for Grandfather."

"Where is he? Where is Grandfather?"

"He is dead."

"What does that mean, dead?"

"That means that he is gone, that he will not come back. Ever. You will not hear him sing again. He will not bless you again."

"Why did he leave?"

"Because God has called him."

"And when God calls, one must come immediately?"

"Yes, immediately."

"And what if one doesn't feel like it?"

"One goes anyway. One has no choice. One does not die at will. We are in God's hands."

"Why does God want man to die?"

"You will grow up and you will know."

28

On her lap she held a book of Psalms she was reading absentmindedly. Her thoughts were elsewhere, with Grandfather, somewhere in the kingdom where the dead gather around God, saying: You have called us, here we are. I wondered whether her thoughts would come back and when. Tomorrow, no doubt. That was the word my mother often used to reassure me. Tomorrow I would no longer hurt. Tomorrow I would play in the yard. Tomorrow I would welcome the Messiah.

"Why this black cloth over the mirror?" I asked my mother.

"It's a sign of mourning. When we are sad we don't care about our image in the mirror."

My mother. I had never seen her so beautiful nor so sad. I looked at her and felt like crying. It wasn't her sadness but her beauty that made the tears rise into my throat.

"I still don't understand the candle," I said obstinately.

"And yet it's simple: it burns awhile and then goes out. What happens to the flame? It rises to heaven. Like the soul. You will grow up and will understand that fire is a symbol both for the living and for the dead."

"What's a symbol?"

"You are too young. One day you'll understand."

"Not before?"

"Not before."

"When? Tomorrow?"

"Yes, tomorrow."

"Tomorrow is far away."

"All right, let me explain to you. A symbol is a word you use in place of another."

"Why would I do that?"

Mother didn't answer and I didn't insist. That night Grandfather appeared to me in my sleep. Surprised that I could see him, I asked him to explain. After swearing me to secrecy, he said: "Your mother thinks I'm dead; she's

29

wrong. Your father too is wrong. And you will be my proof. As long as you live I shall be alive."

"But . . . What if God calls me?"

"Tell yourself that God's call is not necessarily the call of death. It all depends on you."

His voice, I can hear it still. It is that of my first dreams. My mother died soon afterward and I too had to light a candle, then another and another. I can see them still. Their flame rises and goes on rising. And here it is, immense and greedy, no longer symbolizing the soul of a person but that of a town, a region, a vanished kingdom, and like it, ephemeral and invisible except to the dead.

My mother is sick. Her heart, she says. Nerves, says the doctor. This is where it hurts, she says, pointing to her heart. Nerves, says the doctor, shrugging his shoulders. No matter who is right, my father feels guilty. So do I.

One day I questioned my father: "Did you read? The trials of the war criminals are turning into a farce. The killers listen to the witnesses' testimony and roar with laughter as though they were at the circus. How can they?"

Pale, his eyes half closed, he answered me in a barely audible voice: "They can, they can."

Another time: "I don't understand. God's role in the camps—explain it to me."

"You couldn't understand."

The gap between us was wide; it seemed unbridgeable.

"Both executioner and victim," my father went on, his voice unsteady, "have reason to doubt God."

And then the question that was burning my lips and that I never dared ask before: "You. And Mother. Both of you. How did you do it—how did you survive?"

Sometimes I would watch my father from my corner and feel anxiety creep over me. What did he look like

31

over there? *What does he do when he is not doing any-thing? Whom does he see when he is staring into space? The more I observed him, the less I understood the nature of his ailment.*

"You think I am suffering," Moshe had said. Moshe, my mad, my saintly friend lying helpless in his blood. "You believe that I am succumbing to pain. You are wrong. I observe myself, I see myself suffering. The part of me that is watching is not suffering, or else is suffering in a different way. And it is not complaining."

"But doesn't this place affect you at all? Aren't you sad, angry? Wouldn't you like to go out, meet friends, stroll through the streets, be with your wife?"

"You're too young to understand," he had said, grimacing. "My body is in prison, I admit that. Naturally. But my innermost self is free. More than ever. Would you rather it were the opposite?"

He had stopped abruptly, crumpling over even more, turning his head to the right and to the left as though to discover an invisible intruder: "There is something I haven't told you, something you should know. I am cold. I didn't tell you that I was cold. I mean really cold. Totally. All of me. Not only my body. But me. I mean my innermost self. We are cold.

"A man in prison learns to say we. For there, you see,

you are alone; for there you really freeze. If in the street you notice a passer-by shivering with cold, a stranger in need of warmth, know that he has spent time in prison."

They were all cold in Kolvillàg. In the cellars and outside. In the jails and in the houses. All the Moshes of the town, and not only of the town, were shivering with cold; all needed warmth so much they wished for fire, fire everywhere, in the prisons and in the forests, fire on earth and fire in the sky, ruling and avenging all of creation from one end to the other. Sometimes I think that Kolvillàg burned simply because Moshe, my foolish, my saintly friend, was shivering with cold.

"Let's walk, get warm."

Lead him away from here, the old man reflects. Bring him back, make him understand. Don't leave him alone, not yet. Don't let him sink into silence. Grab hold of him, pull him along. Speak, make him speak. He resists, answers reluctantly. His life in general outlines. Lonely childhood, the usual studies. A feeling of emptiness, waste. Go ahead, answer: Why this? Why that? He reacts badly to all this questioning, but at least he reacts; that's better than nothing. Terse, breathless answers. Why this taste for solitude. And this curiosity about politics, religion, science. And why the one-year stay at a kibbutz did not produce the expected results. And why he feels uprooted. Go on, continue. Have you no real problems? An unhappy love affair perhaps? They walk side by side, cross streets drowned in neon lights, empty squares, come back to the waterfront only to leave it again immediately. Go on, continue.

The old man is tireless, insatiable. To save a man, one must think like him, feel what he feels, see what he sees and what he refuses to see. To save him, one must want

35

to die like him. One must be he. Except that he will never be like me; he has never known Moshe the Madman, he has never inhaled the conflagration's smoke.

"Speak, for God's sake. You read books, don't you? You go to movies, you have friends, you flirt, don't you? I want to know everything, everything, I tell you! When you see a pretty girl, doesn't your body respond whether you like it or not? When she smiles at you, don't your cheeks flush?

"*My* cheeks were flushed at the touch of a woman I considered pretty and immodest. I was ten years old, not quite. We were spending our summer vacation in the mountains, near Kolvillàg. Each family had its own cottage but for meals we all gathered in a large rectangular dining hall. Our neighbors at the table were my schoolmate Bernard and his mother. She was constantly laughing in a provocatively infectious way. An invitation to pleasure, happiness, sin, that was her laughter. Jealous, the other women prattled on and on about her. She was doing things, Bernard's mother, things; I had no idea what kind of things. Terrible, no doubt, for in my presence they were referred to cryptically. I was curious and kept my ears perked up. In vain. Nothing.

"After days and days of watchfulness I was no further ahead. My nights were sleepless: what was it that made this beautiful and joyous woman a sinner? She frequently disappeared after lunch followed by an old bachelor who sang well. They would come back an hour or so later, breathless, red-cheeked. And our dear busybodies, seeing them thus, would wink at one another knowingly. And so I learned that there existed a link between the color of cheeks and sin. I learned more than that the day my table companion had the outlandish idea to interrogate me about her son. I answered politely, respectfully, but there was so much light, so much blue in her blue eyes that I had to veil mine; I lost my composure, became confused. There-

36

upon, in order to encourage or reward me, she smiled at me and started to caress my cheeks, which at her fingers' touch, caught fire. It was infinitely pleasant and infinitely painful; I became dizzy. And like her partner, I too was breathless. And like Bernard's mother, I too knew sin.

"And you? Have you never loved anyone? Are you immune to desire? What are you, saint or idiot?"

He plagues him with questions, tries to elicit confidences. In vain. The young man is too shy, too puritanical perhaps. Well, no matter, Azriel muses. Since you refuse to speak about it, I will. My love stories always have sad endings, but all stories end sadly, don't they? Mine, I can barely remember; they took place so long ago. Prague, Berlin, Vienna. The mad, exuberant years between the two wars. Student, laborer, vagabond. A Wandering Jew, learning languages and trades, carting his nightmares from country to country, from setting to setting, finding no respite anywhere.

The old man remembers the only woman who mattered in his exile. Rachel: confidante, accomplice, ally. She had the knack of amusing him. He fell in love with her because she made him laugh. And from that moment on, she rather made him feel like crying. One day she kissed him on the mouth. He confessed his innocence in matters of women. "A man who waits so long must have his reasons," she said. "I would like to know them." — "Impossible, you can't." — She gave him a long look and kissed him again. "No?" she said. — "No. It is better to leave it at that. You keep your secrets and I will keep mine." She never spoke of it again.

Rachel: his conscience, his imagination, his home port. Sometimes when he had no place to sleep he would stay in the studio where she gave piano lessons to girls from well-to-do families. And then, whenever he fell in love— which happened frequently not to say constantly—he would rush over to her to make his report. She would weigh the pros against the cons, pronounce a favorable or adverse opinion, advise caution or daring, console when things went wrong—they were forever going wrong—and tease him gently when at the height of euphoria he floated on clouds of eternal, redeeming love. With one sentence, or even a single word, she would bring him back to earth, sobered.

Then he would compensate with the help of philosophy, his second passion. In his flirtations he considered it indispensable to call upon Plato, Maimonides, and Spinoza. When the stakes were considerable, he would fall back on Ibn Gabirol and Rabbi Moshe Haim Luzzato. With Rachel he would on occasion ramble on for hours, discussing the meaning of existence, the purpose of creation, the limits of perception, freedom or infinity. She would listen with a smile and conclude: "Boring, all that." — "What? What are you saying? Boring?" — "Well, yes, my poor Azriel. What can I say? I find your infinity frankly boring, or if you prefer, infinitely boring." He would get angry, sulk awhile, and forgive. Rachel had all the rights; she could do no wrong. He took the blame on himself; he should not be bothering her with his studies. Rachel preferred his confessions.

He suffered from a need to love. To be loved was less important to him. And so he chose his love objects somewhat haphazardly, or, more precisely, he let himself be chosen. An engaging smile, an insistent handshake were enough to set him off. Spellbound, tormented like a schoolboy, he slid in and out of infatuations with disconcerting ease, yet he would have deemed it immoral—and puerile —to maintain two simultaneous affairs. Purely platonic affairs, to be sure; the women in question had no inkling that he desired them with such violence—or that he desired them at all—or even that later he abandoned them.

His painful shyness made him unhappy. He would sometimes flee the very woman who for weeks had robbed him of his sleep. Blushing like a scolded child, he would stammer incoherent banalities, unable to understand himself what he was trying to communicate. In the presence of the beloved, or beloved-to-be, he assumed a guilty behavior.

He would have preferred loving women for what, in his opinion, was their spirituality. To be sure, the mere sight of a bare shoulder caused him palpitations, but he repressed them. As soon as he summoned up the courage to respond to their advances, he would launch into lengthy and complicated scholarly discourses so as to persuade them that as far as he was concerned, their physical charms scarcely made an impression. Convinced that he did not appreciate them sufficiently, they took offense. This in turn greatly chagrined him, particularly since he exaggerated both their beauty and their intelligence.

As he exaggerated their purity. This was an obsession which shaped his behavior and rendered him ridiculous. To his consenting, impatiently waiting partner, he would recite poems and sermons complete with footnotes and commentaries. The more burning his passion, the more compelled he felt to conceal it. Instead of embracing his companion, who would have been only too pleased, he outdid himself trying to demonstrate why it was important to sublimate one's feelings and forgo their fulfillment. There were those who simply told him to go away, and those who became aggressive. He complained about both kinds, which moved Rachel to remark: "You are as fond of complaining as you are of loving."

An accurate observation. Common sense personified, that Rachel. She spoke to the child in Azriel; she loved it and yearned to protect it. A man in love becomes a child again; this is what makes him susceptible to loving. Any woman who fails to understand that will know a confused, false and necessarily incomplete love.

For the child in Azriel, every woman he loved was

immaculate, the better for being willing to wait. She lived in renunciation and anticipation. That she might have had lovers before him never occurred to him. In love, every time is the first time; repetition excludes love, and vice versa. Azriel was for the vice versa.

Convinced that the union of the flesh mirrors that of the soul, which in turn stems from the primary mystery of creation, he refused to reduce it to the level of the senses. To prevent this sacrilege, he pursued the unavowed goal of uniting beings while circumventing their bodies. With Rachel he succeeded on occasion, but not with the others. He spent the night with a young widow, the mother of two beautiful children, and decided that she was a virgin and therefore not to be touched.

Rachel knew this and was amused. She knew about everything. And yet, and yet. Not even she had succeeded in penetrating Kolvillàg and violating the sanctuary. Gracious Rachel, poor Rachel. She could not drive away the Marauding Angel. Nor could he. Had he married her, he might have saved her. But she had refused all compromise. The night she died Azriel remained at her bedside, watching her face, trying to discern the first signs of death, sure that he would succeed, even at the last moment, in annulling the decree. Toward dawn a long tremor tore through her, ripping her apart. She uttered a hoarse cry, charged with terror, a cry springing from the depths of her childhood, or perhaps already from the land of the dead. A cry of farewell, of distress. She changed color at a dizzying, unreal speed before settling into immobility and pallor. Then she fell quiet. A whisper: "No, Azriel, no . . . don't . . ." And because he wanted to absorb every word, every sound, he let the moment go by. By the time he had regained his senses, the Angel had already struck. Was she aware of leaving a world which until then had turned around her? Possibly. Azriel does not think so. The last glance cast is still that of a living conscience. The eyes of the dead are empty.

Azriel and his companion turn back to the waterfront. It is getting late. Empty, the terraces. Dark, the cafés. The buildings along the street are no longer streaked by shafts of light. One last couple embraces one last time before separating; the woman pushes the gate and disappears, her friend waits a moment before turning to go home. A hobo stares at his empty bottle; his companion sneers. Over there a solitary stroller converses with himself, shaking his head from side to side: he disagrees with his thoughts, his life style, his role in society. He disagrees with his fate.

And Azriel wonders: Send the boy home? Tell him never to try again? How can one be sure? One should get a good grip on him, make him come to his senses. One should, one should. Have I lived and survived only for this encounter and this challenge? Only to defeat death in this particular case? Could I have been spared in Kolvillàg so I could help a stranger? Were I younger, I would suggest a pact of friendship: Whatever I can do for you, I shall try to do with you. We shall share adventures, face enemies together; we shall learn to rule them without their knowledge, obtain obedience without raising our voices, explore the universe without moving. But I am too old.

"Listen," he says. "One day the famous Rebbe Moshe-Leib of Sassov received a visit from his friend, the well-known miracle maker, the 'Seraphin' Uri of Strelisk. Finding him sad, dejected, he asked him the reason. 'True, I am depressed,' the visitor confessed. 'For weeks and weeks I have traveled through the land, knocking at every door, imploring every faithful in every hamlet, harassing the rich and reasoning with the less affluent to extract

41

from them a few coins. I need money to marry off orphans, free prisoners, feed homeless children. I don't know what else I can do, to whom else I can turn. And these poor people waiting; I am their only chance, their only hope. How can I help being distressed?'

" 'I understand you,' said Moshe-Leib of Sassov, 'how I understand. It often happens to me. I ache and I feel like howling with helplessness. We are not rich, you and I, we attract only the poor who come to pour out their grief. I would love to help you, my friend, I would love to do something for you, only I myself need help . . . If you only knew how happy I would be if I could lighten your burden . . . But how?' Over and over he repeated these last words. And then he began to cry, to meditate. After what seemed an endless time, he shook himself and shouted, struck by sudden inspiration: 'Uri, my friend, I've got it, I've found the solution, I know how I can help you, friend! I shall dance for you, my friend, I shall dance for you!' "

Azriel pauses, a smile on his face. "Would you like me to dance for you?" He laughs. "No, don't take me at my word. I am too old to dance. But I can tell stories. Would you like me to tell you a story?"

And to himself: Yes, that is the best method; it has been tested and proved. I'll transmit my experience to him and he, in turn, will be compelled to do the same. He in turn will become a messenger. And once a messenger, he has no alternative. He must stay alive until he has transmitted his message. Azriel himself would not still be alive if his father the chronicler, his friends and his teacher Moshe the Madman had not made him the repository of their tragic and secret truths. By entrusting the Book to him, his father doomed him to survival. So this is the example to follow, Azriel pondered. I shall hold him responsible for Kolvillàg. But I shall have to be careful not to go afield, not to trespass. I shall have to watch myself more than before, to be certain that in speaking of the dead, I shall not betray them.

In his anguish, Azriel closes his eyes, only to see, almost immediately, a wide-eyed adolescent who questions: Where were you? What did you bring back from your explorations? Why this quizzical look? You are here, that is all that matters; the rest is commentary. As long as you respond to the call, everything seems possible. One day you will no longer come and I shall be alone, irrevocably alone, a lonely wanderer like you, often a stranger in my own memories, where all passers-by resemble one another, as I resemble you. One day you will no longer come and it will be the end. I will no longer call.

He gropes through his recollections, divides them, chooses them; he questions familiar and strange faces and sinks deeper and deeper into the singed memory of a boy who finds himself in Kolvillàg, alone at first, terribly alone, and then surrounded by the living and the dead, and all rebuke him for having brought a stranger, an intruder.

Quickly, let us leave. Not a moment to lose. Let us slip away immediately. Without asking for forgiveness, without even explaining that we entered inadvertently. Quickly, let us surface again.

"I am cold," says Azriel.

The town was burning but he was cold.

"I was younger than you. Sick, more than you. Alone, much more alone than you. I had just left my family, or rather, they had just left me. I had nobody to lean on. My possessions were few: a Book filled with symbols, a memory filled with images. Like you, I was adrift, floating in time . . ."

Azriel pauses, bitten by remorse. Be careful! You are coming too close to the forbidden zone! And your oath, are you forgetting your oath? Do you want to get yourself excommunicated after so many years? Destroy everything now? Better to have done it right away. Anyway, that is what you wanted, wasn't it?

"Rebbe, what am I do to? Advise me, guide me. The night ahead of me is black and dense, it opens unto horror and ashes. Where do I fit in? What is my duty? To whom do I owe allegiance . . . Rebbe, I beseech you, don't turn away from my plea!"

We were alone in the room. Outside, in the ante-chamber, thirty-six followers were awaiting their turn to enter and pour out their troubles: health, family, business. Among them were those who, yearning for fervor, complained of their excessive serenity; then there were those who told of recurring storms that caused them to lose their footing, too often for their liking. Yes, he knew how to listen, Rebbe Zusia of Kolomey. You entrusted him with your soul and he gave it back to you assuaged. To him you could reveal what you tried to conceal from yourself: your fears and regrets, the temptations repressed and the sins already committed. I alone was unable to make him lend an ear. He gazed and gazed at me and I was shaken.

But let me tell you about this Rebbe Zusia of Kolomey, who, to be sure, did not reside in Kolomey. Disciple of a Master blessed by the Seer of Lublin, he had steadfastly refused the rabbinical crown; all he wanted was to study and meditate. He used to say: "I am too weak, too poor to change mankind or even to help any community whatsoever; I am barely able to protect my own soul." To the Elders arguing that they needed a Master, he quipped: "What about me? Don't you think I need one too?" And he went on: "You may think that I have resolved my difficulties and disarmed my assailants. Or that I have reached the end of the tunnel, and sure of myself, am heading straight for the light of dawn. But no! Not at all! I am seeking, and seeking, and that is all I can do." To which they replied somewhat shyly and only half seriously: "Precisely, Rebbe. We don't even know how to seek." In the end they crowned him against his will. "You will rule over us; such is our decision and it is irrevocable. We shall follow you even if you refuse to be followed." — "So be it," he mumbled, displeased. "Nobody has the right to oppose his will to that of a congregation of Israel. The community has rights over the individuals that constitute it. Only, I warn you: I am not, nor shall I be, a maker of miracles or a dispenser of indulgences. Don't look upon me as a substitute for study or prayer or as a mediator between you and heaven. If you are seeking someone to lighten your task of being a Jew, then look elsewhere. Easy solutions are not my way. I warn you: I shall not tell you what to do, nor shall I tell you which goals are desirable and which are not; I shall not give orders nor shall I provide remedies. All I promise is to be present. And listen."

He could claim neither the glory of the Wizhnitzer Rebbe nor the scholarship of the Gerer Tzaddik. And yet he drew crowds. People flocked to him from the most distant of villages. For an hour, a Shabbat, a week. Some, particularly the young, stayed months, from Passover to the New Year. It is said that during the High Holy Days nearly a thousand faithful crowded into the temporary structure where he celebrated services. Yet he did not see himself as either cantor or preacher. He recited only one prayer aloud: the one that precedes the blowing of the shofar. Legend has it that whoever heard it was sure to repent in the year to follow, and that in the Tzaddik's presence visitors came to understand their innermost motives, even recalling gestures and thoughts from earliest childhood. In his presence walls erected to shield lies and hypocrisy crumbled. To face him was to be stripped of all defense. He plunged into one's soul as into the iciest of waters.

"Rebbe," I said, stifling a scream, "please help me. You alone are capable of showing me the way that does not lead to the abyss."

"What is the problem, young man?" he asked, gazing at me sternly.

Suddenly I felt incapable of formulating a coherent sentence. The words began to buzz in my mind, to tumble about in my mouth. What was I about to say? Wordless, beseeching, I stared at him; he had to guess, he had to understand my silence.

"What then is the problem, young man?" repeated Rebbe Zusia of Kolomey with increased severity. "What is it you wish to discuss with me? What sort of dilemmas? What is this procession trailing behind you and what do you expect me to do about it?"

And when I did not answer, he continued harshly, accusingly: "Or did you just come to look at me? Or perhaps put me to the test?"

Silently I shook my head in denial. I barely breathed. My body weighed heavily on me; it crushed me. I thought: I am lost. If the Rebbe does not sense the meaning of my plight, I shall never speak of it to anyone again.

But he did. When he spoke again, his gaze was more penetrating, his tone more cutting. "The things one has no right to say, I have no right to hear. Why have you come to bother me? To prove to me my own impotence? To disturb me? You have succeeded. Now you may leave."

"Rebbe," I said.

He cut me short. "No! Not a word! You see me, I see you, that must be enough."

"One question, Rebbe," I said very softly. "Just one. Listen to it. That's all I ask of you. It is the sole reason for my coming here. And you already know it. What am I to do? Keep silent? Forever? Till the end? But till the end

of what? The end of my life? Then say so. Command me.
The burden will remain the same, but I shall carry it in a
different way."

Rebbe Zusia of Kolomey stood up and began to stride
back and forth across the room, oblivious of my person.
Only after what seemed an interminable hour did he
return to his armchair.

"I know how to read but I dare not understand," he
said. "I know how to look but I am afraid to see. A man's
destiny is written in his eyes, and yours make me shudder.
Here is what I propose. Stay with me a few days. I shall
let you know. I want time to think before I pronounce
myself. Be patient. Wait for my call, but keep away from
my people. Don't associate with them, don't talk to them.
Don't kill the joy they believe to have found under my
roof; for them it is necessary if not indispensable to pre-
serve this joy. Will you obey me?"

"Yes, Rebbe. Of course, Rebbe. I shall do as you say."

Thus I was able to spend Shabbat at his court. During
services and meals the Hasidim sang and praised the Lord
for having made the seventh day into the soul of creation.
As for me, I remained on the sidelines so as not to disobey
the Rebbe. I was too sad to mingle with the others, anyway;
their rejoicing was not mine to share. I was slowly giving
in to gloom, convinced that nobody noticed me. But I was
wrong. During the third meal, the one that is marked by
mystery, while the disciples surrounding the Rebbe hummed
a nostalgic, throbbing melody, one of the Hasidim came
over to my corner and asked why I was not participating.
It was Gdalia, one of the Rebbe's favorites because he
dared to contradict him. Tall, emaciated, intense, he was
called the "Somber One" or the "Loner," though in fact
he was neither. An erudite Talmudist also well-versed in
Kabbala, he was treated as an equal by Rebbe Zusia in
private and even in public. The Rebbe loved to tease him.
"The best proof that I am not Rebbe," he would say, "is

that Gdalia is my Hasid." To which Gdalia liked to answer, a gleam of irreverence in his eyes: "The difference between the Rebbe and myself is that I don't feel compelled to prove myself."

"You have blasphemed," Gdalia said to me. "Shabbat, the only Holy Day sanctified by God, deserves all your efforts to liberate the song within you. Sadness denies Shabbat, which signifies joy."

"Not for me," I answered.

"Are you excluding yourself from the community?"

"Only from this one."

"There is no such thing. Whoever situates himself outside one community, repudiates them all."

"Wrong. At least I hope so."

"Who are you? What are you doing here? Are you wanted by some enemy?"

"I have no right to answer you."

"Maybe I can help you."

"I have no right to answer you," I repeated, blushing.

We had to interrupt our conversation. The third meal was coming to an end, Shabbat was withdrawing. After the ceremony of *Havdala*, marking the division in time between the sacred and the ordinary, between light and darkness, between Israel and its foes, the Rebbe retired to his rooms. Young Talmudists gathered to start the week with study, while at the other end of the hall, old men sat around in a semicircle reminiscing: one had seen the great Arieh-Leib dancing at an orphan's wedding; another remembered the cry of pain and anger uttered by Gershon the Cantor one festive night that was to be the eve of his death. "I shall tell him," he had roared before collapsing in the midst of a delirious crowd. They had danced around him for a long time; they had danced with such fervor that they had failed to notice the lifeless body on the ground. "I shall tell him, I shall tell him." Him, who? Nobody will ever know.

I went out into the courtyard to get a breath of air. My heart was heavy. I was angry with the whole world. With the Rebbe who belied his legend; he did not listen. With his disciples who rejoiced even though Kolvillàg had ceased to exist. Where was I to turn? I was angry even with the dead; they would have done better not to exclude me. I was of no use to them. I was too young, I lacked experience. A more worldly, more mature survivor would have known how to behave. I felt stupid, useless, at sea. Someone was calling me: "The Rebbe wants you."

It was Gdalia. He had been walking next to me for some time. I hadn't noticed. "The Rebbe is waiting for you," he said in a neutral voice. "He will listen to you now."

From the depths of his armchair, the Tzaddik of Kolomey looked at me with troubled and disapproving eyes. During Shabbat he had appeared much younger. Now his back was stooped, his features drawn. From time to time his hands, resting on a thick volume, trembled. The flame of a kerosene lamp drew shifting shadows on the ceiling and wall.

I remained standing, afraid and at a loss. This man before me, would he be my judge or my defender?

"You went against my orders," the Rebbe scolded me. "You are sowing black thoughts in my community."

"I have said nothing," I protested, "absolutely nothing, I swear it!"

"Never mind. It is possible to spread fear without opening one's mouth. It is possible to deprive man of his right to consolation without saying one single word. You did it, I watched you."

"But . . ."

"But what? You want to tell me that you suffer? Is that why you came? To tell me that? To unload too heavy a burden? If so, if your shoulders are flinching under the weight, then your presence here is undesirable. There is

49

no room under this roof for anyone who cannot control his sorrow and prevent it from affecting his fellow-man."

"That is not the point, Rebbe," I protested with difficulty.

"No? Are you sure?"

"Yes. Suffering does not frighten me. I don't try to set it aside."

"But then . . . what is this about?" he muttered as he moved his heavy, bushy head closer toward me.

He was asking for an answer I could not provide. Never had I felt so helpless. How was I to speak of what defies language? How was I to express what must remain unspoken?

"Rebbe," I said softly, "it is about a trap bolted on all sides. And it is dark inside."

"And you want to come out, is that it? To go where? And do what?"

How could I explain it to him? I could not. Impossible. It had been a mistake to come, to hope. I felt weariness creep over me, invading my mind. I made one last try. "Rebbe," I said in a whisper, "others have sealed my lips. You alone can open them. Tell me whether I should speak or keep my peace."

"I don't understand," he said with a sigh. I was about to go on, when he stopped me with a wave of the hand. "I don't understand. I didn't know it before but I know it now. I know that I have no right to understand. I also know that you will cause me pain."

"Possibly, Rebbe. Much pain."

I saw his eyes, I saw the flame in his eyes and I thought: Yes, I shall cause him pain.

"The story that is mine, I have been forbidden to tell. And so, what am I expected to do? I should like to be able to speak without betraying myself, without lying. I should like to be able to live without self-reproach. I should like to remain silent without turning my very silence into a lie or a betrayal."

With his head lowered, he was listening, holding his breath. I paused. A flame ravaged his eyes and I wondered what they were seeing. Suddenly he sighed and narrowed his mouth as though pondering a decision. His body tensed.

"Say nothing more," he roared, shaking. "Not another word! You are bound to secrecy and I forbid you to violate it! I shall not be your accomplice! Nor shall I be misled! Not another word, or you shall be damned in heaven and on earth!"

Standing before him, I felt my knees buckle under me. There was no way out: the will of the dead cannot be defeated. Along the walls, the shadows seemed to be rocking, stretching and chasing one another; they were making me dizzy. The blood was pounding in my temples, my vision was blurring. Where Rebbe Zusia of Kolomey had been standing, there now stood the Tzaddik of Kolvillàg, the madman of Kolvillàg, my friend Moshe. And in his eyes there was the fire of Kolvillàg, the end of Kolvillàg.

"I can't," I said, not knowing what it was I couldn't.

His fist came down on the table; the lamp flickered. Choking with indignation, he stood up, his finger pointing to the door. "You are insolent! Get out!"

I was stunned. I couldn't understand his anger. "I can't, Rebbe," I repeated breathlessly. I could find no words to justify my presence.

He sat down, shattered. Then he invited me to sit down facing him. I felt my thoughts take leave of me; they went to join me at the other end of the table, which found itself transported to another room, in another house, set in a charred world of ashes.

"So be it," said Rebbe Zusia. "I shall listen to you. In my own way, not yours. Without words. I shall listen to what they conceal. You will look straight into my eyes and you will tell me everything. Without moving your lips, without thinking about the words you will use. You will relive everything before me, and the old man and you will become one. Go on, begin."

And so, with my mouth open, hands folded in front of me, like his, I began to rethink, to relive the events I was carrying deep inside me since my escape from Kolvillàg. I rediscovered the town only to see it reduced to ashes once more. The last holidays, the last meeting of the Community Council, the last night. I experienced again the ceremony of the *Herem*—excommunication—the wait, the fear. Slowly I retraced my steps as Rebbe Zusia followed with bated breath, grief-stricken. Only his eyes— dark shadows dancing in them—seemed alive. He listened in silence, listened to the silence welling up inside me with every image as though to stifle it; ultimate total silence suffused with twilight, the deadly kind that rises from wilderness at dusk. And then came the black and luminous hour that marked the last convulsions of the last night, the wedding by fire and the end of Kolvillàg.

"I don't understand," whispered Rebbe Zusia. "I still don't understand. You hurt me and yet it brought you no relief."

He rested his head between his hands and remained thus for a long time. A bluish light filtered down from the sky and glided over the windowpane. The shadows withdrew into the corners, behind my back, as though to watch me.

"You will leave here this very day," the Rebbe said without changing position. "You will be *Na-venadnik*, in perpetual exile, a stranger among strangers. May you be the silence between words, the dead forgotten by the living. Reveal yourself to no one, attach yourself to no person. Since you carry a secret world inside you, watch over its inhabitants. You have been entrusted with a key; keep it. It belongs only to you, it belongs not even to you."

His head moved but not his hands. I could see his eyes: more somber than before. And I, in turn, listened. I listened as I had never listened before. I could hear the sound of my blood flowing in my veins and that of night retreating before the approaching dawn.

"I send you on the road to the unknown so that you may lose yourself before finding yourself again," Rebbe Zusia continued. "You will live under new skies, in a changing landscape. One gives, one gives oneself in order to forget; it is in order to forget that one speaks. Try not to speak, my poor friend . . ."

Exhausted, he paused, repeating "my poor friend" over and over, shaking his head to express his sorrow and his sympathy too.

"Yes, I shall impose on you the restlessness of the wanderer. You will walk, you will not spend two nights under the same roof. How far? How long? You will know when the time comes. In the end, the ways of heaven and man coincide. Not only in the hour of death. It all depends on your attitude toward death and toward each hour. Some men do nothing but die throughout their journey; others succeed in snatching a few days, a few weeks of life. The goal of the *Na-venadnik* is to keep the book open."

He stood up, and so did I. He escorted me to the door and put his arm around my shoulders in a tight embrace. "Remember that God is everywhere and that He is everywhere the same. Not you. In truth, there are thousands and thousands of Azriels inside you. It is your task to find them and to bring them together; when they shall have become one, you shall be free."

"Free to speak, Rebbe?"

"Free not to speak." And after a pause: "Freedom, what is it exactly? You do everything you did before, only you do it freely."

53

I had expected a blessing, but was disappointed. He gave me leave without even shaking my hand. He seemed solemn and determined, but the fire in his eyes was gone. It was almost daylight and the town was no longer burning.

The nomad life did me good. Rebbe Zusia had been right. Not being tied to any place or person modifies your relationship with others and with yourself. You are the former prisoner who constantly turns around to look at the prison, and in that way, knows he is free. Master of your body and your imagination, you answer to no one. With no landscape of your own, all landscapes are yours. In your search for time, you conquer space. You are at home everywhere and your house has no doors, open as it is to the four winds and the stars. With your every move, you shift the center of the universe.

Roaming from town to town, from country to country, the *Na-venadnik* gives of himself and becomes the richer for it; the more he gives, the more he extends his powers. By helping strangers live, he himself lives more fully, more intensely. He speaks with his eyes, listens with his lips. For him every word is a call and every call is an adventure; his purpose is to discover not the world but the soul of that world. His feet, at the touch of the earth, reveal to him its incandescent riches. They warn him to flee a particular hamlet or, on the contrary, to set down his walking stick and bundle and take the time to breathe. Indeed, the *Na-venadnik* needs but sniff the air in the marketplace and look over the first person to cross his path, in order to guess whether the locality is friendly or hostile, poor or prosperous. That is one of the privileges of the *Na-venadnik*. Because he constantly moves from place to place, he knows these towns and hamlets better than their own inhabitants.

And yes, all these hamlets seen from the outside resemble one another. *Sadna d'araa had hu,* states the Talmud: all cities come out of the same workshop. The same cottages everywhere—some of them sad, others friendly and streaming with light. The same peasants and woodcutters, framed by the same trees: huge ones reaching into the clouds, frail ones burrowing in the grass. Fields of wheat, rye, corn. The sap rises. Everything blooms. Meadows, fords, haystacks. In the distance, a mountain covered with pine trees. Villages and hamlets, large and small, animated by the same pulsation. Every village has its own church and pointed steeple—pass by quickly and avert your gaze lest you get into trouble for visual blasphemy. Every little town prides itself on its fair, where the same sellers shout themselves hoarse to overcome the same suspicious surliness of the same buyers. Offers fly back and forth; people yell, quarrel, make up, kiss and curse in Russian, Ruthenian, Hungarian, Romanian —and Yiddish. The language of the fair is universal. One horse is traded for another, a bolt of cloth for a calf, cheese for candles. The boys woo the young peasant girls, who in turn provoke them, laughing and rolling their hips. Their benevolent parents do not interfere. Sometimes they even set the example. Here and there couples lie down in the grass. Others, to save time, cling to each other standing up behind the barn. Frequently tempers run high: a lovers' quarrel, an offended father, a jealous husband. Too daring a young man, too reticent a girl, and lo and behold, participants and spectators brandish their daggers, and the blood flows. An hour later they all meet again in the tavern, where Itzik or Sender or Yoske becomes their referee. Or scapegoat. One downs a few glasses, one beats up a Jew—and everybody feels better.

Every village has its taverns, and in every tavern you will find, in front of the wine cask, an Itzik or a Sender or a Yoske for whom pain has become a matter of habit, of livelihood. These innkeepers resemble one another the way the Jewish communities dispersed between the Dniepr and the Carpathian Mountains resemble one another.

Cut off from the outside world, these timeless Jewish kingdoms are private worlds, with their own princes and minstrels, fools and beggars, poets and workers, celebrations and mournings. They do not communicate with one another, or rarely, yet all observe the same ritual and all fashion for themselves the same tomorrow. On Friday nights, before the arrival of Shabbat, they all intone the same melody to invite the angels, carriers of the same peace. In my daydreams it sometimes was not I but the village—always the same one—that was roaming the roads in search of help and redemption, and I was but a link.

With the years, I became a hyphen between countless communities. News was gathered from my lips. Intrigues at the Hasidic courts, clashes with the Mitnagdim. Being well-informed myself, I informed others. The schemes of the clergy and the politicians, the rates for so-called official protection: I was up-to-date. I knew who was trying to intercede with whom on which family's behalf—and at what price. I was newsmonger as well as messenger.

Of course, I occasionally would travel through large cities. Thus I visited Lemberg, pushed as far as Prague, spent a night in Kiev. I even lived an unforgettable Shabbat in Vienna, where a rich merchant, a friend of the governor, offered me hospitality. He resided in a building

ELIE WIESEL

crammed with rooms and stairways, enough to make one
lose one's way. It was teeming with servants who all
looked alike. To reach the top floor, one had to take a train
that traveled upward. I refused to board it, as I found even
ordinary trains not too reassuring. Why do people insist
on making themselves the slaves of machines? I wondered.
In their eagerness to arrive quickly, they forget where
they are going. But the vertical train, in my opinion, was
infinitely more dangerous. How could one be sure that it
would actually halt at the ceiling? And what if suddenly
it felt like continuing, higher and higher, to the very stars?
Can you imagine me suddenly appearing before the
celestial tribunal in a train? I fled that capital as quickly
as I could, running faster than the train, thus deeply distressing my host. Poor benefactor, he was seeking a tutor
for his children, and had hoped to impress me. I thought:
He'll manage. Surely he will ferret out a tutor who likes
machines; as for me, I prefer the stars.

Offers abounded; I had but to choose. Some propositions
were tempting: lodgings, a home, respectability. I was
begged: Stay, we need you, for we tend to forget, become creatures of habit, lose sight of our sources. We no
longer hear the call, please don't abandon us. And everywhere I answered: No, thank you, thank you, no. Resisting
temptation was easy; stability held no attraction for me.
For a *Na-venadnik* belongs to the communities he visits
and his role is precisely that: to visit them, not to settle
in them. Once the flame has been kindled, the wanderer
takes his candle and moves on.

There was another reason, a personal one I could not
discuss. I was haunted by Kolvillàg; it held me tightly in
its grip.

I remember one particular incident. It was Shabbat. The
little town where I had ended up the day before had a
tradition of inviting one of the wandering beggars to give

58

a sermon. Even if the choice fell on a dunce or a madman, he was still given the honors due a celebrated scholar.

So here I was in the midst of a packed synagogue. The entire congregation was crammed into it, eagerly waiting, ready to listen to me, to admire me and perhaps even to follow me. With words, nothing but words, I could have shaken them, renewed their bond with the living tree of Israel. I was on the verge of doing it, the sermon was all set in my head. Suddenly I realized that the hall was identical to that of Kolvillàg, only larger. The rapt faithful below; the women out of sight in the balcony. The children on the steps leading to the Holy Ark. A thought crossed my mind, petrifying me: I am still in my native town, I have left it only in my dreams, I have done nothing but changed dreams. To recover my senses, I studied the faces lifted toward me. The rabbi's head was resting on his right hand, his arm leaning on the lectern. The beadle, practical and efficient, was making sure that the head of the community was seated comfortably. An emaciated young student was keeping his eyes lowered so as to hear better—or not hear at all. A speech delivered to this large an audience could not possibly be distinguished; important teaching can take place only in a limited circle. A taciturn old man was shoving a neighbor too noisy for his liking. The school-teacher, combing his bushy beard with his fingers, was counting those of his pupils who were stealthily edging toward the exit.

The more I looked, the more I doubted my sanity: What if I were indeed still at home?

The beadle tapped me on the arm, pulling me out of my daydream: "What are you waiting for?"

"I don't know . . ."

"Well then, begin!"

"Everything is getting mixed up in my head," I muttered by way of excuse.

"Start, the rest will follow."

"I don't know how."

"Say anything," the beadle insisted. "Say that the sanctity of the Shabbat must be observed; that's not complicated and makes a good impression."

"I don't know how," I said stubbornly.

"Say that we must praise the Lord for having given us his Law. All the preachers say it, you won't be taking any chances!"

Our whispered discussion could but intrigue the audience. The rabbi lifted his head and looked at us questioningly. The beadle rushed to inform him that fate had played them a nasty trick; this particular Saturday they had happened on an idiot. The distressed rabbi was about to rise and come to my aid, when I began to speak.

"*Morai verabotai*, my revered teachers," I said, rocking forward and backward. "I ask you to forgive me if my words are brief. I could lie to you. I could pretend feeling dizzy. I could feign ignorance. But one does not lie in the presence of the Torah. The truth is different: I am not here to speak but to hold my tongue."

And I returned to my seat.

This happened time and time again, whenever I was about to speak in public. The speaker became speechless. Everywhere I saw the same faces, the same expressions; I moved in the same setting. How could I offend the good people of Kolvillàg by telling them their own story, the very one they had forbidden me to reveal?

Yet sometimes it happened that I did useful work. In the small hamlets, mostly, far from the centers. There I brought back lost sheep to the fold, preaching repentance, showing the way. I jostled the self-righteous, the rich, the proprietors, the merchants. I encouraged the humble. As for the poor, I communicated to them the pride of calling Israel's past their own. I made them sing after services, during services and even instead of services. On the side, I settled disagreements and quarrels between rabbis and notables, butchers and ritual slaughterers; I interpreted the Law so as to reconcile the minds it had divided. It would not have taken much for me to fall into the trap of vanity and consider myself important, indispensable, irreplaceable. People praised me, feared me. They saw in me one of the hidden Just Men whose mission it is to sanctify space with their ephemeral presence wherever man tries desperately and unsuccessfully to approach the Almighty. They took me for the prophet Elijah, who, like me, visited and consoled lonely beings. They whispered that I was a Master in disguise. Before revealing himself, the Tzaddik must undergo trials of renunciation in anonymity. By helping strangers, I became a stranger in my own eyes. Having convinced my fellow-men, having guided them, I persuaded myself that language was omnipotent as the link between man and his creator.

So as not to break my oath, I told all sorts of stories but my own. Inventing them, I gave my imagination free rein: to wit, the one about the pickpocket who decided to steal no more. And to stop living in fear and shame. Not so easy to rebuild a life, an image; not so easy to inspire respect after having aroused contempt: he becomes the community's laughingstock; even the floor-sweeper at the synagogue guffaws: "You here? What are you doing among these honest people? Changing victims, are you? What brings you to this holy place? Say, is it God you are going to rob from now on?"

"I want to repent," says the thief weakly. And the faithful begin to sneer: "That's a good one! Not so stupid, that fellow! Now that he's getting old, he's putting his affairs in order! Shrewd, that fellow!" The former thief, a sincere though naïve penitent, protests that his motives are pure and honorable: "I have truly decided to give up stealing; I truly wish to please heaven. I swear it. Trust me. I have but one wish—to be one of you." And they all laugh and applaud: "Perfect, perfect! The thief has seen the light, bravo! He is retiring, bravo! Only he has neglected to settle his accounts! Let him return what he has pinched since the day of his birth. How many rings? How many snuffboxes? How many wallets . . . ?" They tear at his clothes, first in jest, then in earnest. Bewildered, he thinks: And I wanted to deserve them, imitate them! How foolish I was! A spring inside him snaps. He distinctly feels it. And so he offers no resistance; too late to turn back, to open another door. A thought crosses his mind: I am going to die, in this very post, a few steps from the Holy Ark. And he begins to run; he runs, he runs until he is out of breath, he runs toward the light, toward the darkness beyond the light, he is expected there, they are calling him. Then a shout: "He has stopped moving!" And a reply: "He is dead. The thief remains a thief to the end; he has just robbed us of our dignity!"

Or the one about the sleeping man who awakes with a start. Standing in the wide-open doorway there is a stranger who asks him: "Are you afraid?"

"Yes, I am afraid."

"Of me? You are afraid of me?"

"Yes, of you."

"Do you wish me to go?"

"Yes, I do."

"You'll stop being afraid?"

"Yes, if you leave me alone, I won't be afraid."

"Are you sure?"

"Absolutely sure."

"Not I," says the visitor, withdrawing.

And then the sleeper is overcome by panic. He realizes that he has just met, for the first time, the stranger who has always lived inside him.

Or the one about the dreamy-eyed young man whose

path I crossed one autumn morning on the embankment of the Vltava in Prague.

"What do you want of me?" I asked him.

"I know who you are," he said in a solemn voice. "I recognize you by the scar on your forehead."

"But I don't have a scar on my forehead!" I protested.

"That proves nothing."

"What do you mean?"

"I recognized you. That is the best proof. I know who you are. Admit that I know."

I shrugged my shoulders and wanted to be on my way, but the dreamy-eyed young man blocked my path. "Don't go away, I am hungry. Come and share my meal. I am poor, but surely you like the company of the poor. Don't turn me down. If you go away, my curse will accompany you, do you hear?"

One may not offend the insane; their voices rise to heaven, straight to the Throne. And then, they all remind me of my holy friend, my mad friend, Moshe. And so I sat down next to the young man, in the middle of the street, and was preparing myself to break bread by reciting the customary blessing, when suddenly he seized the pocketknife and with a swift move, wounded me, marking my forehead with a scar.

"May I ask you a favor?"

"Go ahead, try."

"Promise not to refuse."

"Oh, no, I promise nothing. I am too old. I make no more promises; I couldn't keep them. Past a certain age, man should no longer speak in the future tense."

"Too bad. You would have given me pleasure."

"By doing what?"

"By marking my forehead with a scar."

Make him dream, that's what I must do, the old man ponders. If I succeed, he is saved. One doesn't kill oneself while dreaming, not even while dreaming to kill oneself. To dream is to invite a future, if not to justify it, and to deny death, which denies dreams. Not so simple. Today's young people are choked by the sterile world that is theirs. For them, there are no more distances, everything is made easy; they no longer need their imagination, and so it atrophies. The past is too far removed, the future not far enough. What need is there to imagine distant places when they are within your reach? And how is one to worship a heaven splattered with mud? What is the good of prolonging a civilization wallowing in ashes?

And a poor world it is, with little room for either the young or the old. The former are born old, the latter are forever dying; too slowly for some. All are to be pitied. This century is cursed.

And why do you want to die? What mistake are you seeking to atone, to denounce? Oh, I know—everything disgusts you. The gilded altars and the false priests, the sullied sanctuaries and the corrupted sovereigns. Yes, I know, there are a few too many innocent men massacred in a few too many lands. And then, the cheating, the lying. Words lie, men kill and go on lying and go on killing. You want *your* death to be a genuine act in a world where all is fake.

Oh yes, I understand, you are so young, so desperate. Born after the holocaust, you have inherited the burden but not the mystery. And you were told: Go ahead, do something with it. Only it is too enormous, too heavy, it eludes and transcends you. A treacherous situation, one cannot possibly disregard it, yet one cannot possibly continue without disregarding it. Dealing with it poses as many problems as turning away.

And yet, and yet. I must speak to you. Convince you that death, on all levels, is not a solution but a question, the most human question of all.

What if I told you about Kolvillàg? It contains a lesson that might benefit you, who are incapable of living simply, or simply of living. Kolvillàg: contagious hate, evil unleashed. The dire consequences of a commonplace, senseless episode. The importance of unimportant things. Breaking his chains, the Exterminating Angel has turned all men into victims. Moral: it is dangerous to use his services. Do you hear me? Despite the innumerable eyes that characterize him, he is blind; he will strike anywhere. In every family. Decimating every tribe. Filling every cemetery. And no one will know why he perishes or why he is spared. Kolvillàg: the culmination of fanaticism, of stupidity. The ultimate chastisement, affecting equally victims and executioners. Moral: whoever kills, kills himself; whoever preaches murder will be murdered. One may not accept any meaning imposed on death by the living. Just as every murder is a suicide, every suicide is a murder. Yes, the story must be told.

"I saw him again," said my sick mother.

She had just awakened, covered with sweat, frighteningly pale. As every morning, glassy-eyed, her voice slow and faltering. As at all her awakenings, she had once again parted with a ghost.

"I can't go on," she said in a toneless voice. "I have reached the end. Next time I'll go with him."

We stood at her bedside, my father and I, and looked at one another in consternation. Lately the patient's condition had worsened. These nightmares. These fits of remorse. Every night she plunged into the turmoil again.

Her first husband. Their son. The war, the journey, the arrival at the camp. The selection. The refined and oh so cultured army doctor questioning the small boy: "How old are you? Five years already? Go and play over there, go quickly, like a big boy." One tear, one shove later, my mother found herself separated from her husband and son. Forever.

"I should have rushed forward, gone with him. He was so small, so far away."

"Try not to think about it any more," said my father.

"I can't."

"Make the effort; you must. You can't go on like this. You have no right to. What you did, others have done. By accusing yourself, you condemn all the mothers who did what you did. You are unfair to them."

Her head was tossing on the pillow. "No, no," she said. "I did not behave well. I should have understood. And refused to be separated from my little boy." Though awake, she was still following her ghost and her breath was halting. "He is five years old. He has not grown up. He will be five years old forever."

I should have liked to know this little brother, both younger and older than myself. Whom did he resemble? My mother? I should have liked to see her the way she must have looked that night, surrounded by barbed wire. But even while I listened, I could not help thinking: And I, where do I fit in? I suffered with her and for her, but I could not understand. Where do I fit in, where?

Woe to those nameless orphans who believe in nothing but the brotherhood of the dead. Woe to those ghosts we keep expelling from our memories. Woe to this generation which sees everything and understands nothing. Woe to those who, like yourself, await death and expect nothing else. You have not yet lived and already you hate life. You have not yet confronted your fate and already you are bored. You want to die and you don't know the reason. How can one help pitying you?

At your age I went from wonder to wonder, despite the ghosts pursuing me relentlessly, despite the proximity of the abyss. I fought with life every morning and with darkness every dusk. I explored every direction and intercepted every call. I spoke and I listened, I taught and I learned, I received and I gave, I yielded and I stood fast, I laughed and I cried—often for the same reasons—and I regret nothing. I could have not lived any of these experiences; I am glad I did. I could have not met any of my companions; I am glad I did. People, events, discoveries; I could have arrived a year earlier, a year later, I could have chosen the path leading to the right rather than to the left and not have known them. I am glad I did.

I remember: a winter night, a sleepy inn. Muffled up in my cape, stretched out behind the hearth in the spot reserved for impecunious travelers, I was reviewing, as I did every evening, the events of the day gone by: the people met, the words pronounced, the moments wasted. A balance sheet I imagined drawn up and inscribed in the *Pinkas,* the Book which never left my side.

It was dark. And so I had not noticed my neighbor lying at the other end of the hearth. I could not tell whether he was young or old. I only knew that he was *Na-venadnik* like myself. Like myself, he was not asleep. Like myself, he barely moved. After a while we began to speak softly so as not to disturb the proprietor. We traded impressions and anecdotes, but no precise, personal information—such is the law of wanderers in exile.

His was a warm voice, inviting trust and comradeship. He claimed this was his last year of wandering. Had he had his fill of dusty roads, barking dogs and criminals infesting the woods? I asked. Was that why he wished to return home?

"No," he said, "that's not it. Some sinners prolong their penance because it links them to their sins a little longer. Penance can become a trap. I prefer to halt; I choose not to reach the goal."

He confided to me the origins of what he called his "offenses." Forbidden readings, mystical projects. Exorcism through fasting, mortification of the soul and invocation of the Names. Frankly, he had not been mature enough or sufficiently prepared for the task. Of course he had had a Master, but he had turned out to be a clandestine Sabatean who aimed to redeem the world through sin. His Master spoke of the Messiah but was really referring to the imposter; he glorified the Shekinah but described her in terms of a sensual and vigorous woman, his own. While ostensibly initiating his disciple into the splendors of the secret tradition, he was in fact awakening him to forbidden lust and sensual play. "I who aspired to purity, I who saw my body as an obstacle, here I was, letting myself be lulled by sinful visions . . ." I told him I envied him. He had set a goal for himself, I had not. His exile was limited, mine was not. Every day brought him closer to deliverance.

"How do you know?" he muttered impatiently. "Man's goal is not defined by man. We are all too weak, too ignorant to foresee the outcome of our plans. True encounters are those set in heaven, and we are not consulted. Look, what if I told you that the sole purpose of your wanderings was to hear me speak on this winter night in Dragmuresh?"

I started. "Dragmuresh? You say we are in Dragmuresh? And here I was thinking I was in Petrova."

I am not sorry I mistook one village for another. Just as all suffering is a test invented by God, the sorrow of having been subjected to it is an invention of the devil.

Another encounter, elsewhere, with another kind of *Na-venadnik*. Abrasha, like myself, wandered from one Jewish community to the next, though not as a penitent but as an agent of the Komintern. His mission was to arouse the youth, organize and activate it, arm and integrate it into the international revolutionary movement. A speaker of talent, a born activist, Abrasha succeeded so well with his recruitment campaign that every police force of the region was at his heels. There was a price on his head; his description was posted on every wall. He slipped through their nets with the help of his sympathizers. But he still had to reckon with parental hostility. Pious for the most part, parents fought emancipation and assimilation as much as atheism. To them communism represented both aberration of the mind and repudiation of the holy tradition. Therefore, it had to be opposed with vigor; all the more since the young, yearning for freedom, eagerly listened to its message.

"You could be of real help to me," Abrasha was saying. "You could take charge of a sector which as an outsider is closed to me: the Yeshivoth, the Talmudic schools. This is unbroken ground, unjustly so. My instinct is sure, infallible, in this domain. There are, inside the Yeshivoth, numerous, unsuspected comrades. They are waiting only for a signal, a first contact, to join us and militate with us. They are waiting only for you."

We had met at the outskirts of Batizov, a tiny hamlet in the mountains. Chased by an unfriendly dog, we were crossing the forest together. I had not disclosed to him who I was nor whence I came; as for my destination, I knew as little about that as he did. To him I was one of those mystical vagabonds he termed the true outcasts of the earth.

"You could keep up your way of life," he said. "You would be my double. Together we would accomplish—I was about to say miracles, but no—useful, important things. We would help our fellow-men, transform them into free and happy creatures. We would abolish slavery and injustice. We would build a new society, create a new man . . ."

"All that?" I exclaimed. "Aren't you overestimating my abilities?"

"Therein lies the beauty of the revolutionary ideal. You and I must change the world. You and I—that is a lot. You think we are alone? The movement has many comrades like you and me."

Robust, energetic, dynamic and obstinate to boot, he impressed me.

"All that is very nice," I said, "but . . ."

"But what?"

71

"You want me to be your double? You must be joking. Did you take a good look at me?"

"Appearances, you worry about appearances." Abrasha was annoyed. "You surprise me. More than anyone, you should know they don't count. It's what's behind the appearances, right? Take them away—and what remains, tell me? Two people. Equal. We eat when we're hungry, sleep when we're tired; we laugh when we're amused, right?"

"No," I said, thinking of Kolvillàg.

"What do you mean, no! Without your beard you would be me; and I with your beard would be you."

"No," I said.

"All right. The beard is not enough. Add the clothes. And the upbringing. And the faith. All these may be acquired. You see? I could easily be you."

"No," I said. "You will never be me."

He assumed that I was indulging in dialectics and took pleasure in beating me at my own game. Excitedly he began to use a vocabulary strange to my ears. From time to time I would catch a more or less familiar word, which then remained isolated and opaque without becoming integrated into a complete sentence or an intelligible idea. Meanwhile Abrasha spoke on and on with a fervor not unlike that of a Talmudic student grappling with a difficult text. I waited for him to calm down before I mentioned that I had understood nothing of his tirade.

"All right," he said. He was not discouraged. "Let's start all over. I am a communist . . ."

"What's that?"

"A communist is someone who states that all peoples, all men form one big community. Do you agree with that principle? Let us continue. The communist declares that man owes it to himself to abolish evil and suffering, hunger and poverty, social injustice and war."

"Your communist seems to take himself for the Messiah, right?"

"Why not? You want to know what communism is? Simple. It is messianism without God, just as Christianity is messianism without man."

"Words," I said. "You don't make sense. A messianism without God is like bread without flour, dough without yeast, a body without life, a life without sunshine. If that is your most convincing argument . . ."

Nevertheless Abrasha, knowing human nature, intuitively found the right words to overcome my resistance: "You don't understand, you can't understand. You have lived as a recluse, preoccupied with your own salvation. And the others, what about their salvation? Those who cannot afford the luxury of a purely metaphysical struggle, those to whom a loaf of bread represents unattainable riches. Do you ever think of them? The farmers reeling under their debts, the overworked laborers, the starving children, do you happen to think about them sometimes?"

"That's irrelevant," I said.

"Oh, but no! Communism is precisely that: the theory of relevancy. It demonstrates that every phenomenon relates to all others and that—"

"A theory, another! I have no use for your theories! I don't understand what they're about!"

"You interrupt me, you listen badly and you demand that I explain to you what you don't know. Do you think that is fair?"

"All right," I said gruffly, "I am listening."

But he knew better; I was in no way ready to listen. "You seem angry," he said. "I'm sorry. I was wrong to annoy you with my philosophical riddles. A simple definition should suffice: communism is a theory for some, a dream for others . . ."

A dream. Changing tactics, Abrasha described it to me with childlike simplicity. A society based on justice and predicated on work, with no overlords or servants, no criminals or executioners. No man would bow to any other; no man would experience shame or fear. Finished, poverty. Abolished, terror. Down with the superstition of bigots. Long live liberty. Imagine a happy Isaiah. Imagine Jeremiah appeased. Imagine our prophets reconciled with the people and their God. That is the communist dream. Imagine our peasant brothers no longer forced to plow sixteen hours a day to make the local landowner richer. Imagine our poor less poor and less ignorant. Imagine our children less frightened and their parents less weary. Imagine Jewish men and women freed from all anguish, all threats . . .

Oh yes, he knew, good old Abrasha, he knew how to handle me. I became his accomplice, his brother-in-arms. Together we visited dozens and dozens of communities, outwitting police and thwarting informers, recruiting new members, training militants, extending the borders of the clandestine network from province to province, from region to region. We had our tasks divided: he took care of the working circles, I was in charge of Talmudic schools. While he distributed pamphlets and tracts among the tailors and shoemakers, the apprentices and clerks, I attended the places of worship, participated in the services, then in the studies. In the evening I would detain the best students to delve with them deeper into this complex *Sugya* or elucidate that obscure commentary, and soon the cell was ready to function. I don't remember how many schools I seeded. Only once did I face danger —a rabbi, the head of a rabbinical school, caught me in the act.

It happened late one night, in a mountainous village buried in snow. We were in the middle of a cell meeting. The comrades in caftan were leaning on their desks, swaying forward and backward, listening to me, concentrating on my every word as though they were attending an ad-

vanced course in Talmud. The very idea that they could
consider me a sage robbed me of my usual earnestness;
there was in this scene an element of the absurd. Several
times I had to repress a violent urge to laugh. I quickly
lost that urge, for suddenly the door opened with a bang.
The police, I thought—we are lost. No, it was only the
rabbi. Nevertheless we were lost. There he stood—tall
and erect, fierce, personifying power and implacable
will. He stared at us, and then, without uttering a word,
he went from student to student, sizing them up, curling
his lips, as though taking stock of the extent of the betrayal: You too, you too. Then, with one motion, he
sent them all away. Like reprimanded children, they left
humiliated, their heads bowed. In less than a minute we
were left face to face, he and I, he and his cold anger,
and I, curious, waiting for what was to come. I was somewhat intimidated but I managed not to show it.

I chose a direct, frontal attack. "My compliments," I
began. "Bravo. You are tough. You terrorize your students. They are like slaves. The same fear, the same obedience. Are you proud, proud of your power? Are you
proud of crushing spirits so as to rule them? Is that
your concept of Judaism?"

His eyes would not let go of mine; they were taking
possession of me. Only at the price of great physical effort
was I able to hold my head high. There emanated from
his person such strength that he canceled my will. What
was he going to do? I felt the blood rushing to my face.
I was swimming in fantasy. One of us was out of place.
I knew I ought to break up this strange confrontation,
and disentangle myself before it was too late. But my
body obeyed him, not me. I gripped my desk, knowing
I was defeated, without recourse. And all this time the
rabbi was not saying a word. Why was he staring so?
What punishment did he have in store for me? Was he
planning to hand me over to the authorities? He guessed

my fears and shook his head. What was the meaning of this no? That I had nothing to fear or nothing to hope? He began to speak and the gentleness of his voice stirred me to the core.

"And so once more a stranger comes to bring us the good news: salvation is possible and its name is communism. If what he says is true, then our lives so far have been mistakes and lies. The future would matter more than the past, progress more than inherited values. Is that what he came to teach us? That in order to build the future, we must destroy the past? Or in other words, that man will continue his work of destruction until the end of time. And he dares call that a message of hope! What else does he tell us? That man is cast into the world and forgotten? That there is no eternity for him? That work is more valuable than meditation and slogans more important than prayers? That happiness negates faith, knowledge kills mystery? This is what he tells us. And he wants us to believe, this stranger, that his truth is more just than ours and his justice truer than ours. He claims to be able to explain everything, even suffering, even Jewish suffering.

"Well, if he doesn't understand that knowledge is a mystery in itself, that a man without a past is poorer than a man without a future; if he doesn't understand that the miracle lies not in the beauty of twilight enveloping the forest, but in the eye of man beholding and sharing that beauty. If the stranger fails to understand that, then I pity him as I would pity anyone who lived alienated from his people and from all creation. For us there can be no salvation outside the community. Yes, the stranger has just told us that in order to save man, one must annihilate the Jew in man, and that our people must disappear so that mankind may prosper. His mouth betrays his ignorance. Whoever opposes man to himself becomes his enemy; whoever opposes man-as-a-Jew to mar repudiates both. If the stranger wishes to help us, let him remain in our midst. Let him eat at our table, participate in our festivities. A Jew's place is among Jews. If the stranger agrees, I'll see him tomorrow at study time. If not, I won't see him again. If he decides to leave, let him leave right now; he has a long night before him."

Thereupon, without waiting for my reaction, he left.

For one moment I was stunned. Mad thoughts whirling through my mind. Should I accept the invitation— stay, lose myself in studies and friendship, start all over? This time it was I who shook my head. I would not be tempted. I could not remain. A *Na-venadnik* must not remain in any one place. What had the rabbi said? That I had a long night ahead of me? Was that a threat, a blessing? I left the village with a sense of failure. I never returned.

Later, in a nearby village, I learned that Abrasha had been summoned to Moscow. I waited for his return, in vain. Much later I learned why Abrasha had not come back. A victim of the first purges, he was killed by a bullet in the neck in the name of the dream he had awakened in so many hearts. This marked the end of my activities on behalf of the revolution.

I don't regret having believed Abrasha, nor having helped him. At my age one doesn't regret the dreams that have carried us—and that we have carried—all over the world. They are what is left of a lifetime.

The thing is that as a child I believed that the Messiah would deliver us all from solitude. It was dark and I shivered with fright. I contemplated the stars and heard nothing but the thumping of my heart, heavy with growing fear and anticipation. Fool that I was, I was convinced that at the end of night there lay redemption. But

Satan interfered and man stood by idly. Man is strange; he is waiting for the Messiah, yet it is Satan he follows.

And yet, and yet. I, an old man with one foot in the grave, persist in believing, in proclaiming that the world needs the Messiah, that men cannot survive without the hope that one day he will come to judge and free them—judge them in their freedom—so that the game may end, once and for all. He will come. Sooner or later. Oh yes, he will come, but it will not be a man—no, it will no longer be a man—who will redeem us. Mankind no longer deserves to be redeemed by God, but only by a demon, an evil angel. Man is strange—he clamors for the Messiah, yet it is death that fascinates him.

A fierce sadness closes in on the old man. Abrasha shot; his dreams murdered. So many men betrayed by so many false prophets. So many promises flouted by so many idols. And yet, and yet. He recalls his father, his comrades, his mad friend, his mad friend most of all—for it was he who had personified for him the messianic dream in all its ardor and serenity. He had never showed his truest smile, saving it for the great day; he had never sung his purest song, reserving it for the same occasion. He died, my mad friend, without knowing that the great event was not the one he had expected; it was a conflagration and not a celebration. But I do know—and what good is that? Tomorrow I shall die and my knowledge will die with me.

What then is the significance of this mute testimony deposited within me? An invisible force compels me to walk a stretch of road, my head bowed or held high, alone or at another's side—and we call that life. I look back, and we call that conscience. Someone smiles at me and gives me his hand, and we call that love. Someone offers me his support and his complicity, and we speak of friendship. I close my eyes, and that is called questioning. And then if one finds oneself a few steps ahead, a few encounters later, at the side of the road, at the entrance to night, at the edge of the precipice, one says: That's it, it's over. And all the wealth of this existence, all the mystery of the *I* vanish in one sweep: a man has lived.

Is that why you want to put an end to your life? To prove—prove to whom?—that you are not like the others, that you withdraw from the game whenever you choose? You want to write the last act of the scenario? As for me, you see, I have no need for that sort of proof. I am older than you, but I go on. Step by step I move closer to the abyss, behaving as though death itself is part of the adventure, as though, beyond death and in spite of it, eternity exists inside me, around me, as though it were me. I eat, I sleep, I walk, I search, I read, I question the days and the nights, I answer the curious who want to know whether old age is a blessing or a malediction and whether I am frightened at the thought of death. No, it makes me ashamed. A key word, one more: shame. If you die, I shall not feel guilty, but ashamed. I think of Kolvillàg and shame comes over me. An understandable, normal reaction. Man is incapable of imagining his own death; he imagines that of his fellow-man. The survivor resents his survival. That is why the Christians imagine their Savior expiring on the cross. They thus situate him outside the circle of shame; he dies before the others, instead of the others. And thus the others are made to bear his shame. The Messiah, as seen by the Jews, shows greater courage; he survives all the generations, watches them disappear one after the other—and if he is late in coming, it is perhaps because he is ashamed to reveal himself.

For us, the living—therefore the survivors—the great shame is that we claim to be brothers when we are nothing but wild, solitary beasts. I could force you to accept life, but you would remain alone. I could save you from death, but not from yourself. What are you to yourself: savior or wild beast? Both perhaps? You are proud and ashamed at the same time? One does not cancel the other, I know. But then, where is the solution? I don't know. Perhaps there is none, but what of it? Is that sufficient reason to want to die? Who says that the solution lies in death and not in the refusal of death?

When I was your age I already knew that the world was guilty and doomed; I was already convinced even then that man labored against man and that the Messiah himself was against him. Don't you think I wanted to die? Only I couldn't. Worse—I had no right to speak of dying.

I remember the last time I let my eyes wander over the landscape plowed by death, ruins over which a black and pestilential smoke still hovered like a network of highways encrusted in the clouds. I was leaning against an oak. I could not tear myself away. My legs were riveted to the ground, my eyes fixed on the dying embers. The fiery wind had run out of breath, and was now retreating. What was left was a devastated, ghostly cemetery. I gazed at the ashes and was overwhelmed by a feeling of solitude that has never left me. Another feeling, darker, angrier, welled up inside me: my uselessness. All right, I thought, I'll go. You rejected me, excluded me, you chose for me. I would have come to hate you; the easiest to hate are the dead.

What helped me to stand fast was the Book, the *Pinkas* of Kolvillàg. If I used all my wits to stay alive, it was to save it, to protect it. A matter of duty. I had no right to die. One night, a few weeks or a few months after the conflagration, I found myself on the verge of suicide. Friendless, without any resources, I roamed from forest to forest, not knowing what to do with my past and my future. Where was I to go? What help was I to solicit and from whom? I was young, I had no experience other than that of death. A kindly peasant woman offered me shelter and food on one condition: that I become her son. A priest declared himself ready to take me in on one condition: that I become a Christian. A forester insisted on teaching me to shoot at animals; when I refused, he set his dog on me. I had had enough, I could not go on. I called the dead, I called death to come to my aid. From beyond sleep I could hear Moshe scolding me: "You must really have fallen low to want to debase yourself further, and I had such hopes of attaining the highest summits through you!" He winked and confided to me that there was no possible escape from Kolvillàg: "Up there, there is a city like ours, only bigger; and it burns incessantly, just as ours did. Except that you are absent. Too bad for you. Imagine the Master mingling with the sages and telling them stories—our stories." Before bidding me farewell, he added: "I am not releasing you from your oath. On the contrary. With the years, it will grow in significance. For your silence to have meaning, you must stay alive."

But what if I didn't care if my life had meaning? What if I didn't care about life at all? I owed my survival to an error. And yet, and yet. To survive by error is perhaps the equivalent of being killed by error.

Sometimes it made me laugh. Laugh until I cried. Like one possessed. I remember and I cannot forgive myself.

The little monsters. Like obscene visions, they appear out of nowhere. Impossible to hold them back. I am dreaming, I told myself. These crippled dwarfs flocking toward me, surrounding me, are not living creatures; they move only in my imagination, deranged by an old madwoman who, having glimpsed me at the inn at Rinkabar, the village of the holy fountains, had shouted: "A Just Man! A saint! I recognize him! He is endowed with powers, such powers! He is a miracle maker! Thank you, Lord, for having sent him, thank you, thank you for having pointed him out to me . . . !" The insane old hag. Known as such. Dreaded as such. She terrorized the region.

Responding to her shrieks, the villagers came storming into the inn. When I saw them head straight toward me, I feared the worst. They are going to kill me, I thought. Sender the Innkeeper apparently thought the same, for he tried to intervene. Three punches later he was on the floor. Alone, defenseless, I prepared to die. Imagine my astonishment when they grabbed me and carried me on their shoulders all the way to the asylum at the other end of the village. There they set me down in the midst of a dozen or so scrawny, resigned inmates.

"Since you make miracles," the men who had carried me explained, "go ahead! As you can see, you'll have plenty of work here!"

Off they went to bring more cripples from the surrounding villages. Soon their numbers multiplied. I was hemmed in on all sides as though a formidable hand was driving this twitching, moving mass toward me. Fifty, sixty, one hundred and twenty ageless creatures minus arms and legs fidgeted on their stretchers and rolling carts, performing grotesque circus acts. Every hopeless, incurable case of the region had converged on this spot. Wide-eyed young boys, mutilated, patched-up adolescents, bony women and girls with distorted limbs, all of them staring at me fixedly—God must have invented them in a moment of cruel fancy; they were playing with Him and He with them.

Once I was over my initial fright, I tried to go around them, then to jump over them. I almost trampled them, so anxious was I to break their hold, to escape before I lost my mind. In vain. They had blocked all avenues of retreat. In the end I stumbled and let myself fall. I remained mute, motionless. I remembered my conversations with Abrasha: every truth that shuts you in, that does not lead to others, is inhuman. Between these living wrecks who took me for a miracle maker and myself who knew my limitations, between their destiny and mine, there did exist a link, a kinship that imposed a role, not to say obligation, on me. Since I did not share their predicament, I was identifying myself with the powers that had reduced them to their condition of victims.

"Well?" the villagers were shouting outside. "Hurry up! Show them to us, your gifts! Prove to us that God is listening!"

"He's a saint!" the old madwoman was screaming. "He knows how to force the Lord's hand! Cures for our dear ones, he's the one to get them! Your requests, give him your requests!"

"My husband is paralyzed," cried a peasant woman with a black kerchief on her head. "I have five mouths to feed! Give me back the father of my children!"

"I have three," roared a giant, a horse dealer by trade. "Three small boys. They are in there, do you see them? There, with crutches! If God refuses to cure all three, let Him cure at least one!"

Meanwhile the crowds were getting larger, outside and inside the asylum. Soon the building, then the village, the river, the horizon were hidden from my view. The excited wretches used their elbows, shoved and pushed to get a closer look at me. Dazed, my head on fire, I wanted to speak, explain to them that I myself was helpless and poor, with no powers either on earth or in heaven, and that I considered myself their fellow-man, their brother, also nothing but a freak, a useless mouth. But the words were lost, dissipated in my throat. I could only look, remember and keep quiet while the monstrous bodies pressed around my own rigid body in successive waves, uttering weird,

barely human sounds. While they gesticulated and performed their dances, they eyed me not with hate, but with
curiosity and infinite seriousness. In all their lives they
had never seen a miracle maker, a Just Man, who had
taken the trouble to come to console them and intercede
on their behalf. Except for the villagers, I was the first
whole man they had ever seen. Unwittingly I was offering
them a new spectacle, heralding a probable event, holding out a possibility of hope.

I experienced a sharp, urgent need to do something,
say something, but I could control neither my muscles
nor my voice.

"He is meditating," the old hag screeched, "he is con-
centrating! Look at him! He is sending his soul to heaven!
In a moment it will be up there with your requests! Hurry
up! Entrust him with your sorrows, your suffering!
Quickly, do it quickly! Seize the opportunity, it is unique!
Quickly, quickly!"

Pandemonium ensued. Everybody yelled at once, trying
to outdo all others, trying to be heard above all others.
The scene might have been a howling contest, with life
or death as the prize.

"Blessed man, bless us."

"Reverend Sage, come to our aid! Lend us your ear!"

"A miracle! Just one! I am the mother of seven starving
little girls! Mercy!"

"Don't forget Benish! Benish the Tailor!"

"And the welldigger! Holy man, a word for the welldigger!"

"And the tax collector's widow, are you forgetting her?
The girl behind you! She's my oldest! Consumptive, that's
what she is! Have mercy, mercy!"

"He has powers," the old madwoman growled. "Let
him use them!"

"Quickly, quickly!"

"Have mercy on us!"

I do not remember at what moment I began to laugh. I was laughing and did not know it; I could not hear myself laughing. In the deafening roar one had to either join the crowd or seek refuge within oneself. Unconsciously I chose escape into laughter. I became aware of what I was doing only by the way the creatures stopped in their tracks and exchanged glances. The sound was so new to them that they received it with drawn-out, almost languid whispers, followed by prolonged and uneasy silence. Never before had these men-puppets heard human laughter; they didn't know it existed. A black glimmer lit their eyes. They were convinced I was a divine messenger; more than that, a human god who had forsaken his home to share theirs.

"More, more," they clamored. "Continue!"

"More, more!" The old madwoman was screeching, jumping up and down. "Look, look! He's laughing! The holy man is laughing! That's a good omen! Do you hear? It's a good omen! He's happy! He made them listen up there! Watch him! It's important! More, more!"

"Louder, louder!" the poor monsters bellowed, their eyes gleaming darkly, insistently.

"He's laughing! Thank you, heaven! Thank you, Lord! Thank you, ancestors! The holy man will help us, he has already helped us!"

I am dreaming, I thought. I am not here but elsewhere, I am not myself but another. I find that I cannot see what my eyes are showing me; that I cannot hear what my ears are perceiving. I dream of a dreamer who haunts my dreams. And here my goal is attained: I am present while my "I" explodes, I shall be present when it disappears. I brush against nothingness almost stealthily. And I shall penetrate the void. I am Azriel. I am not Azriel. I come face to face with his victims and I laugh. I come face to face with naked misery and I laugh. Sitting here, I contemplate injustice at its ugliest and I laugh. Suddenly I remember the features and expressions of my mad friend

Moshe. Moshe in prison. Moshe facing me. As he faced me long ago. I open my mouth to give free rein to laughter. I am dreaming your dream, Moshe. It is you who are laughing.

Then ecstasy takes hold of my audience. Bravo, bravo! More, more! Louder, louder! Whenever I stop, they protest vigorously, indignantly: More, more! And the old madwoman flings herself about, wildly shrieking: "Go on! Don't let him stop in the middle! As long as the holy man is laughing, the gates of heaven are open to him!" And the villagers yell: "Mercy, mercy!" And the cripples pick up the cry: "Yes, more, yes, mercy!" Everything is spinning inside my head, which swells and swells until it becomes a caricature. I double up with laughter when I see it. Brave, Moshe. Now I understand your teachings. In the valley of tears we are left one weapon, the last. Now I understand you. I will laugh like you. I am laughing louder and louder, louder than the noise of the mob and of the valley below, the noise of life and of heaven, I laugh with all my strength and I know that this time it is not your doing, it is mine. With my laughter I drive the living to life, the dead to oblivion. With my laughter I bring together earth and sea, hell and redemption, enigma and light, my self and its shell.

I am ashamed just thinking of it. I had transcended my own person and I did not know it.

"What is that? A diary? May I see?"

In my hands I held a thick bound notebook, the old-fashioned kind. Black cloth cover and narrow long pages. It looked like a ledger. With an abrupt, angry motion, Azriel tore it from my hands and clasped it to his chest as one might a threatened or recovered treasure. He was behaving like a father with his child, or a child with his toy.

"Don't touch that," the old man said harshly.

We had gone up to his garret; he wanted to put on warmer clothes. While changing coats, he had taken the notebook out of his pocket and laid it on the table.

Why this harshness in his voice? What was so special about this notebook? I felt an irresistible urge to know. The rest no longer mattered. My mother and her ghosts, my father and his air of resignation—there was nothing on my mind except the notebook.

I surveyed the room; it was almost bare, half monk's cell, half hotel room. A bed, a table, a chair, a tiny bed lamp, a wardrobe. In the wardrobe, a metal trunk. What does it contain? What treasures, what documents? Is it

87

locked? What does he see from his tiny window? A piece of sky, two chimney stacks towering over five roofs? How many hours a day does he stay here? With whom? To do what? My eyes wandered back to the notebook. Dimly I sensed that it contained the answer to all the mysteries surrounding his person.

"These pages intrigue you," Azriel said, nibbling at his lower lip. "That's fine. A man who searches does not kill himself . . . You want to know what they contain, don't you? All right. After all there is nothing extraordinary about the Pinkas except . . . the ending. I shall stop before."

The Pinkas: a collective work extending over many generations. The last author to consign events to its pages was Shmuel, father of Azriel, official registrar of the community. His predecessors go back to the famous chronicler Matityahu the Judge, a native of Cracow, who came to Kolvillàg to be married and found his bride-to-be drowned in blood. Matityahu described the scene and added a terse observation: "In these days exile is becoming ever harsher. To have hope in God is to have hope against God."

His successor Meir of Podoli liked to link his name to maxims. On hate: "Self-hate is more harmful than hate toward others. The latter questions man's relationship with man; the first implicates man's relationship to God." On encounter: "Man changes whenever he confronts his fellow-man, who, in turn, undergoes an essential change. Thus every encounter suggests infinity. Which means: the self is linked to infinity only through the intermediary of another self, another consciousness."

In the following century an anonymous scribe took up Matityahu's theme: "When stricken unjustly, man theoretically should have the right to decry divine justice. But knowing the value of theories, he will not use that right."

In 1851 a certain Itzhak, son of Israel, an enlightened

and literature-loving man, confided his despair to the Pinkas: *"All has been said, I can only repeat . . . In the beginning there was the word; there no longer is. We no longer say 'light' to simply name it, but to replace it; we say 'love' not because it is present, but because it is not. Every creation, on the individual level, implies a void, that is to say a gap, a sin, a failure. Doomed to repeat himself, man resorts to language for atonement."*

Twenty years later his son Israel ben Itzhak took an interest in mysticism: "The 'I' of man is the 'I' of the individual, yet the converse is not true. The first is situated in time, the second in consciousness. My mind seeks the individual, my soul flees from him. The mystic in me knows that he must fall in order to see and recognize himself; that he must touch the bottom of the abyss to aspire to the heights. The 'I' dissolves before it fulfills itself."

Two generations and fourteen pages of chronicles later, a lonely bachelor called Akiba the Sleepwalker set down an astonishing thought: "The sum of all men is not God, whereas my innermost self is."

The next pages were written in Shmuel's own handwriting. I tried to imagine him bent over the notebook, at night. Leafing through the Book, Azriel explained:

"My father loved to write, erase, erase some more, condense twenty words into a single word or preferably into a comma. Did he suffer? Surely. But he was too proud to show it. His life? Total identification with the heroes and characters of the Pinkas, *his only reading matter. Look at his legible, precise handwriting. Every sentence is definitive. He chiseled his words and fitted them like stones into a gigantic tower, until they burst apart, like so many dismembered bodies tumbling into the precipice."*

I thought: Now I know what a Pinkas *is—a precipice.*

Blackened pages, images torn from death, undelivered messages. I plunge into the whirlwind, at random I reread verdicts, indictments, anecdotes, complaints, notes taken on the spot. Now that I am old, I see them more clearly than I see myself. Here I am treading on familiar ground. I know everybody and everybody smiles and waves to me. I engage others in conversation; I communicate to them what I have acquired, I explain the inexplicable, I fear neither lies nor cunning. I understand and make myself understood, I love and am loved, and it gives me neither pride nor remorse. Here everything is simple and genuine; everything is past, unalterable. These characters have lived their quests before they transmitted them. And I? I shall take mine into the grave with me. What you have written, Father, nobody will read. What you have accomplished, Moshe, nobody will know. And it hurts me, I admit it. Ten Just Men could have saved Sodom. One man by himself can justify the hope of mankind. I learned that from you, Moshe. What is the Messiah, you said, if not man transcending his solitude in order to make his fellow-man less solitary? To turn a single human being back toward life is to prevent the destruction of the world, says the Talmud. Do something good and God up there will imitate you; do something evil and suddenly the scale will tip the other way. Let me succeed in diverting death from this boy and we shall win. Such is the nature of man, you told me: whether he celebrates joy or solitude, he does so on behalf of all men. Would you want me to end my life on a defeat? Are several decades of silence not enough for you? Release me from my oath, Moshe. My mad friend, my dead friend, give me back my freedom. I don't want to die defeated.

And I can see my father taking up the notebook from which emerges my mad friend, who winks at me as he did long ago in prison. He voices his displeasure: "Hey, what's the matter, are you letting yourself go? A man ought to control his grief, stifle it and hold his tongue. Have you forgotten? To cry when one hurts means to succumb! Don't you remember? The tears one does not shed are precious and fertile. The silent prayer is the only one heard . . ."

He has not lifted the injunction. Neither has my father. And you, do you still want to end it all? You are staring at me. Why? I suddenly find a strange resemblance between you and Yancsi, that little hoodlum who was the cause of all our woes. And what if you were he? Quickly, let me dismiss this foolish thought; you would now be as old as I. Quickly, let us turn the pages. Thank you, Moshe. Thank you for showing me the way, thank you for restraining my impulses. Don't worry. Your haunted, fiery gaze, so harsh, so impenetrable and yet so human, I carry it inside me—it is me.

Now do you understand what makes me so anxious? I am afraid to lose my mind by expressing the ineffable, by naming the unnameable. I am afraid to say that which ought to remain unsaid, that which cannot be said. I am afraid to die mad. Like my friend, long ago, over there. Like him I know that whoever sees his innermost self must perish; whoever discovers his madness goes mad. Mad with fear, mad with cold. Perhaps I already am just that. The proof? Moshe, my mad, my dead friend. I see him everywhere. Don't tell me that's normal. I know he stayed behind, dead among the dead, and yet wherever I go I find him; sometimes he is there even before me. As though he were expecting me.

It's the same for Kolvillàg, I admit. I know that little town has disappeared, dispersed with the smoke, swallowed by the flames, carried off by the enemy—yet I go on seeing it and even living in it. Destroyed by fire, Kolvillàg has become a town of fire. Except for this, it has hardly changed. I dwell there and warm myself in its blazing houses.

Madness, this vision of Kolvillàg, I admit. Madness, this tale and the tale of this tale. Sheer madness, of course. Madness if I dreamed it, madness if I survived the dream. Do you want me to tell you? Moshe is not dead, I am. And all the rest is commentary.

So go ahead, Moshe. Speak to us. Speak to us of man's distress, of the scandal of existence. Tell us why life is worth living. Explain to us why—height of injustice— misfortune must also be ugly. Tell us why, having chosen knowledge over immortality, man is subjected to the punishment of exile. Go ahead, Moshe. *You* speak, since you have sworn me to silence. Tell me why the old man in me must live while boys are drawn to their death, lured by beckoning rivers.

One day you said to me: If man speaks to God through man, that's good; if he speaks to man through God, it is not. And so I ask you, Moshe: whom are you addressing through me? Is it to express yourself that you have made me mute? Is it to take revenge? But you have already taken revenge. I am no longer who I was. Older than my body, I have forgotten what I am supposed to do down here. I listen to the sounds of a new day breaking and of night retreating. I strain my ears to hear the song of the weeping mother and her desperate son who is sinking into the slow, contagious insanity of violence and disintegration. That's all, nothing more. News items do not concern me. Sundry riots, scientific discoveries, changes of regimes here and there no longer affect me. I have seen too many.

War will never be eliminated, nor evil, nor crime. No matter what he does, man cannot win. There is nobody left to speak to but the children, the wounded children. But I feel sorry for them, so I spare them. Why sadden them? Why burden them with this weight you bequeathed to me? What is the good of dragging them into the cursed universe you have entrusted to my care? Better for them not to listen to me, to avoid me completely. I bring bad luck. Had this boy met someone else instead of me, he would be saved. Yes, I carry bad luck inside me as I would a cancer. Step aside when I pass, run. Whoever approaches me risks freezing at my touch. For I am cold, I am cold in my veins, in my guts. The way you were cold in your cell. There I was your freedom; here I am your prison. Is that why you were laughing? How you laughed! And so did I! More, more, you ordered me, louder, louder! And laughing, I left you. Laughing, I made my escape.

I remember. I gaze at the Book and I remember. Daybreak. My eyes follow the Angel of Death as he labors to level the strangely hushed town. My lips begin to whisper on their own: I don't understand, I don't understand, no, I shall never understand.

Strangely, all this horror was not without a certain beauty, a certain hallucinatory grandeur whose meaning escaped me, if meaning there was, for it turned to ashes before my eyes. There was no afterwards; I had expected as much. The dying town was taking along its secret, its survival and everything that linked it to the outside world; that too I had expected. And then I was gripped by the peculiar sensation of being present at a misunderstanding, a farce, both monstrous and inhuman. God refused to play His role and so did man. Listening intently, I thought I heard a cry for help so powerful it almost took my breath away. I felt the urge to laugh but did not dare. I clung to the tree and closed my eyes. It was then that I saw a boy who opened his. He smiled at me, gently, politely. "Don't cry, sir. Don't be sad, and above all, give up your illusions. Haven't you learned anything?"

"Who are you, boy? Where did you come from?" I asked him.

"No, no, you mustn't ask me that. Haven't you been told?"

"Who are you?" I asked again, furious because I suddenly understood that this most crucial of all questions would haunt me to the end. "Who are you and who am I? What do we have in common? What divides us and what sets us one against the other? Tell me if it is your story that lives inside me, or my own. Tell me if I must obey and whom."

"You are shouting," the boy said reproachfully. "At your age you still don't know that a man losing his temper is not a pretty sight? You should smile and make believe."

"And Kolvillàg?" said the boy, surprised. "What is it? Never heard of it."

He looked at me, annoyed. I had displeased him, I had been wrong to mention that town with its mysterious and sealed past. The boy was right. He was wise, wiser than his elder. Standing before him, on those heights overlooking the conflagration, I felt small, intimidated, lost. He had a sense of humor, that boy. He had understood that the destiny of this particular town had farcical overtones.

And you know why, Moshe. Better than I. Go ahead, speak. I beg of you, Moshe, speak. It's our only chance.

This young man must not be allowed to die because of one madman's silence, because of one madman! He mustn't be allowed to die mad. Go ahead, Moshe, open the sanctuary, open the *Pinkas*. Speak, Moshe, speak.

"Nerves," said the doctor, "that's what it is."

"The heart," insisted my mother. "Memory, conscience, the past, fate—God. I am helpless against God."

She had just spent another bad night. You could tell from her distraught features, her livid complexion.

"He comes, looks at me and goes away. I run after him, but the distance between us does not diminish. And so I shout, I scream. He stops and so do I. He waits until I am calm again, and tells me: You mustn't follow me, it is forbidden; they will not let you in. I begin to shout again, to scream, but he has already disappeared. He is angry with me, I know that he is angry with me. I shouted too late."

"Nerves," said the doctor.

"Do something," my father pleaded. "Is there nothing you can do? Nothing, really nothing? There must be something you can do. Please?"

"I shouldn't have," said my mother, looking at me from far away.

Poor child, the old man thinks. He must be helped. Moshe, you alone can pull him out of this. He thinks he can do it by abdicating. I am old and know that isn't so. Man's nature is to fight even though at every moment he is given confirmation that he will not prevail. It is man's nature to think of himself as immortal. Is that good, is that bad? Both, no doubt. It cannot be helped. "The dying man who recites his last prayer is paying respect not to death but to God," said Meir of Podoli in one of his chronicles. "Therein lies his strength and his greatness."

And then, while leafing through the Book while conversing with his mad friend, the old man understands that the young man is unwittingly helping him by putting him to the test. He is forcing him to reinvent a meaning to his quest. On the very threshold of death, the old man is still fit for battle.

He had lost sight of that. It had all become a burden, a matter of habit. He had lived too fast; he was exhausted, his sensibility blunted. With Kolvillàg as a landmark, the present seemed pallid, puerile. He had felt no want, no pain for a long time. He was neither happy nor unhappy.

Nothing surprised him, nothing offended him. Nothing moved him, nothing tempted him. Having lived inside the Book so long, he ceased to be touched by the outside world, and floundered into boredom and death.

Thank you, my boy. Thank you for disturbing me, shaking me. Thank you for crossing my path. I desperately needed you. Thank you for forcing my hand; you did it in time. Oh yes, I was living inside the closed world of memories. I liked my exile. I knew things by their names. I had lost my innocence, my need for worship that had been racking me for years. Worse, I no longer felt pain. A stranger to myself, a stranger to my own story, I was a poor participant in that of others. No more remorse, no more regrets, no more nostalgia. Nothing but indifference. A matter of age, no doubt. "May God save you not from suffering but from indifference to suffering," my friend Moshe had wished me. A wish that almost didn't come true. That is why I shall speak to you in spite of everything. Out of gratitude. I shall break my oath not only to save you but also to save myself. I may be old and weary but I am not yet dead; I want to live my own death after having lived that of Kolvillàg. And though I am older than the old men I watched being murdered, I am still capable of recalling their childhood and mine. I am still capable of borrowing their voice.

PART TWO

The Child
and the Madman

I WAS A BEAUTIFUL DAY, promising to be mild, almost warm. Clear sky, invigorating breeze. In the distance, long rows of pine trees bowing to the sun. Nearby, stone buildings and wooden cabins casting off their shadows. The familiar sights and sounds of a provincial town awakening: pails drawn from the well, animals being led to the drinking trough. First gestures, first meals, first decisions. The daily miracle was renewed; earth once again was beginning to live. Oh yes, it was going to be a peaceful day, bearing offerings, the kind that reconcile man with his fate and even with that of his fellow-man.

I was returning from the *mikvah,* where I had performed my ritual ablutions, and on my way to the House of Study to participate in the first morning service. I was sixteen years old and planned to change the world through prayer.

I was hungry and thanked God for my hunger. I was tense and feverish, and I blessed God for that fever and that tension. I rediscovered my body, as I did every morning, and resented its coming between me and myself.

101

I decided to treat my body with even greater severity; I would nourish it less, drive it harder. I customarily fasted on Mondays and Thursdays. I would now push my resistance even further. From Sunday to Friday. Following the example set by the great ascetics Moshe had taught me to revere. I wanted to resemble them, I wanted to resemble him. Impossible to elevate and enrich the soul except at the expense of the body.

Moshe was already at the *Beit-Hamidrash*. Wrapped in his tallith, his phylacteries on his forehead and left arm, he was staring into space with an intensity close to pain. He had not seen me come in. I withdrew into a corner and put on my phylacteries, picked up a volume of *Mussar* and read a few passages on things to do and not to do, on impulses to unleash or to restrain, on goals to attain or transcend, and also on agony, chastisement and the future of the illusory world men persist in wanting to conquer, embellish and possess as though they could take it along to the grave. After a while eight more worshipers filed in and we could begin the service.

At the end of the last litany a voice was heard: "Is nobody saying *Kaddish?*"

"Nobody."

That particular day none of the faithful worshipers had a dead parent to commemorate.

"Wait," said Moshe. And he began reciting the prayer for the dead. His voice was harsher, more deliberate than usual.

Now I know that I should have recognized it as an omen.

Back home, I found Rivka the maid busy in the kitchen, a rueful look on her face. Father was in his room, already at work; I caught a glimpse of him bent over the table, his Book before him.

"I have a premonition," Rivka said while pouring me hot coffee.

Rivka was forever having premonitions. When things went well, she expected the worst; when there was trouble, she radiated optimism.

"A premonition?" I said, smiling. "Another?"

"Yes."

"A bad one, I expect?"

"Very bad."

"Then why worry about it?"

In vain, I did not succeed in cheering her up. Never mind, in another hour her mood will change, I thought. It wouldn't be the first time, nor the last. Our maid was flighty, extremely unstable in matters of premonitions.

"You're making fun of me," she complained as she wiped the table. "You're wrong. I know I'm only an ignorant woman. I know my head is empty. But my heart is full . . ."

I smiled. She was telling the truth. She was kind-hearted, compassionate, warm. She had taken care of me and the house since my mother's death. I loved her. Very much.

"I know men of whom one could say the opposite, Rivka—full heads and empty hearts. I prefer you to them."

"You only say that."

"Because it is true."

"Then why do you make fun of what my heart predicts?"

She seemed vexed. I apologized and rose to go. "Will you be in a better mood when I get home?"

She shook her head, refusing to answer. Fate took it upon itself to answer in her stead.

God needs man to manifest Himself, that we know.

103

Whether to affirm His power or His mercy, He does so through man. He uses an intermediary to express Himself and an emissary to punish. We are all messengers.

The one He designated as the instrument to chastise my little town was called Yancsi—a troublesome youth who loved wine and the outdoors, animals and girls. And whatever he loved he felt compelled to hurt. When he was five he plunged a knife into his mother's arm; she was late preparing his food. When he was ten he roamed the streets at night assaulting solitary strollers. He loved to frighten, he loved to hurt.

He was not an enemy of our people, no more than of any other. He was a far greater foe of the birds, who, I remain convinced, were aware of it. They avoided him. No sooner did he appear than the sky became empty. But Yancsi pursued them, caught them, tortured them and threw their mutilated bodies into the brackish, poisoned pond.

And so when he disappeared and there was talk of murder, my first thought was: It's an act of reprisal vengeance. The birds had surely condemned him to death. Now they had carried out the sentence. Which would explain the disappearance of his corpse—the executioners had carried it away.

Unfortunately, the authorities leaned toward a less judicious explanation. For the first time in her life Rivka the maid had accurately foreseen the terrors to come. For the first time in her life her premonitions were about to take shape.

It's an old, old fable. And a foolish one at that, though it has proved its worth. So black and blinding was its baseness, that wherever it was invoked, bloodshed followed. In its aftermath, love of God turned into hate of man. A hate that fell into the same pattern everywhere, nurtured by a variety of instincts, superstitions and interests, constantly adapting itself to the requirements of the times and the environment. Nothing has changed since the first "ritual murder." Again and again the same corpse served as pretext; over and over the same child has been assassinated to provoke the same abominations.

This time there was a difference. Usually these slanderous rumors began to circulate around Easter time. And this was October. We had just finished celebrating the last of the High Holy Days, that of the Law, Simhat Torah. And then, too—there was no corpse here.

There was only the disappearance of a hoodlum, the fourteen-year-old son of a stableman. After going for an outing with the horses two weeks earlier, Yancsi had not returned home. When it was reported that the horses had been seen in a neighboring village, a cursing Dogor went to bring them back.

At first people thought of it as an escapade. What schoolboy, particularly a dunce, does not dream of running away? Surely he would show up, meekly anticipating the thrashing that Dogor, his colossus of a father, a gruff and bloodthirsty man, would not fail to give him. But Yancsi had not reappeared.

When another three or four days had elapsed without his being able to punish his son, the stableman took issue with his wife, who obviously was responsible, for without her this cursed bastard would not have come into this world, therefore would not have run away, therefore would not have caused this trouble. As the blows rained on her, bloodying her face and back, the woman began to scream so loud that for once her neighbors decided to go and have a look.

"That son of a whore," the enraged man was shouting as he trampled on his legitimate victim, who was shrieking like a madwoman. "That son of a whore has taken off! And I have to stay with his whore of a mother!"

"Leave her alone, Dogor," the neighbors tried to reason with him. "It's not the woman's fault . . . She had nothing to do with it . . ."

"Oh yes, she did, oh yes. It's all her fault. Like mother, like son. Vicious dogs, both of them! She, too, thinks of nothing but running away. I'll kill her first. The slut, the tart. I'll kill her!"

"Leave her alone, Dogor."

But Dogor, obstinately bent on his task, continued to strike his victim, aiming for her head, her belly, her hips, as though determined to kill her.

"Dogor, Dogor, good Dogor, that's enough," the neighbors pleaded. "Think of this—dead or crippled, she'll be of no use to you!"

"Let her croak! Good riddance!"

Foaming with rage, the stableman relentlessly battered her inert body. It took four peasants to subdue him.

Dogor was still struggling and swearing. "Slut, whore, tart! She and her bad seed, I should have killed them long ago!"

"May God forgive you, Dogor," said one of the neighbors. "You speak without knowing. To kill is a sin, a crime the law does not look upon lightly. You want to go to jail? To the gallows?"

"You are unjust," his spouse echoed. "You have married a woman worthy of you. No, you are the one not worthy of her. Poor woman. She is devoted to you, she works harder than you. While you are busy running from tavern to tavern, she slaves away. Poor woman. While you are rolling under the table, she takes care of your home. You should thank God for having chosen her for you."

"To hell with her!" Dogor was not to be distracted. "Her son too, to hell with him! Whores, the lot of them!"

"Your mouth and your thoughts go different ways,

106

neighbor. Fortunately for you, God hears and forgives you. Otherwise *you* would go straight to hell."

"She first! And her son with her!"

"After all . . . why are you making such a fuss? He'll be back, your son. In the end they all come home."

"Who cares! Let him appear under my roof and he'll be sure to leave feet first! I'll kill him, with my own hands I'll kill him!"

A search party went out to comb the surrounding countryside. One of three things: he had lost his way (no, he knew every footpath, every cavern); he had fallen asleep (no, nobody sleeps that long); he had been wounded by a wolf (no again; he would have wakened the dead with his cries for help). Only Yancsi could have explained the circumstances of his disappearance; and he was not to be found.

Finally the men grew weary. With not one lead to follow, they decided to give up. It was senseless to continue. At nightfall they took the road home, frustrated and bitter. They would not admit it to one another, but they were angry with Dogor for having made them waste so many hours. His offspring hadn't come home, so what? And what if he had felt the urge to run away? To build a new life for himself elsewhere, with a beautiful gypsy perhaps? You would think that Dogor was an exemplary father. Nothing could be further from the truth. Lazy, drunken, idle, evil, violent; he cared as little about his family as about theirs. The only thing that mattered to him was his belly. To make all this noise for that clod of a son he didn't even have the excuse of loving, really, he was going too far. They had no inkling, these men of Kolvillàg, that Yancsi was not just any adolescent. God had specifically chosen him to light the fire and unleash the flood. Heaven's messengers are revealed only after the fact.

Night had fallen by the time the stableman's devoted

friends reached the square in front of the church. They were about to part company, impatient to get back to the warmth of their homes. Suddenly they froze. In the silence around them, they perceived weird sounds. Not far from here, there was singing.

"The Jews," a peasant grumbled.

"Who else?" an itinerant peddler added. "Our problems are no concern of theirs. We have nothing in common with them. Enemies of the Christ, the lot."

"Always the same," the first peasant went on. "You beat them and they sing. You spit on them and they beam with joy."

"It's against us," a stableboy said. "Everything they do is directed against us. Those Jews, I know them. I've worked hard enough for them. They love to make us angry."

Meanwhile the song was wafting toward them, above them, as though coming from the mountains, bearing their mystery.

"The Christians are suffering and the Jews couldn't care less," complained one farmer. "They're having themselves a celebration. If it were one of their own, lost without a trace, they wouldn't be singing."

The priest, who had come out to get the news, thought it proper to remain moderate. "True, it's their religious holiday, but they exaggerate; they could show more discretion, more respect for our grief."

Windows were being opened. Bystanders joined the circle.

"So? Yancsi?"

"Nothing."

"And they are singing with joy!"

"What lack of respect!"

"Are you surprised? They respect nothing!"

"And nobody! They didn't even respect their own Saviour, the Christ!"

The priest, his hands clasped over his belly, seemed to be meditating out loud: "Still, it's odd . . . Very odd . . . I get the impression they are singing louder than last year. I wonder . . . if they are doing it on purpose."

"On purpose! Yes, on purpose! Certainly on purpose," several voices cried out.

"Odd," the priest continued as though talking to himself, "all this seems very odd . . ."

By now a rather considerable group had gathered around him, preparing to listen in awe, as they did on Sunday in church. Forgotten their animosity toward Dogor, forgotten their eagerness to go home. Everything is forgotten when it comes to being entertained at the expense of the Jew. One word from the priest and the synagogue would be without a single windowpane. But the priest remained silent.

It was Cuza the Woodcutter, with arms like a strangler's, who led the way by clapping his hands: "I'd give a lot to know whether by some chance their religious holiday has some connection with—with our grief." He had been on the verge of using another word, but the word "grief," used earlier by the priest, seemed to fit neatly.

"I wouldn't be too sure about them," someone volunteered. "They are capable of anything, everybody knows that."

The priest, whose experience had taught him caution— every pogrom began with this kind of talk—tried to retreat. "Brethren, brethren, you are losing your tempers . . . We have no proof. To accuse the innocent is a sin, even if they are Jews!"

"You're defending them? You, our priest!"

"Brethren, listen, I defend only the Christ and those who believe in him. But what if, by chance, the Jews were innocent in this affair?"

"Innocent? Did you say innocent? The Jews? Didn't they kill our Lord? Oh yes, they crucified him! You re-

109

peat it to us often enough. Well, having killed once, why wouldn't they kill again?"

"Don't tell me that Yancsi is Christ." The priest was smiling.

"Did I say that? Did someone suggest that? I only said that the Christ's assassins are all alike."

A weighty argument, and one the priest was unable to refute. He limited himself to a few innocuous but pious remarks about the Christian virtue of forgiving those who trespass. His appeal for moderation had an effect on these peasants, who though used to shedding Jewish blood in the name of Christ, preferred to do it with official approval. Without it, nothing would be undertaken immediately.

Finally the mob dispersed; it was late and some of the villagers had an hour's walk ahead of them. Dogor and his neighbors took the road back home, accompanied by the priest. They halted in front of the synagogue, and through the half-open windows, watched the Jews dancing and kissing the Torah, carried away by the ecstasy of their song.

"Well now," Cuza the Woodcutter grumbled. "I have one of these urges to go in, and that, I swear, would be the end of their celebration!"

"Quiet," said the priest. "No scandal, please. Nothing proves that they are guilty . . . or accomplices."

"You can see it on their faces. Just take a good look."

"I, the servant of Christ, see nothing but lost sheep."

"Ah, just let me catch one and I'll cut its throat," threatened Cuza.

"Bite your tongue," scolded the priest, getting worried. "And stop talking like that. Go home. All of you, go home. Night will bring counsel. Who knows, by morning Yancsi may very well show up. If God so desires, he will come back."

"I bet he won't," said the stableman, suddenly a grief-stricken, concerned father. "Yancsi is dead and they are alive. That's why they're so happy. And you, priest, don't tell me there is no connection. They're in the midst of celebrating the death of my son, my only son, that's what they are doing."

Dogor was drunk, as always. Usually nobody took his ravings seriously. Now, of course, one couldn't help thinking that while he was not entirely right, it could be that he was not entirely wrong. After all, he was the father of the missing boy. How was one to know whether, after all, he did not sense the truth? Unfathomable, the heart of an unhappy father.

"That's enough," the priest said with authority. "Go home, and be quick about it! Otherwise . . ."

The priest knew that he had to act decisively if he was to prevent an imminent disaster. Fortunately, he commanded respect and obedience. Dogor and his confederates, unhappy though they were, dreaded his temper too much to go against him. Grumbling unintelligibly, they left. The priest returned to his quarters, pleased with himself. He had intervened in time.

Nevertheless the very next day a campaign of rumors got under way: gossip pregnant with double meanings and insinuations. The Jews considered the story so absurd, they did not bother to deny it. How does one go about challenging antiquated lies that are insults to both intelligence and reason? Jews may sometimes know how to disarm evil, but in the face of stupidity they are helpless. And so they decided to do nothing, leaving the problem for the authorities to handle.

An inquiry was conducted. Yancsi's classmates, teachers and neighbors were interrogated. No, they knew nothing of the circumstances surrounding his disappearance. The last time the schoolboys had seen him, he had been in the midst of a fight in the playground. He had hurt three boys; there had been no provocation.

111

Three essential questions faced the investigators: Who was Yancsi's best friend? His worst enemy? Who might have wished to do away with him? They gathered the following answers: Yancsi had no friends; the entire school, teachers and pupils alike, hated him. He lied, he cheated, he stole. But no one person could have taken him on by himself. Did that mean there had been a conspiracy?

Dogor's confederates made no bones about stating their opinion of the inquiry. A waste of time. The assassins were to be found not in the school but in the synagogue; that was where the investigators should look . . .

The Jews only laughed. "Our enemies lack imagination. Really, to accuse us of ritual murder, us! In the twentieth century! Ah, if ridicule could kill, they would be their own victims . . ."

And yet, the social and emotional climate of the town was rapidly deteriorating. Jews and Christians were on their guard; they no longer talked to one another. Jewish children no longer played in the streets. One could feel the approaching storm—seething, dark and bearing evil.

The town crier, girded with the drum reserved for solemn occasions, his legs planted far apart, his mien severe and forbidding, recited the phrases he had memorized. The poor wretch could not read.

"Hear, hear, notice is given to the entire population of the town named Kolvillàg! Listen to me, all of you, listen to me with all your ears! Not to listen is to break the law! And to break the law is to oppose the will of His Majesty the King! And that is a grave offense!"

The hunchbacked dwarf was full of himself, he adored dramatic gestures, lengthy preambles. He spouted them at every street corner. The children, delighted, followed him, howling his announcements with him, before him.

These youngsters made his life miserable. Hopping about on his short legs, flushed with rage, he choked at the very thought of them. Half puppet, half clown, he preferred to perform his official duties during school hours, in front of an audience of adults.

"In the name of the Prefect, who, in turn, speaks in the name of the government, which, in turn, expresses the wishes and intentions of His Majesty, our beloved King, I have the honor of reading to you an extremely urgent appeal addressed to you and to yours. A serious event has just taken place . . ."

Yancsi, murdered. Insinuations, clues. The inquiry was following its course. No suspects, not yet. Suspicions, yes, only suspicions. The people's cooperation was solicited.

". . . We ask the honorable citizens of the town Kolvillàg," concluded the dwarf, "reading" the lower part of the scroll in a martial tone, "to do their duty, obey justice and help those in charge of public order to unmask and arrest the criminal. All this in order not to be unworthy in the eyes of His Gracious Majesty . . ."

The Christians listened and sulked. The Jews listened and shrugged their shoulders.

Father was rubbing his forehead with both hands, as though to wipe away a headache—a sure sign of anxiety.

"If people would only listen to me," he said in a mock-playful tone of voice. "I would mobilize every Jew of the region to find Yancsi."

"Do you mean that?" I asked, surprised. "Does this affair really concern us?"

"Your father always means what he says,"' Rivka interjected, "and so do I. I haven't closed an eye since the other day. I have premonitions . . ."

"A Christian child that runs away," said my father, "is of more concern to us than to his parents. We have the

113

history of our people to prove it and make us remember. If people would only listen to me, we would establish a Jewish Society for the Protection of Christian Children."

But nobody was asking for his opinion. He was only the scribe—the chronicler—of the community. His role was to listen, not to speak; to record decisions, not to make them.

On that particular evening, sitting in front of his Book, he seemed to be suffering from an unusually violent migraine. He rubbed his forehead for hours, even while he spoke of other things.

Three days later there was news. Davidov, the president of the community, had been summoned by the Prefect and informed that serious suspicions had fallen on one or more of his fellow Jews.

"Suspicions?" he growled, looking blank. "What suspicions? What and whom are you talking about?"

Davidov was in his fifties, heavy-set, squat, with an aquiline nose. His surprise was not feigned. Unquestionably, the official statement took him unawares. During the many years they had known one another, the Prefect and the rich lumber merchant, owner of sawmills scattered throughout three provinces, had maintained business relations, meaning, that when the Prefect found himself short of funds, he could count on Davidov. In return, he saw to it that the Jewish community felt more or less secure. What was troubling him now? Could he be needing money? So soon? Two months after the last payment?

"Far be it from me to implicate you personally in this distressing affair," the Prefect continued, lighting an aromatic cigarette. "I merely wanted to keep you up-to-date. It's best to be forewarned, isn't it? I am acting as a friend, and as a friend it is my duty to give you the following advice. Do all you can to help us uncover the culprit. The sooner he is caught, the better it will be. Believe me, he must be apprehended soon, before the situation gets out of hand. Tell that to your co-religionists. To shield a criminal, an assassin, is a serious crime. We are in agreement on that point, are we not?"

"You are jesting," said Davidov, incredulous. "You must be."

The Prefect usually enjoyed references to his sense of humor. "Jesting?" he replied, settling deeper into his dark red leather armchair. "No, my dear friend. I am in no mood for that. Not today. What we speak of here is murder, not comedy."

"Then . . you have decided to frighten me."

"Perhaps. Fear can be a useful tool. Fear loosens tongues. At least, that is what I am hoping. For your sake. An assassin is on the loose—yes or no? Until he has been placed under lock and key, none of you—excuse me, none of us—will be safe."

There was a scar on the Prefect's forehead, a pale, ugly scar. His eyes were like those of a fish. And Davidov thought, irrelevantly: Funny, in all the years I've known him I never noticed he had eyes like a fish.

"How much?" he whispered, leaning across the table.

The Prefect wrinkled his brow, and the scar became larger, uglier. "A great deal, my friend, a great deal. More than before. More than ever. And even at that, I am not sure that it will do much good . . ."

In a calm, detached voice, he explained the situation: fourteen denunciations had been recorded at police headquarters, mine maintaining that Yancsi's assassin was Jewish, four insinuating that the crime had a ritual motivation.

"It's stupid," the Prefect said, looking chagrined, "but I can't help it. I cannot ignore it. Especially since it represents a general state of mind."

"I don't believe my ears," said Davidov.

"That's life, my friend. It never ceases to surprise us."

"How well you put it," Davidov said, annoyed. "Life is full of surprises. Especially for the Jews."

"What you mean is that I disappoint you."

"All right," said Davidov, stiffening. "You disappoint me. I did not expect such an attitude on the part of a friend whom I considered loyal. After so many years . . ."

The Prefect abruptly rose to his feet. He arranged his tie and dryly commented: "Let us set aside our personal feelings, if you don't mind. They are not pertinent here. I am doing my duty and I strongly urge you to do the same!"

Davidov also stood up. All these years that I have known him, he thought. What an actor! He felt himself growing pale with shame, rage, and also apprehension. He understood that it was more serious than he had suspected. Never before had the Prefect spoken to him in such a hostile tone. Of course, he did lose his temper at times, especially when under the influence of alcohol, or when his spouse badgered him with her constant demands for money. But those outbursts were always quickly forgotten. He would laugh about them later and everything would be all right again. This official, impersonal tone was not a good omen. And then, those expressionless fish eyes. No, he was not jesting.

"What do you expect of me, of us?" Davidov asked glumly.

"The same that I expect from every citizen. The loyalty to the crown must be greater than the individual allegiance to a clan, to a tribe. If one of your people is withholding useful information, he would do well to hurry up and communicate it to us. Otherwise he runs the risk of seeing himself indicted. As an accessory to the crime."

"You seriously believe this fable of . . ."

"I? I only consider facts. But the people believe it. That is a fact."

"Insane! They are all insane!"

"You had best watch your language, Davidov! To call the Christians of our town insane denotes tactlessness on your part. You are living in a Christian country, must I remind you of that?"

This is really bad, thought Davidov. This is when I should be saying something true, definitive, convincing. But his head was empty. He dared not open his mouth again. He bowed imperceptibly and waited for what was yet to come.

"That's all for now," said the Prefect. "I thank you for coming." He showed his visitor to the door, and without moving his lips, whispered: "See you tonight, at your house. Lower the shades." And aloud: "Justice before everything, Mr. Davidov. It is in the Jews' interest to help justice and those who implement it."

Out on the street, Davidov inhaled the fresh air and wondered how high a ransom it would be this time.

In the next hour Davidov visited the most prominent members of the Jewish community. All were of the opinion that there was no reason to panic. The Prefect would have his money and all would be forgotten. What was the use of sounding an alert? After all, "ritual murders" were a thing of the Middle Ages. In Kolvillàg, Jews and Christians were living in harmony. People helped one another, even sent one another presents on holidays. One would have to go back four generations to find traces of any major incident dividing the two communities. Why should the situation change now?

Also, the Jews relied on another powerful ally: the Count who ruled over the town and the surrounding villages. He was an enlightened and charitable squire. His Jewish overseer, Leizerovitch, had obtained various favors from him, including the one to build, on the estate, his very own synagogue. The Count's father, of blessed memory, would have let himself be carved up for his Jews, and here is why.

One day, the story goes, he had himself announced at the Rebbe of Vozhidan's house. "Saintly man," he told him, "I have come to confide in you. It is not the devout Christian who is imploring you to intercede, it is the father, the unfortunate father of an even more unfortunate son. He is five years old, my son, my oldest, my heir. He is wasting away. Death is lying in wait, asserting its claim on him. The physicians say it is hopeless. Pray for him, I shall reward you. Pray for him, you shall not regret it."

"Why do you come to me?" the Rebbe asked gently. "You should address yourself to the priest of your own faith."

"I have, saintly man, I have. I have seen monks, ascetics, inspired healers; I have obtained blessings from the most illustrious names. I have supported many charitable works, I have lit twelve times twelve candles for our saints, I have promised to build a chapel. All in vain. You are my last resort. People admire you, they say you can work miracles," concluded the Count, embarrassed.

"They are wrong," the Rebbe said, smiling. "Only God brings about miracles. Our task is to announce them and, above all, to deserve them."

The Count insisted: "Don't send me away, holy man. Pray for my son. Even if I don't deserve it, he does. He is so young, so sick. At his age religion does not count, should not count. A five-year-old child is neither Jewish nor Christian; he is only a child who is sick. Make him live. I shall never forget it." He fell to his knees, shaken by sobs.

The Rebbe of Vozhidan made him rise. "You must not, you must not . . . God Himself doesn't want to see man on his knees, humiliated. Our tradition demands that we stand when we address Him." Then he pulled on his overcoat and reached for his cane. "You want me to pray for your ailing son. I shall do better. I shall go with you to his bedside. On one condition: that your bishop accompany us there. Together we shall pray for your child to be cured and grow strong."

When the child recovered, the bishop's gratitude was matched only by the Count's. And during their lifetime the Jews enjoyed their double protection. At the Count's death, the son inherited his title and fortune—and his father's debt. If the Jews should need his help, he would be ready. So why worry over the rantings of a few fanatics sick with hate.

For greater security, certain preventive measures were decided upon. Leizerovitch would mention the matter to the Count. The youngest of the Katzman brothers would take care of the priest; a favorable sermon the following Sunday could do no harm. Joelson would have a chat with his gentile associate, Petrescu, a well-informed, influential personality.

As for Davidov, he awaited the Prefect's visit with impatience. The latter arrived late, a heavy cloak concealing his uniform covered with decorations and gold embroidery.

"One can never be too careful," he said, removing the cloak.

That too is new, mused Davidov, nodding his agreement. "Indeed, there is no lack of gossips around here."

The visitor sat down at the table, emptied two glasses of *cuika*. "You are not angry about this morning? I had no choice. I played it well, didn't I?"

"Marvelously well," said Davidov.

"What could I do? I had to take the first step. Ready my rear guard. Act the clown. My enemies already accuse me of loving you Jews too much. Tomorrow they will call

119

me a traitor. That would be my undoing and would hardly
do you any good. I know that you agree."

The Prefect loved long introductions. Davidov let him
soliloquize. "Of course," he said as a matter of form.

The Prefect picked up the bottle, studied it attentively,
uttering small appreciative cries. "Quality brand! Confound
you, Davidov! You are a connoisseur! A true native! And
yet your ancestors had other preoccupations than drink
. . . You know how to adapt yourself, congratulations!
Well done, Davidov!"

He emptied another glass. "Congratulations, Davidov!
This stuff makes the blood boil; it would revive a
corpse. Speaking of corpses, if only I could put my hands
on Yancsi's, I'd make it fit for the military in no time
. . . Yes, but . . ."

"But what?"

"I don't . . . have my hands on him!"

"But you have the bottle, which isn't so bad. Do you
like it? Take it. And the eleven that go with it. I was just
about to offer them to you."

Cat-and-mouse play that went on until well after midnight. Determined to win, Davidov tried hard to appear
relaxed, almost carefree. I'll stay up till morning if need
be, he thought. The Prefect wants something—well, let him
say so. I have time. My wife is in bed, and so are the
children. And as for myself, I can do without sleep.

"Your cloak suits you beautifully," he said. "And with
winter around the corner . . ."

"Oh yes, it will be an awfully cold one, this winter."

"We'll have snow soon."

"Yes, we will this year. Winter is at the door."

And so they talked about everything and nothing. As
though this were a friendly visit with no purpose other
than toasting each other's health.

The Prefect was the one to capitulate. "So . . . What
do your people think . . . about the affair?"

"What affair?"

The Prefect flashed a bewildered glance at Davidov, then slapped his thighs. "You are funny, Davidov. You are clever. Not all the Jews are funny, but they are all clever. A little too much."

"What good does that do us?"

Suddenly serious, the Prefect examined his glass at length, played with it, making the pleasure last. "You are clever but blind. You feign indifference. You have made believe for so long, you don't sense danger any more. Yet it exists, believe me, Davidov. It does exist. Blood will flow and you do nothing. The sword has been unsheathed and you refuse to see it. You, for instance, have nothing else on your mind except those silly victories you are winning over me—your friend. How can a people such as yours, so educated, so mature, adopt so childish a behavior when its own fate is at stake? That is beyond me, I confess."

At last he emptied the glass in one gulp. "Could you be unconscious, friend Davidov? Could all of you have been struck blind? Don't all of you see? Don't you, Davidov, see what is hatching? Those evil, subterranean forces, can't you feel them? The vise is being tightened around you, tighter and tighter with every hour. And you claim to know nothing? The rabble is in an uproar, thirsting for vengeance, rediscovering passionate and long-dormant hates. It clamors for your blood, your death—and you go about your daily lives as though nothing were amiss? Have you no eyes to see, no ears to hear? And your celebrated sixth sense, where is it? The ground is shaking under your feet and you don't feel it? How does the most tested, most alert people on earth manage not to discern the writing on the wall? I should like to understand, Davidov. Explain it to me."

Shattered, the president of the community tried to remain casual. "Oh, you know, we are used to it. This has been going on for centuries, eternities. Our enemies are

121

numerous, so numerous that we prefer not to count them. So as not to lose hope. Or our sanity. We choose to bow and avert our heads."

"That is an understatement. When it comes to averting your heads, you certainly do avert them. I'd even venture to say that on that score, you are unbeatable. This time, though, you risk losing them."

Careful not to show any emotion, Davidov smiled and shrugged his shoulders. "Oh, we have seen worse."

"You don't believe me?" The Prefect was losing his temper. "You are making a mistake, Davidov. You will regret it, you will hate yourself for having doubted me and my warnings. You may think I am exaggerating, lying on purpose, expecting to squeeze a larger sum out of you. You are making a mistake, one that may well be your worst. Irreparable, that one. For you see, Davidov, you will be offering me more money than I have ever asked of you. Let us hope it will serve some purpose. Let us hope it will not be for naught."

Abruptly he got to his feet, slipped into his cloak and headed for the door.

"Listen, Davidov, I like you. Believe me, I am not your enemy. You have helped me for years. I owe you what one friend owes another—his presence in times of need. That is why I came tonight. Not to discuss money; I don't need any, not now. I have come to put you on guard. The people here are going mad. Yes, Davidov, you were right this morning—it is insane. I have never seen them like this. The signs do not lie; the troublemakers are preparing something. And that something has a name: pogrom. Their hatred is deadly. And all-pervasive. The storm is rumbling, Davidov, it is rumbling. Sooner or later, in a week or a month, who knows, it will break over all of you, and then may God keep you and protect you—for my help, to my great shame, will not suffice."

And without waiting for an answer, he rushed outside, into the quiet night.

That same evening the chronicler noted in his Book:

> Hoodlums have broken the windows of our main synagogue even while *Minhah* service was under way. Zelig the Brushmaker and Haskel the Porter went out into the street, sure of finding it deserted. It would not have been the first time. Urchins sometimes come to throw their pebbles and disappear. Not today. There were a dozen of them; not one took flight. There must be a connection with the Yancsi affair. A sad, dismal story. It will be discussed tomorrow by the Council. Our leaders seem serene. As for me, Shmuel son of Azriel, I admit to not sharing their optimism. Rivka's influence? I have begun to have premonitions. May I be mistaken, amen.

For the first time I attended a night session. Father had taken me along over Rivka's objections. She was constantly worrying about my frail health.

"Sleep is something one can always catch up on," my father said, cutting short the discussion.

"And if he gets sick? Who will take care of him?"

"You, of course."

"And who will take care of the house? Do you think I have four arms?"

We reassured her. We would come home early. She need not worry. Let her prepare some tea. In an hour or two we would be back.

Once outside, my father gave me instructions: "You will look, you will listen. You will remember. Try not to be noticed."

I promised to do my best. I was excited at the thought of watching my father at work. And also at being present at an unscheduled, extraordinary session of the Community Council.

All the participants were punctual. They took their seats around a rectangular table. As for me, I found myself a spot in a corner, tried not to breathe and did my best to remain invisible. As far as this assembly was concerned, I was. Nobody paid attention to me, so preoccupied were they by the impending threat which with every passing minute grew more ominous. The tension in the room became palpable. Now they believed. Not like the night before.

Each emissary made his report. Failure down the line. Neither help nor consolation. Nothing. Total isolation. One could count on nobody.

"We must expect the worst," said Leizerovitch, the Count's overseer and confidant. "Mark my words, I said the *worst*."

Leizerovitch, elegant, a pedant, had studied engineering at the University of Vienna and liked to recall it at every opportunity: "I, who have traveled all over the world . . ." It cost him visibly to admit failure.

"I who know the Count intimately, I who enjoy his complete confidence, I tell you that his refusal to grant me a personal interview—I stress personal, not business —means that a disaster is imminent. Otherwise he would not have rejected my request. This is no whim on his part. No, it is more serious than that. I must confess I am alarmed."

The youngest of the Katzman brothers, having been admitted to see the priest, was told: "I am ready to pray for the salvation of every Jewish soul, that of the murderer included." Nothing more? Nothing more.

"If the priest offers us nothing but his prayers, it is bad," said Joelson. "His prayers—let him keep those for his flock."

Joelson: pointed goatee, twinkling blue eyes, his voice thin and high, like an adolescent's.

"And Petrescu?" he was asked.

"He and I had a rather painful, not to say nauseating, talk. He advised me, in the interest of our partnership, to avoid any subject not directly related to the operation of our business."

"I don't understand anything any more," moaned Hersh the Greengrocer.

Hersh: lined face, the head of an old man. He was clasping and unclasping his fingers, unable to control his anxiety. He trembled like a hunted animal.

Then came Davidov's turn to do the summing up. "We are exposed and alone. That is clear. Our neighbors are turning away from us. Our few allies are hiding. Nothing like this has ever happened to us—I feel that no help will be forthcoming."

There was a hush. Everyone present was undoubtedly thinking about his business and social ties with the Christian community: men they had met with day after day. Of their meetings, of the words they had exchanged, nothing remained.

"And your friend the Prefect?" asked Leizerovitch.

"I saw him again an hour ago, before coming to the meeting," said Davidov. "He claims that he cannot trust his own militia. Those men would not obey him even to halt a massacre. They would probably be pleased to participate."

"I don't understand anything any more," moaned Hersh the Greengrocer, trembling. "Did the Prefect use the word . . . massacre?"

"That's not all," said Davidov.

At this point my thoughts wandered and came up with the image of Job. Whenever a witness ends the narration of an event by saying "That's not all," one is reminded of Job. Job: tragedies in succession, disasters begotten one by the other. Job: solitary grief in the face of God and man.

"The Prefect is of the opinion," continued Davidov tersely, "that any steps we might undertake in the capital would prove unproductive, useless. The die is cast. Help will come too late."

Too late, too late. Now it is the character of Isaac that I see before me. A Midrash claims that divine intervention on Mount Moriah took place too late. The appearance of the angel and the ram solved nothing. Abraham rejoined his servants, alone. Too late, too late: the leitmotif of Jewish history.

"I tried to reason with him," continued Davidov. "I was convinced that he was taking too bleak a view. When I told him so, he flew into a rage. He swore, insulted me, blasphemed. He shouted that we would all be strangled and that it would serve us right. They would drown us in our own blood, and it would serve us right. To my question as to what remained for us to do, he answered with one short sentence, cutting like the lash of a whip: 'See to it that you find me a culprit.' Without giving me time to protest, he added: 'And preferably a Jewish culprit. Nothing else would appease the beasts now.' I protested as best I could. Sheer waste. I have never seen him in such a state. 'The King himself would be unable to help you,' he shouted. 'Not even God Himself could save you any more. Nothing but the murderer, real or fake, could make a difference. I need him, do you hear? I need this murderer, and soon, otherwise I guarantee nothing, or rather, yes, I guarantee one of those pogroms, one of those massacres that will dwarf all the others in your history, that's what I guarantee!'"

As Davidov came to the end of his report, there was heavy, questioning silence. All eyes were glued to the lamp suspended from the ceiling; it seemed to flicker, ready to fall. Murderer, pogrom, massacre: harsh, definitive words. How were we to drive them away, disarm them? Their stifling presence was everywhere. Sadness had taken possession of this room, this town. One could hear the wind dancing over the roofs and through the bare trees under a sky gleaming with black, evil stars.

Finally a voice was heard whispering: "He is generous, our Prefect . . . Always ready to help us, except when we need him."

"And to think that we made him rich," another added.

"I don't understand anything any more," groaned Hersh the Greengrocer.

"A culprit! He needs a culprit! And where are we to find this murdering Jew, hmm? To please our enemies, should I begin to kill . . ."

"That's enough!" Davidov said with authority. "The Prefect is a friend! I offered him money, he refused! He sincerely wishes to help us. But he is the only one. He is our *only* ally."

He was right and they all had to admit it.

"Woe to us," said Leizerovitch. "Woe to us if our salvation hinges on one man alone, be he the most honest and most just of men."

The discussion ceased. Davidov suggested dispatching an emissary to the capital. Agreed? Agreed. Tomorrow, by the first train. Other suggestions: To telegraph the Chief Rabbi, the Governor, the King. Agreed. To issue an appeal to public opinion, stir the conscience of the nation. Agreed. Until then, who knows, they might lay their hands on Yancsi or the real assassin. To gain time had to be objective number one. Agreed? Agreed. Above the voices I could hear a pen scratching the paper: Shmuel the Chronicler, silently writing, omitting nothing of what was being said around the table. Each fulfilled his role and my father his. I was sad for all of us and proud of him . . .

The clock ticked off the hours and I wondered whether he was recording them in his Book.

Now I know that he was. We were caught in a race against the clock; time progressed and chose to be on the enemy's side, on the side of death. What were we to do? What were we to do right here, in the town? If the Prefect was right, there was nothing to be done, nothing to be attempted. If the Prefect was right on one count, he was probably right on all others. Therefore we had to accept his conclusion. Not dumb, the Prefect. Not stupid, his solution. Radical, direct, though outlandish, unthinkable, unlikely—and above all, impossible. A culprit, fine, good idea, excellent idea. But where in the world were we to find him?

In the heat of the deliberations, none of the participants had noticed an intruder, dressed in rags, who had arrived an hour earlier. Only I was aware of him crouching in his corner, motionless and tense, listening intently. It was only when he began to speak that all heads turned toward him in amazement.

"I believe I can help," he said. And after a moment's silence: "I have the solution. And also the man we need."

And the dumbfounded members of the Council discovered their savior in the person of my mad friend, Moshe.

Moshe: forty or so. Haggard. Unkempt, bushy beard. Somber, haunted eyes. Intimidating and intimidated, harmless. Subject to depressions and alternate fits of rage and enthusiasm. At such times only Leah his wife could calm him.

Moshe, my mad friend, my dear friend. I see him now. I recall his outbursts, his silences. I know now what I did not know in those days: that the relationship between

Master and disciple is as mysterious as that between father and son.

At our first meeting, after a Hasidic evening, he had asked me who I was.

"Azriel. My father is in charge of the community *Pinkas*."

"His name is Shmuel, isn't it?"

"Yes," I said, proud that my father was well known in all circles.

"You go to school?"

"Of course."

"To what purpose?"

"To learn."

"Learn what?"

"Torah," I said, growing uneasy.

"Torah is life, and life must be lived; it cannot be learned from books, between four walls."

"I thought," I said, "that Torah is more than life, since God Himself submits to its commandments . . ."

"God too must be lived, my boy. You must live Him, not study Him in books, between four walls!"

My composure was deserting me. I was lost in a labyrinth of sentences and sensations. This beggar both frightened and attracted me. Who was he? What did he want of me? I was at a loss.

He must have noticed, for he put his hand on my shoulder to reassure me. "If you promise to see only what I show you and to reveal it to no one, no one, I shall make you discover things, sublime and secret things. I'll turn you into a Jacob's ladder, such as angels in search of a mission dream of. I'll fashion you into a link with the celestial spheres, where language is made of white fire and thoughts of red fire. Do you promise?"

"Who are you?"

"Do you promise?"

I wanted to repeat my question. Instead I heard myself say: "I promise."

"You will not even tell of your promise. If you do, you will forget, you will forget me. And your language will beget oblivion, your thoughts will beget remorse."

"I promise. With all my heart I promise."

"Perfect. I need a disciple. Not even Moses could do without one. Why did I choose you? Because you have just turned thirteen, because you are innocent and have just entered the community. And then, because you are the son of Shmuel, the man responsible for the Book. I like your father. He and I are trying to attain the same goal. Only our methods differ. He takes care of the past, my domain is the future. He trusts memory, I prefer imagination. I rather like the idea of having his son as my disciple."

Strange eyes, dark and red—oddly staring, unfathomable. Eyes that went straight to the core of things, seeing nothing but their essence, tracing reflections back to their source, back to primary wonder, back to the first agreement and disagreement between the self and its conscience. I remember his eyes, I can see them still. Whoever gazed into them belonged to them, whereas they belonged only to him, and even that was not certain. Therefore, one had to take care not to expose oneself to their light; one risked being left speechless. Those were the rumors and I believed them. With Moshe, everything was possible.

"When things go badly for you," he said, "close your eyes and think of mine; when things go well, also. As for me, when I close my eyes, I see the great Mordecai, of Rubashov, who saw his Master, the Tzaddik of Karlin, who remembered the Maggid of Mezeritch . . . so, there you are, linked to the Besht, the Holy Lion of Safed, the sages and prophets . . . Your eyes gazing into mine contain the first gaze of the first man, that is to say, the light that Adam received from God, blessed be He."

Only later did I follow his advice. At the moment his words simply intrigued me. I mumbled: "May I ask you . . . ask you a question, Moshe?"

"Of course. I like questions."

"Listening to you . . . If I am to believe you, our people's history would be filled with men whose eyes are closed . . ."

"Never mind, you will understand one day. This world is not beautiful to behold. You will come to prefer the one you carry inside you."

Though I continued to attend school, from that moment on, my mind never left Moshe. My hours of leisure were spent at his side. Rivka, as usual, did not hide her displeasure: "You will get into trouble, you will become mad like him." But my father knew how to appease her: "Moshe is a madman unlike any other."

Mad like Moshe? Why not. I accepted the risk, the challenge. I went so far as to desire it. I liked to join my gaze to his and rest it on faraway heights, on limpid or ominous clouds, to order it to illuminate that which is closed to light, to search the darkness and bring back its last flickering spark. I liked to do whatever he did. I liked being silent with him as his eyes scanned the craggy mountainside. Thanks to him, like him, I fell under the spell of the inaccessible. Thanks to him, like him, I yearned to climb high, higher than any peak, higher than the clouds. I aspired to trace new paths. I hoped to influence destiny, as Moshe was influencing me. Was he—Moshe—my destiny?

I remember a whispered conversation between Moshe and a wandering beggar, no doubt an anonymous Just Man. It was late at night. The two men had met in the attic of the House of Study, where torn prayer books and discarded scholarly volumes were collected before being buried—for written works are like people: they deserve the respect due the dead. We children avoided the place. There were rumors that knowledge-thirsty ghosts congregated there to consult the yellow, ragged pages. I myself would never have gone near it had I not heard voices and recognized Moshe's. But who was in there with him? A thought chilled my blood: he was conversing with the dead! I went up the stairs. The door was ajar, enough for me to see—no, Moshe's companion was not a ghost but a *Na-venadnik* with staff and bundle. He bore a certain resemblance to my Master; their voices too were similar, almost identical.

"I know who you are."

"Who am I?"

"The one who seeks."

"And whom would I be seeking?"

"The one who seeks."

They fell silent, and I opened my eyes wider to see who would move his lips first; it was Moshe.

"There was a time when I was a wanderer like you. In a way I still am. You roam without respite, so do I. The difference between us? You are seeking because you have not yet found; I have found and yet I continue to seek."

Later, in the prison cell where I went to visit him, I asked: "Are you still seeking, Moshe?"

He lowered his head and grumbled: "As long as the heart bleeds, it seeks. And yet . . ."

"And yet?"

"The heart disappoints me; it should know."

"Know what, Moshe?"

"Man's heart is the heart of the world. Man's death reflects that of creation. That is why the Messiah will not die. He is our link to eternity."

Though I was used to his elliptical style, I did not fully understand this concept. I told him so, but he paid no attention.

"The Messiah," he went on, "the Messiah. We seek him, we pursue him. We think he is in heaven; we don't

132

know that he likes to come down disguised as a child. And yet, every man's childhood is messianic in essence. Except that today it has become a game to kill childhood. Thus it is hopeless. Even I give up."

"Why, Moshe? Why prison? Why death? Why so much resignation? Why the martyrs?"

"Why, why," he flared up. "And if I knew, would I tell you? If I die, will you die? And if the Messiah were at our gates, would man let him enter? Men, these wretches, consider that his mission is to save them from death. Wrong. He would save them from boredom, from mediocrity, the commonplaces of routine! If he calls, will you follow him? Even into prison? If he does not call, will you call him? Yes? For what? For whom? To offer him what haven, what consolation? And what if I decided not to call him? Not to be his herald?"

Moshe my mad friend, my Master with the tormented face. I have but to lower my eyes and out of deepest night he suddenly appears to claim me.

He was the town's most famous, most respected madman. The most mysterious too. There was not one home where he was not discussed, not one traveler who did not wish to meet him. Forgive the interruption, but he is the principal character of this tale. His story, not mine, deserves to be told.

An only child, he was five years old when his parents were carried away by an epidemic. He was adopted by Pessach the Tailor, and soon thereafter gave evidence of a strikingly precocious intelligence. He learned Bible and Talmud simultaneously, entered a Yeshiva, but did not stay there long: he outshone his instructors. Consorting with the great of the Hasidic movement, he befriended a few of the initiated, crossed Central Europe, stopping only wherever he found a Master worthy of himself. People predicted a career for him that would make the most illustrious envious. On his return to Kolvillàg, he was received with respect and warmth. People flattered him, showered him with honors and even gifts. Davidov, as president of the community, arranged to have a set of phylacteries sent to him from Jerusalem. Leizerovitch had cut logs delivered to his house, enough for the whole winter. People worried about his health, brought him milk, butter and freshly baked bread. Nothing was allowed to hamper the rise of his star, for his glory reflected on a grateful community. His name was pronounced as though it were a benediction.

Things went wrong when he plunged into Kabbala. Little by little his behavior changed. He became taciturn. Almost never did he visit the House of Study. When he did, he behaved strangely. He rose when everybody was seated, sat down when everybody stood. He laughed at odd times, moved his mouth without saying a word. People respected him too much to question him. Geniuses are eccentric, that is common knowledge. They let him do as he pleased. One beautiful morning he left the town and settled in the woods, to live there as a recluse. Despite the wolves and demons abounding there, he spent hours in a place known as the Bandits' Cave, which nobody else dared enter. From time to time, especially for the High Holy Days, he would wander into the town but no longer seemed to recognize its inhabitants. He confused names, barely responded to greetings.

His adoptive father was alarmed. He took him aside. "When you are absent, my son, I wonder where you are. Even when you are present, I am not sure."

Moshe looked at him, looked at him and did not answer.

"You're not saying anything, my son. Why don't you say something? Have you taken a vow of silence?"

Moshe looked at him, looked at him and shook his head: No, that was not it.

"If I were your real father, I should order you to speak, to explain your behavior. But I am not. And yet, Moshe, even if in your eyes I am not your father, in mine you are my son."

And so, in order not to grieve him, Moshe explained: "I have chosen solitude and silence. Because I had your interest at heart. It is for your good, believe me."

"I don't understand."

"You are doing well, aren't you?"

"Very well. I have never had so many customers, so many orders. But I don't see the connection. On the contrary . . ."

"On the contrary?"

"Yes . . . Lately, people look at you askance, exchange glances . . . They don't know what to think. Neither do I."

"All right, then," said Moshe. "If I live far from society, it is in order to protect it. And it is for the same reason that I remain silent. If I began to speak, people would not be pleased. I have acquired certain powers: I know how to see through masks, I see the lie hidden in every truth, I uncover what people conceal from me."

Pessach the Tailor was incredulous. He did not voice it, but he wanted some proof—powers, powers, words that are easily said . . .

"All right," said Moshe. "I'll give you proof."

"But . . . how did you know . . ."

The tailor already regretted having spoken, having suspected. He scratched his head, pulled at his beard, wiped his lips. I wanted proof, I have it. Let's not discuss it further. And yet, this is not *really* proof. Moshe is not stupid, far from it, he must have guessed, anybody would have guessed . . .

"I will tell you what you thought about this morning

135

during prayer." And he told him. "You wondered why Zanvel the Milkman has not yet paid you for the caftan he ordered for his youngest daughter's wedding."

At that, the tailor felt faint.

"And if that is not enough for you, I will remind you of the dream you had last night." And he did. "You were traveling in a luxurious coach drawn by four horses. You crossed an unfamiliar village. It was empty and you were frightened."

"Yes, yes," stammered the tailor. "I had forgotten . .".

"And if you are still not convinced, I shall reveal to you all that you have seen and done since the day you were born . . ."

"No, no," sighed Pessach, "say no more!"

Unfortunately, Moshe forgot to caution him against divulging his secret. Before the evening service had come to a close, the whole town had been informed. The news traveled from gathering to gathering, from circle to circle, from court to court; people commented, evaluated, embellished. Moshe had been a respected scholar, now he was a saint. He was not yet performing miracles, but that would come. He was already a seer; he saw the invisible, foraged the depths of the soul, delved into the very roots of consciousness, guessed and unveiled unformulated thoughts and intentions: a true Tzaddik!

There were those who suggested crowning him Rebbe. But the Hasidim protested. Rightly so. For that would have meant a break with their own Masters. Luckily for all, the idea was quickly abandoned, for Moshe would certainly have ridiculed it.

He was already the object of too many tokens of respect and affection. He was the pride of the community. People rose when he approached, interpreted every one of his gestures, anticipated his every wish. Even the Elders treated him as their superior. On Rosh Hashanah, he was assigned the choice benediction: *Maftir*. On Simhat Torah eve, he was given the best place in the procession, next to the Rebbe and the president. And why not? Kolvillàg did not have many celebrities. From the surrounding villages, people came to admire him; some simply stared at him in wonder as though he had three eyes and two mouths. With him as a center of attraction, perhaps Kolvillàg would at long last know prosperity.

The fact is that his influence was salutary. Evidently awed by his gifts, people became better, or at least made an effort. The professional preachers catigated themselves before they judged others. The merchants lied less, the grocers adjusted their scales. The butchers, the millers no longer cheated—or at least, cheated less. The beggars' lot improved; no sooner did they extend their palms than copper or silver coins were dropped in them. People decided it was better to be careful than risk public humiliation. The synagogues had never been so well attended, the officiating rabbis and cantors so respected. Satan must have been bursting with jealousy and spite: a whole town rejecting discord and sin. Never before had there been such a thing. Of course, such an accumulation of virtues is often marred by a flaw, always the same, that undermines and cancels them. When people are virtuous day after day, they tend to slide into self-righteousness and pride.

There were those in Kolvillàg who wallowed in vanity, expecting compliments and congratulations. In public, of course. Why not? Since Moshe had uncovered evil, he should recognize good as well. And just as people feared his reprimands, they now anticipated praise.

But Moshe did nothing of the kind. He refused to play the game. He exhibited the same indifference as before, remained unaffected by the change in morals. In vain did people wait for him to notice them, to smile at them. He continued not to see them.

And so the vexed townspeople vented their frustrations on the tailor.

"What a joker, your son. He made a fool of you, and you of us!"

And: "A breach of trust! We cover you with gold and you deceive us! Both of you are ingrates! Hypocrites!"

And also: "Like father, like son! Shameless liars both!"

The poor bewildered tailor was shattered. He realized his blunder, but how could he erase it from people's memory? He literally fell ill. At first he equivocated, hoping that things might work out. When this hope failed to materialize, he poured out his heart to Moshe. "I have become the laughingstock of the town. I don't dare go to services or even out on the street. People point at me, spit in my face. I don't know what hole to crawl into, where to hide my shame. I don't sleep any more, I don't eat any more. I wish I could die . . ."

Moshe listened, surprised. "What can they want of you? What do they have against you?"

The tailor, forced to confess, began to sob. "It's my fault, I know . . . I talked too much. I shouldn't have. Forgive me . . ."

Moshe forgave him everything. But that was not the end of it. The tailor was convinced that his adopted son could reverse the trend. It was so simple: all he had to do was to repeat in public the performance given in private. A demonstration for strangers. Once, just once. A few words. And the people would know that the tailor and his son were not liars.

Pessach lamented so much and so long that once again Moshe gave in to pity. He promised to save his father from derision. Yes, he would demonstrate his powers. The following Saturday. Before the reading of the Torah. Now was he satisfied? Yes, Pessach the Tailor was satisfied.

He rushed to the marketplace, from there to the ritual

baths, on to the Yeshiva, announcing everywhere that the hour of truth was at hand: he would be vindicated. The news created a sensation. The town was excited. *He* would speak at the synagogue. *He* would perform in public. What would he say? Would he keep his word? Would he rise to the occasion? The rest of that week he was the topic of conversation in every family. Opinions varied, but few were favorable. The consensus: it would be a disaster.

Moshe, my friend, I shall always remember your speech. I have read it and reread it. I often do. My farsighted father recorded it in the Book. Let us open it, shall we?

This is what took place on that particular Saturday in Kolvillàg, and what Moshe the Seer said to its assembled citizenry.

"You are forcing me to speak, very well. But I find your motives repugnant. Because I have eyes to see, you fear me. Because I see through your veils, you feel threatened and draw closer to one another. Yet God sees better and further and more clearly than I—and Him you do not fear? May He in His kindness have mercy on you. You do not deserve His love, only His compassion!"

The congregants bowed their heads as one. The Rebbe nodded his approval; he always agreed with visiting preachers. Up in the balcony, the women uttered sigh after sigh. Some cried as a matter of habit, not knowing why, nor caring.

"I leave and I come back," Moshe continued in the same sharp tone. "I sleep and I awaken, I plunge into darkness and re-emerge, leaving behind some part of me. I pray and take stock of my failings, I pray and I count my sins. And you are afraid of me. Of me? And God, where does He fit in? Are you afraid of Him? As much as of me? Do you tremble with fear lest He unmask you? No, of

139

course not. You do not fear heaven's judgment, and
I shall tell you why. Because you believe in His love.
An appeasing, reassuring concept: God is our judge
but He loves us. You cling to that comforting
thought, and that too is natural. But are you sure
of it? Yes? What makes you so certain? What makes
you think that God indeed loves you? And what if
I told you that the Creator of past and future worlds
is to be found in fear and not in mercy? In anguish
and not in grace?"

Moshe seemed transformed by passion. With his
eyes, his voice, he turned the universe upside down,
modified the relationships between words and their
meanings, between beings and the Being. All of us
present held our breath.

"And why should you fear me?" Moshe continued,
aggressive, merciless. "Because I see through your
disguises? Because I know when you go astray? As
a matter of fact, I am aware of your little schemes,
your wiles and petty machinations. You don't believe
me? You only half believe me? Never mind, I shall
prove it to you. The merchant who squandered his
father-in-law's fortune unbeknownst to the latter—
does he want me to name him? The broker who for
three months has been cheating his partner—would
he care to have me go into details? Oh yes, I know
your guilty secrets. I could expose them here and
now, and shame you, all of you without exception. I
choose not to, not to strip away all sham.

"Why such indulgence? To spare you? To keep
alive this community which without your convenient pretenses would fall apart? Perhaps. But there is
something else: I use my powers not to observe you
and even less to judge you, but to observe and
judge myself. I use them to reach the core of my
quest, to perfect my tools. For you must know that

every adventure is an inner adventure. Let one being rise above himself, free himself and attain fulfillment, and history will change its course. By working on himself, the individual influences the universe that opposes him. When I seek myself, it is for you I am seeking, for you that I walk the tightrope between splendor and oblivion, between ecstasy and damnation. Let me attain my goal and it means deliverance for us all. Let me fail and it means night and its abyss for me and me alone. My success or my failure will influence more than my own future. The powers I plan to challenge do not forgive; nobody flouts them with impunity. And so I make but one request of you, and I beseech you, for your own sake, not to reject it—let me build my work; do not encumber me with your worship or your curiosity. Do not come close to me, do not greet me. Since I assume all the risks, you have nothing to lose and everything to gain. My solitude is as essential for you as it is for me. Whoever breaks it destroys me, and all of us."

As he returned to his seat in the first row near the Ark, the entranced congregation stared into space as though in touch with a higher power that should not be disturbed. The Rebbe cleared his throat, signaling the cantor to resume the service. There was a long silence |before the faithful dared look at one another.

This is how my father concluded his entry in the Book.

Strange, but everyone heeded Moshe's request. It was as though he had ceased to exist. People pretended disinterest, and if, perchance, someone forgot and mentioned his name, people reacted by lifting a finger to their mouth.

Why? Did they really believe in his adventure and its chances of success? By acceding to his wishes, were they offering him a chance or simply a ransom in exchange for his knowing silence? Did they refrain from speaking so that he too would not speak? The fact was that both sides scrupulously respected the tacit pact.

But it was only a temporary truce, eventually broken by the community, for whom Moshe had become embarrassing, cumbersome. His presence created doubts and suspicions, made people feel ill-at-ease, their freedom diminished, threatened. They no longer dared drink, sing, laugh or let themselves go. They felt watched, imprisoned. Clearly this could not go on indefinitely. They had to act, take strong measures. No community could live in a constant state of alert and continue to function.

Nocturnal meetings were held in a neighboring village, on the other side of the mountain, in the hope of eluding the dangerous person's clairvoyance. Several dignitaries participated. These secret conferences had but one purpose, though a most arduous one to achieve: to solve the case of Moshe. The slightest false move could provoke the opposite effect. Mystics are so unpredictable. Let Moshe find out about the conspiracy and its aim, and he was capable of shouting whatever he knew from the rooftops. And since he knew everything, what was required now was patience, tact, know-how, caution—above all, caution. Ideally, one ought to have deprived this madman of his powers surreptitiously. Anyway, his messianic hallucinations had never been taken seriously, at least not as seriously as his soothsaying. What difference did it make whether redemption came a little sooner or a little later—well, of course they were in a hurry, but they knew how to wait, they were used to it. On condition, however, not to have to live side by side with a raging madman who disturbed everybody by being different. How was he to be disarmed?

They talked and talked, and at last they thought they had found a way. Since Moshe felt such a need to isolate himself, well, he should be prevented from doing so. By imposing a presence on him, he would be forced to live with constraint, if not deception. It was as simple as the blessing for bread and wine. Since he displayed such a yearning for solitude, all they had to do was take it away. In other words, he had to settle down, take a wife, start a family. Then he would learn the problems of being husband and father, and everybody would sigh with relief.

A stroke of genius, undoubtedly. Everyone agreed. One detail remained. To convince the principal involved. Clearly not an easy task. It was a well-known fact that for years the most prominent families of the region, and even of the country, had been eager to welcome him as a son-in-law. He had refused to listen to all such talk. He was offered a sky of gold, a bride as beautiful and pure as Sarah the Matriarch—to no avail. One father offered to found a special Yeshiva for him to direct—to no avail. Impossible to tempt him, to entice him. Someone invoked the first commandment of the Torah, the one that orders man to perpetuate the species. Others are taking care of it, had been his reply, I have time. Was there any way to make him relent? Perhaps by exercising pressure on Pessach the Tailor, as in the past? No, the tailor, wary and unhappy, would not cooperate, not any more. And what about a delegation of rabbis? Wasted effort. Moshe was not impressed by delegations.

In the end it was Reuven, the cynic of the group, the *bon vivant* with the fleshy, puckered lips, who volunteered: "I have an idea: pity. I'll get him with pity. Let me handle it."

Next day Reuven appeared at Moshe's. "It's wrong of me to disturb you, I know. Your time is precious, your attention sacred. It's inexcusable, but this is an urgent matter. A matter of life and death. Almost. Anyway, there is this poor girl Leah who cannot find herself a husband."

"And that is why you have pushed your way into my house?" Moshe shouted angrily. "What do you want? Money? I don't have any."

"I know, I know. Saints don't need money. But this spinster Leah, she needs it badly."

"But I don't have any! Must I repeat myself? What do you want of me?"

"A miracle."

"What?"

"A miracle, Moshe. Only a miracle can save the poor orphan."

"I do not perform miracles, and I will not! I don't believe in miracles, I don't want them! Do you hear me? Mankind is not ready nor are the times! We no longer live in the days of Moses or Elisha! Miracles and spells are meant for fools, said Mendel of Kotzk! Go away!"

Reuven feigned consternation, despair. "Then it's terrible . . . terrible . . . I don't dare think of it. A tragedy, she'll certainly do something terrible."

"What is the matter with her, this Leah, that prevents her from marrying according to the law of Moses and Israel?"

"That's just the point, Moshe. Leah, stricken by God, has nothing. And nobody."

"Never mind, I'll find a family that will adopt her, a rich Jew who will provide a dowry—and you, off with you! Out of my sight! You are disturbing me!"

Reuven did not protest, instead he put on a worried, resigned face. "Very well, Moshe, I'm leaving. I shouldn't have come, forgive me. I thought I was doing the right thing. Too bad for Leah. She should have known enough to be born into a wealthy, respectable family. She should have known enough to be born more beautiful, more graceful. Let her take it up with God. We had nothing to do with it. Why was the Creator so cruel? The fact is she is ugly, poor girl, terribly ugly . . . She repels even the matchmakers."

"Nonsense! Physical beauty? Nothing but illusion. Nothing but dust."

"Perhaps you're right, Moshe. You probably are. Unfortunately, bachelors, widowers and divorced men all like illusion. Three have fled even while the canopy was being erected, even while the rabbi was ready to intone the first hymn!"

"What! They have done that?" Moshe jumped with indignation. "They insulted, humiliated a poor defenseless orphan? They dared break her heart in public? But who are they? I shall curse them, I shall damn their souls, I . . ."

"You have to understand them," Reuven said sanctimoniously. "If you saw her, you would understand, you would be less harsh . . ."

"Never! To humiliate a poor, abandoned orphan is worse than sin, worse than crime—it is murder! Pure and simple murder! What sort of a community am I living in? Does nobody fear God? Is there nobody to decry this scandal? And take pity on this victim of heaven and earth? And that calls itself charitable and pretends to be a good Jew. That talks of generosity, compassion, and of obeying the laws of the Torah—ah, if you only knew how they despise us up there!"

And Moshe, who ordinarily could read other people's thoughts, allowed himself to fall into the trap. Blinded by compassion, he failed to see the stratagem. The seer became dupe, instrument, prey: he ended up marrying Leah.

This is what my father wrote in his Book:

It was the most astonishing, most impressive wedding in the centuries-old history of Kolvillàg. Thirty-two rabbis from nearby villages participated. The ailing

145

Tzaddik of Dolonik arranged to be carried there so as
to personally honor the bridegroom. Naturally, it was
he who recited the first of the seven blessings; the
others were distributed between the Rav of Kotchima,
the Dayan of Ramrog, the Maggid of Poritol, our
own Rebbe and Pessach the Tailor, who, under the
stress of his emotion, drenched in sweat, stammered
so incoherently that he had to repeat the blessing. For
the customary seven-day festivities they brought
musicians and minstrels from Cracow. Rebbe Zusia
of Kolomey made the long journey just to partake of
one meal. He danced with Leah, sang for Moshe; he
sang and danced one full night. I myself saw him
jump into the air and had the impression that invisible
arms were holding him aloft. He radiated happiness.
At one point, as he rested his gaze on Moshe, his
expression changed. Tears rolled down into his beard.
I feared a scene, but the groom whispered a few
words into his ear and the illustrious visitor recovered
his gaiety.

After the wedding the young couple settled in their
own house, in the street behind the cemetery. To everyone's surprise, Moshe proved to be a considerate, devoted
husband. He was no longer the same. He who had refused
himself to the world, gave himself to Leah without reser-
vation. He who had been so conscious of every wasted
minute, spent hours in her company. Never had any
woman been shown such tenderness. Determined to make
her happy, serene, he covered her with honors and praise.
He called her my queen, my Shabbat. And poor Leah,
transfigured, came back to life. She began to think of her
body without contempt or bitterness. She felt beautiful
because Moshe saw her that way. Never had there been
so grateful or so anxious a woman. She needed her hus-

band, she needed to know that he was close, very close—so as not to slip back into humiliation.

And so Moshe tried to go away less often. There were times when he would pause at the threshold, glance back at his wife—and defer his departure. At other times he would put down the book he was studying, the despair in Leah's eyes having brought him back to reality. He could gamble with his own suffering, but not with that of someone for whom suffering was not a game. He knew that nothing justifies the pain man causes another. Any messiah in whose name men are tortured can only be a false messiah. It is by diminishing evil, present and real evil, experienced evil, that one builds the city of the sun. It is by helping the person who looks at you with tears in his eyes, needing help, needing you or at least your presence, that you may attain perfection. Was his kindness the result of a deliberate decision? No one will ever know. He felt no need to explain his actions. And nobody dared ask him. People were satisfied that Reuven's maneuver had succeeded so well. Better to thank heaven and turn the page.

Except that Moshe had not turned it, not quite. Though he settled down, he avoided mediocrity. He entered madness the way one enters religion. His madness helped him to hold fast. As soon as he felt the flame go down, or its intensity diminish, he plunged back into the past. For hours on end he made speech after speech as he stood at his door or at the nearby cemetery's gates. He made the beggars at the asylum laugh and sing. He transported the urchins into the eerie kingdom of his legends. In summer he would run through the streets, shouting: "I know who it is, I know who it is." People would ask: "Who are you talking about?"—"About you, about me," he would answer and burst into laughter. Other times his lamentations were enough to break one's heart: "I know who it is, I know who it is, but he refuses, he refuses to know."—"Who refuses, Moshe?"—"He, not I, not you, but he . . ."

147

This would go on a few hours or a few weeks, particularly during the August heat waves, and then, abruptly, he became himself again, the tender husband of poor Leah into whose eyes he brought the song of sunshine in the middle of the night.

What did they live on? Leah took in laundry, washed floors in other people's houses. Moshe tutored the boys of poor families. Rich parents preferred not to entrust their children to him: what if madness were contagious?

True, Davidov had offered him a regular subsidy. He had refused, saying: "You wanted me to be a Jew like the others, and so I shall earn my bread like the others, by the sweat of my brow. But I shall give of my time to the children; it seems that they need me." Unfortunately, he turned out to be an inadequate instructor. He was too gentle, he lacked authority. The children did with him whatever they wanted. Never did he punish, never did he scold. All his pupils, even the most ignorant and noisiest, received their share of praise. Their teacher, he? Surely not. Rather, their holiday.

And then the parents decided this was leading nowhere; their children played too much and learned nothing. They took up a collection to hire a genuine tutor from an adjoining village. Out of work, with nothing to lose, Moshe took charge of one single pupil, whom he elevated to the rank of disciple.

A moment that will remain graven in my memory forever: I saw my Master smile for the first time.

He did not see me, his thoughts were drifting elsewhere, into the uninhabited spheres of the mind; he barely breathed. That I was used to. For the last year I had trudged ahead, clinging to him, hour after hour, step by step, page after page. Frequently he became impatient with my slow pace and would abandon me on the way to dash forward, overturning obstacles, brushing aside dangers. All I could do was follow him with my eyes.

But I had never seen him smile.

There were times when he wept silently, like a child baffled by misfortune. Other times he hummed a song and his very body would overflow with joy. And still at other times, he trembled with rage, his fist hammering the table or lectern as though to break not the wood but the very laws of nature, the laws that restrain the body and keep it from flying away exalted and free at last.

I had observed him so long, I had learned to interpret the meaning of his flights. When he shed tears, it was to move the Messiah's heart. When he danced, it was to persuade him. But at no time had the faintest smile ever lit his face. And so for me, it was a unique, privileged moment when I surprised him smiling.

It was winter. It was already dark outside. Leah was in the kitchen, tiptoeing so as not to distract us. An invisible hand was having fun drawing multiple icy pine trees on the windowpane. At times a rasping sound allowed me to catch the hand at work; and then I tingled with joy. It was my Master who had taught me the art of tracking down the presence in our surroundings: all is life, all is symbol. Hold your hand before your eyes and you will hide the universe; take it away and you are re-creating it. Man's secret is within himself and so is the world's. Thence the strength of their bond, the violence of their parting.

Where is he? I wondered that night. He frequently left me like that. When his soul wandered in the high mountains whose peaks are joined together in seventh heaven, Moshe saw nothing and nobody. An instant, an hour— time no longer mattered, no longer moved. When the soul breaks loose from the body's hold and rises toward its source, it forgets space and the slow plodding of the mind and pulse. It goes wherever it chooses, redescends whenever it wishes, and then, the time of a heartbeat, man resembles the half-awake prophet whose fierce and fiery eyes still retain the vision of sacred and luminous things— a vision he tries to detain, but his body rebels and reminds him of his human condition.

But I had never seen him smile before.

At a loss, I closed the book, kissed its cover; without Moshe, I could not go on. All I could do was watch him.

"He is beautiful," I heard a voice say behind me.

Leah too had been watching him. I had not noticed her leave the kitchen. How long had she been standing there, between the door and the table, staring at us with wonder in her eyes?

"He is beautiful," she repeated. "Isn't it true that he is beautiful?"

She was right. His smile made him beautiful, and that too seemed new to me. I had never thought of him in terms of beauty. Only of truth.

He had ventured onto a new path, that was clear. I had, we had, but to await his return. In silence. An evocative, protective silence. I had, we had, but to absorb it, make it our own to justify ourselves with regard to Moshe. And here he was, Moshe, at the end of silence, exhausted but happy. I felt the urge to mention it to Leah, but he was motioning me to come closer.

"I have just met my own Master," he said, "the one to whom I owe much. He lived many, many centuries before us, but I consider him my Master. He said to me: 'Like you, Moshe, I fought for truth, placed it beyond man and could not attain it; I lost my breath at the first try. You, however, will succeed; you did not know it before, now you know. That knowledge will either save you or crush you; therefore I both pity and envy you, but I should not like to be in your place.' "

Moshe was still smiling. Leah returned to the kitchen.

Once again we were alone. I became uneasy when my Master stopped smiling.

"And now," he said solemnly, "we must continue. Together. You and I. For before you didn't know. Now you know."

Davidov was shaking his head, so were the other councillors.

"You are interfering in matters that are not your concern," said the president. "We are dealing here with the authorities, not with God. Mysticism is one thing; politics, another. It is good of you to want to help. Unfortunately, you are not the man we need."

The voice of reason, of common sense. What was required was a murderer, not a martyr. What was required was a hoodlum like Yancsi, not a Kabbalist like Moshe.

"Go home," said Davidov. "Take care of Leah . . ."

Moshe was still huddled in his corner, quiet and motionless. He waited until every councillor had stated an opinion. He had not expected his proposal to gain immediate acceptance. Still, it had the advantage of being the only one.

"If somebody has a better idea," said Moshe, "I withdraw mine. If not, I maintain it."

Davidov and his colleagues exchanged glances. The argument was not without merit. Another idea? There was none. All avenues seemed closed. Sullen faces, rejections everywhere. Only the madman and his mad suggestion. How symbolic.

"But who would believe you?" someone asked.

"The enemy," said Moshe. "The fanatics will believe me. Naturally. I am just what they want, I'll make them happy."

"They'll want to know why, the motive . . ."

"That's one question madmen are exempt from answering."

"They will demand details . . . full particulars . . ."

"I'll invent. I know how. 'My imagination has never let me down."

The men were troubled, excited, desperate. Caught up in the game, they put themselves in the place of the prosecutor, raised questions and objections, tightened the examination, omitting no hypothesis, no contradiction. Moshe defended his position with extraordinary composure. His fabrication held fast. He had an answer to everything. Yancsi and his cruel games. Moshe and his fits of anger. From a madman you must expect the worst. Why not. The madman as avenger, the madman as dispenser of justice. A possible, plausible explanation. The impressed Community Council was about to give its sanction, when the Rebbe, who so far had not said anything, asked to speak.

"You are choosing the road that leads to torture, Moshe. You want to be a martyr, and I think I can guess your motives. But it is contrary to our holy Law. You know that, Moshe. You know it better than I, better than anyone. Man sanctifies life by celebrating it, by rejecting that which makes it poorer. Suicide is murder. Whoever kills himself, kills. You mean to sacrifice yourself for the community? You hope to save us by your death? No individual has the right to set himself up as judge in God's place. You, Moshe, have no right to decide that your life is worth less than mine. *Vekhai bahem*, says the Torah. *Khayekha kodmin*, orders the Talmud. You shall live your life, you shall protect it. Whoever renounces his life, rejects life, rejects Him who gives life."

Only then did the real debate begin. Passionate, stimulating. Not as before. Now they were on familiar ground. They could use quotations, precedents and decisions dating back to the Tanaim or the Gaonim. They knew which doors to open, which questions to ask, whereas before they had been groping in the dark. As though the true object of this meeting was this debate and not the other. This was the real one, the only real one.

Everyone participated. Everyone had something to say. Father had to make a considerable effort not to miss anything; he wrote fast, very fast. Someone rejected the Rebbe's condemnation of martyrdom as too extreme. What about Rabbi Yishmael and Rabbi Shimon in Roman days? Yes, but . . . And Hutzpit the Interpreter? Yes, but . . . A shrill voice: Because Pappus and Julianus, in Ludd, agreed to declare themselves guilty of a crime they did not commit, they are even dearer to God than the saints and the just. A drawling voice: Yes, but . . . It's the same. It's different. And what about the men and women who sanctified the divine Name at the time of the Crusades? After all, commented Joelson, there rest in our own cemeteries scores of pious and brave Jews whom we revere as martyrs. Could all of them have broken the Law?

"The situation is not the same," said the Rebbe, annoyed. "Martyrdom is acceptable to safeguard the Torah of Israel, and that is what our ancestors did, may their memory be a blessing. But in this case the Torah is not at stake as far as I know, it is not in danger. Is the enemy seeking to convert us? To make us kiss the cross? The threat is to the body, not the soul, not the faith. Therefore I repeat: since the circumstances do not warrant martyrdom, I order Moshe to abandon his plan."

A murmur of disapproval ran through the audience. The Rebbe was going too far; this was no time to impose his religious or legal authority. That time was past. They had to act, and act quickly. Since Moshe had decided to to provide no, to *be* the solution—why stop him? But a rabbinical decision is binding on the community. How can it be challenged without jeopardizing authority based on tradition? The obviously displeased councillors shrugged their shoulders, as if to say: Very well, Rebbe, have it your way but the responsibility will be yours.

It was Moshe who broke the ensuing silence. He rose and resolutely walked up to the table, stared into the yellowish flame of the lamp and ran his hand over his face as though to force it into a smile. "The time for discussions is over. *Eit laassot laadoshem heferu toratekha.* We must act, we must save the divine Law even if it places us in contradiction to the Law. No, the Rebbe is deluding himself. Whenever any Jew is threatened, the Torah itself is at stake. Without Jews there would be no Torah, at least not as living law. They are inextricably bound. To the extent that this community is in danger, so is the Torah. Therefore we must safeguard the one because the other has already been marked by the enemy."

He stood halfway in the light, motionless, seemingly belonging to two worlds at once, dominating the one with his words and the other with the silences between them.

"I shall go and give myself up," he continued, "and the Prefect shall have his instrument."

Whereupon the Rebbe, unable to restrain his indignation, began to shout, punctuating each sentence by pounding his fist on the table: "I forbid you! I command you! In my capacity of spiritual leader I forbid you . . . otherwise I . . ."

"For heaven's sake, don't finish your warning," countered Moshe, humble but determined. "Ordinarily I would obey, but these are not ordinary times; these are times when men like me cannot be bound to principles. Morever, I am mad, therefore free. Free not to understand, free not to submit to any will but my own."

He took a step forward, crossed his arms and his voice became pleading: "For the love of heaven and of the Jewish people, don't drive me into open rebellion; I don't wish to disobey you. Don't give me orders I could not carry out. Don't say anything I could not accept! I have made my decision, I shall not turn back. Fate is against us. Let me fight it in my own way. The very survival of this community is at stake."

He looked so vulnerable, so innocent, so sad that the Rebbe felt his anger ebb. Those present looked from one adversary to the other. They seemed so different. And here they were, staring at one another, evidently concluding a strange alliance made of complicity and compassion. At this moment they were promising one another aid and allegiance; the one offering his strength, the other his lucidity. Seeing them face to face, one forgot they were of the same age and shared the same past. Also, that one could not subsist without the other. The resignation of the one and the daring of the other reflected the same call for survival.

"You understand," said Moshe, taking a step backward toward the door, "I have been sidetracked once. This time I shall go to the end."

He made an awkward attempt at greeting the councillors and left, leaving behind, as a pledge, his immense and silent shadow.

The news struck like lightning. At the synagogue, the beadle constantly had to call for order. At the Yeshiva, the students lost themselves in endless analyses while their Talmudic Tractates remained open. Jew Street was buzzing; grocers and customers were arguing, sneering, exchanging words of indignation. The prevailing opinion was that it was all a farce. People called to one another, laughing:

"Tell us that Yancsi strangled Moshe and we believe you. But the opposite? Really, who is going to believe that?"

"A Jew capable of murder? No! Never!"

"Moshe? He wouldn't hurt a fly!"

"Even if he wanted to, he couldn't! If Yancsi but blew at him, he would be flat on his back!"

The whole thing was absurd, unthinkable. But the facts were indisputable. Moshe had appeared early that morning at the Town Hall, asking to be received by the Prefect. He had promptly been sent away by the sentry: "Hurry up and get out of here, and faster than that . . . You have the nerve to think the Prefect has nothing better to do than chat with vermin like you?"

Unprepared for this turn of events, Moshe ignored the insult and began to argue: "It's important, urgent . . . The Prefect is expecting me."

"Listen, you, do you take me for a fool?"

"It is imperative that he see me. Immediately. Even if he is busy."

"He's not here," said the sentry.

"Even if he is not here, I must see him . . ."

"Are you deaf?" roared the sentry. "I am telling you he's not here!"

"Impossible," said Moshe. "He cannot be anywhere else. Tell him . . . tell him it has to do with the murder . . . I am bringing him a vital piece of information . . ."

The sentry reacted like a true civil servant. He rid himself of the nuisance by directing him to another department: "The murder? Unless you're the corpse, it concerns the police."

Moshe had better luck at police barracks. As soon as he announced the purpose of his visit to the sentry, he was pushed into the guardroom in front of Sergeant Pavel, who, notwithstanding the early hour, was already half drunk.

"Suspicious, this Jew. Implicated in a murder. Says he has information. I thought it well . . ."

"You! Back to your post before I bury you!" the sergeant bellowed.

"I thought it well to come with . . ."

"You should have yelled, that's all! A sentry's place is outside, not inside!"

"The information he . . ."

"Information means security and security is my business and my business is not yours, understand? Get back to your post!" Then, his hands on his hips, he continued, addressing himself to Moshe: "What are you doing here? You walk into a military zone just like that? Who sent you? Why so early in the morning? You say you have information. Are you selling or buying? And for which foreign power? Hmm? In whose pay are you? And why are you undermining the security of this country, which should have cut you into pieces a long time ago, if only to render you harmless?"

A matter of habit with the sergeant: he didn't strike right away. He first worked himself into a rage, thus preparing himself a pretext. He always prefaced his blows with speeches.

Moshe waited for him to calm down. How was he to explain that there had to be a misunderstanding somewhere? That the sergeant suspected him unjustly? That he, Moshe, was certainly no spy. Only a simple murderer! Mentally, Moshe was composing a clear straightforward statement. But the sergeant was still carrying on his monologue, punctuated with curses and accusations, persuading himself that this Jew in a caftan had come to blow up first the barracks, then all the military installations of the area, then those of the whole country. It was not Moshe he was seeing but thousands of Moshes, caricatures of Jews with hooked noses and long teeth, all ready to trample on the King's sacred Fatherland, to devour the King's heroic army, to assault the King himself. Overwhelmed by this outpouring of invective, which he understood as little as the military jargon, Moshe tried to interrupt and was promptly rewarded by a resounding slap.

"You dare interrupt a sergeant of the Royal Police? You, a Jew? And in the military zone at that? Can't you see my uniform, my stripes? When I wear this uniform I represent my commander, who represents the military governor, who represents the general, who represents His Majesty the King. You dare, you nobody, to interrupt His Majesty the King?"

Moshe certainly had no thought of lacking respect for the August Sovereign. And so there no further interruptions. The sergeant was able to bring his tirade to a climax, a tirade in which Moshe and the King presently confronted one another in a historic and religious struggle of life and death, honor and sacrilege, truth and deception. The King had but one enemy: Moshe. And Moshe had but one concern: to seize the throne.

Having had his say, the sergeant suddenly calmed down. "Your turn, Jew. If you have something to say, say it fast and say it well."

Moshe breathed. At last. His statement was waiting, ready to go. "Well, it has to do with the murder . . . I must see the Prefect . . . With regard to the murder."

"What murder?" asked the sergeant, returning from the battlefield strewn with Jewish and royal corpses.

"But . . . Yancsi's murder."

Pavel was beginning to emerge from his drunken state. "Aha! You have information?"

"Yes."

"What are you waiting for? Spit it out! Well? You come, you play the clown, you waste my time—and you shut up! Speak, I tell you!"

"I know the murderer," said Moshe very calmly. "Yessir, Commander, I know him. I must add that I am the only one who knows him."

The sergeant stood there with his chest puffed out. He bristled. "Come on! You know who he is! You! A nogood Jew, a mangy dog, you succeeded where the Royal Police failed! Yancsi's assassin, you know who he is, is that right? We look for him, we carry on, mobilize all our forces to find a clue, and you, with your devil's goatee,

your warlock's eyes, you have identified, recognized and
nailed the culprit, is that it?"

"Yes," said Moshe without affectation. "That's almost
it."

The sergeant decided that the time had come to consider the matter carefully. He began to pace the office,
his chin buried in his right hand. Was it possible that a Jew
would know things the investigators did not? He circled
the room several times without ever taking his eyes off
Moshe, as though he wanted to study him from every an-
gle to decide whether to take him seriously or send him
away after a good thrashing.

"I warn you," he said. "If you are about to inform on a
Christian in order to deceive us, divert our vigilance to
protect the real culprit, you will not leave this place alive.
I know your tricks. Your treacherous swindles, your dou-
ble-dealing—I know all about them; I was not born yesterday. So be careful what you say, Jew, or else . . ." He
stamped his right foot, crushing an invisible insect under
his boot.

"The murderer is not Christian," said Moshe.

The sergeant froze, wondering whether he had not
drunk too much, after all. This Jew, a gift from heaven—
here he was denouncing one of his own. His confession
could have no other meaning. *The murderer is not Christian!* That's good. That's wonderful. That smells of trea-
son, of show trial. The murderer is Jewish, says a Jew.
Better and better. Bravo, Pavel, Sergeant Pavel. You
have unraveled a complex, obscure affair. Bravo, Lieuten-
ant Pavel. Bravo, General. We are proud of you, my son,
says His Majesty the King surrounded by his court. You
have served justice, avenged Christianity. You have un-
masked our hereditary enemies, punished the guilty—
bravo, my dear Count. Now tell us how you did it. It must
not have been easy. Jews have a reputation for helping
each other. Tribal solidarity. Common front, shoulder to

shoulder. Still, here we are; here is a Jew who states in the most natural way in the world that Yancsi's assassin is Jewish. Go and figure it out. No doubt an exception. His motive? His purpose?

"Come, Jew," said the sergeant. "Let's talk a little—you and I."

Moshe, his tallith and tephillin under his arm, let himself be pushed into the barracks courtyard and from there into the gymnasium. A faint smile played around his lips. As far as he was concerned, the matter was closed, or almost. He had played his part, done his duty. He had said everything. Another three words . . . three words and it would all be over. *I did it.* And the catastrophe would be avoided, averted. The power of words. *I did it.* One brief sentence, and the destiny of a Jewish community somewhere between the Dniepr and the Carpathian Mountains would be changed.

Pavel closed the door behind himself, went over to sit on the edge of his desk and began scrutinizing Moshe. For a long moment nothing happened. Outside, the rain had started to come down thick and fast, splashing on the red-tile roof patched with blackened metal. A horse neighed. Hurried steps in the corridor. Vaguely aware of the dull sounds coming from the courtyard and street, Moshe focused his attention on the sergeant. He saw him raise his right leg slowly, deliberately, bend it and impassively kick him in the stomach. Moshe was thrown backward but managed not to fall. The sergeant ordered him to come close again, and he obeyed without protest or delay. Another blow to the same place. Panting, Moshe tried to catch his breath. Pavel immediately started all over again. Moshe doubled up with pain but remained standing. What was he thinking about? About the strange need, the strange passion that drives certain individuals to inflict pain on others. A funny kind of game which continues into death, a funny kind of death. What does it prove, being capable of causing pain or death to others?

Moshe tried to study the sergeant's face for a clue to what it meant and what was to follow, but he saw nothing. Nothing. Neither hate nor anger. Neither thought nor passion. Nothing. Moshe could not understand the indifference with which the blows were struck. Nor could he understand the need for this exercise, since he was going to tell all! He was about to comment on that point but was not given the chance. Pavel was now on his feet, slapping him with full force. Moshe clenched his teeth as he swayed back and forth and back again, glimpsing the sergeant only through a misty, dirty veil. Moshe looked surprised, bewildered. And sad, profoundly sad. What was he thinking about? A book he had studied long ago in a Yeshiva in Galicia. A book describing the first torments experienced by the body lying in its grave. The angels and their trials. The traps. The visions of punishment. The wait. The sergeant an angel? An angel in the service of Death?

"Very well," said Pavel. He went to fetch a chair, and straddling it, sat down. "You have had the appetizer. The meal will follow."

A sadistic brute, anti-Semitic in the extreme, he sometimes demolished his victims with his bare hands. Suspects went directly from him to the hospital. And usually on a stretcher. For hard-heads he kept, locked away in a drawer, a riding crop that was not only his favorite toy but also his friend—a living and demanding creature. Pavel talked to it as a whimsical mistress to be seduced and worshiped. The angel and his fiery whip. Pavel, a part of a kingdom beyond the grave?

"We are going to listen to him nicely," said the sergeant, pulling his beloved riding crop out of its drawer. "Isn't that so, my pet? This gentleman—this dirty, stinking rogue of a Jew—is going to tell us pretty stories.

161

We love those pretty stories, don't we, my pet? Stories of blood and treachery—oh, how we love them. So then, what are you waiting for?" he taunted Moshe. "We are dying of curiosity, aren't we, my pet? Isn't it true that we are dying of impatience?"

Moshe felt a thousand needles piercing his chest. His head was bursting. Yet he did not take his bloodshot eyes off the seated figure. The sergeant was caressing his crop with both hands. Do the angel and the dead man in his grave have the same concept of divine and human justice? The problem is not as simple as I imagined, Moshe thought. I took death into account but not the executioner. That book he had read was incomplete; he would have to add his own chapter on the executioner. No, it wouldn't be so simple. Moshe looked sad and bewildered. With his tallith and tephillin under his arm, he seemed to be waiting for a sign to go and pray, meditate, study by himself, far from society, sheltered from its debasing and cruel needs. He seemed surprised that no sign was forthcoming. Could I already be in my grave? he wondered. The angel and the fiery whip. The wait. However, the executioner does not follow the victim, not into the grave. The equation is no longer the same. Not so simple, the equation.

"This gentleman is not very polite," said the sergeant. "We speak to him and he does not answer. We invite him to entertain us and he declines the honor. He lacks manners, isn't that so, my pet?"

Moshe made an effort to listen, to follow the words and remember them, and to control his breathing, his own thoughts. "There is nothing I'd like better," he said, trying to hold himself erect. "That was the purpose of my coming here. I came of my own free will. To beg you to . . . end the search. I . . . I know the murderer."

Three words . . . three words and order will be restored. But how was he to pronounce them? At what moment? In what tone of voice? How was he to present them? When the Messiah will come, said Rebbe Levi-Yitzhak of Berditchev, man will be capable of understanding not only the words but also the blank spaces of the Torah. Yes, yes, they are important, those blank spaces. Man is responsible not only for what he says, but also for what he does not say.

"He knows the murderer," said the sergeant. "Yancsi's murderer, he knows him and it is . . . Who is it?"

Moshe tried, tried with all his strength, to smile, but he failed. Much to his sorrow. It was important for him to smile at that particular moment, while answering that particular question, while stressing those particular words; three small incandescent words branded with a red-hot iron: "I did it."

It had come out a grimace, not a smile, which annoyed him. A bad omen, he was sure of it. Things would not work out only because he had not smiled while saying *I did it*, those three simple and primitive words meant to come between the executioner and his victims.

"Do you hear?" said the sergeant tenderly. "He knows the murderer, he is the murderer. Simple as A, B, C. Right, little one? He is the murderer and he knows himself."

"Indeed," said Moshe. "It was I. I did it. I can explain everything. Why. How. When. I did it . . ."

Yes, he was ready to repeat it over and over, until the very end of this affair—and life: Yes, yes, I know the murderer, naturally, since I am the murderer. He, Moshe, was prepared to make a detailed confession. Yes, he had killed Yancsi. Yes, in the forest. Not far from the river, close to where the stream becomes a noisy, deafening whirlpool. He had made fun of him, Yancsi. Always. Always without provocation. Out of sheer malice. He had insulted him, cursed him, shouted obscenities. Just like that, for nothing. For no reason, without ever a

163

response. Yancsi had thrown stones. Just like that, without motive. And that was when Moshe's blood had begun to boil. Naturally. With one jump he had caught him and with one blow of his fist he had knocked him down. Then he had struck him in the back of the neck with a rock and killed him. And then? Then he had carried and dragged the body to the river, to the spot mentioned earlier. It was dark. He was alone. A shove. Thrown in. Return to town. Dark, it was still dark. That's it, that's all. I did it.

"You see?" said the sergeant, touching the tip of the crop with his lips. "I promised you a beautiful story, here it is. You heard it and it is beautiful, isn't it, my pet? A Jew, who knows how to tell a story. Keep you in suspense. Deceive you. Bluff—a Jewish specialty. Now everything is clear. Let's go home to sleep. The case is closed, goodnight. A good Christian child has been assassinated and the assassin is here, before us, and he looks at us, looks at us ironically, thinking that he fooled us, once again. That's funny, my pet, don't you think that's funny?"

As he spoke he caressed the crop with a sensual, voluptuous, almost religious tenderness, kissing it from tip to tip, rubbing it against his puffy cheeks, his drooping mustache. His voice was quivering, cooing. Suddenly he changed tone and peered at Moshe sideways. "All right. That takes care of your fable. What about you, who are you?"

"My name is Moshe, I live . . ."

A whiplash he had not seen coming cut a channel of fire across the left side of his face. Moshe staggered. Through a haze he heard the sergeant's voice, condescending, calm, methodical.

"Whether you live in hell or elsewhere is of no concern to us, right, my pet? Anyway, Jews have no homes except temporary ones. On the other hand, what does in-

terest us a great deal is to find out who you are, who
you really are. You must not lie to us."

"I told you. I am Moshe."

This time the blow struck Moshe full force. "You are
lying, we don't like that. You are not just Moshe. That
would be too easy, too convenient. Surely you realize
you're not fooling me. Surely you have more than one
name, more than one identity, thus more than one accomplice—and don't tell me I am the one who is lying!"

That buzzing in his head, those needles in his chest.
Moshe's mind was sluggish and getting more so: Where
am I? Who am I? With whom?

"My name is Moshe and I have no accomplice," he
said.

No, dying would not be simple, he thought, wavering
back and forth. He had not foreseen such a development,
such digressions. He had counted too much on the Prefect,
who would have been only too happy to have a culprit at
last. He would not have tortured him. And now? I must
go to the end, not give in, thought Moshe. Hold out, hold
on. Repeat the same formula, a thousand times if need
be: My name is Moshe and I have no accomplice. I have
no accomplice. He did not see the crop dance over his
head before it came crashing down on his forehead.

"He is making fun of us, my pet. A Jew never operates
alone. They taught us that at school and in church. As
part of the catechism. Jews exist only in the plural. Together they plot their crimes and together they carry
them out. Together they dream of our death and hope for
our demise. Together they crucified our sweet Lord Jesus
Christ. The Christians are alone just as Christ was. He was
alone, Christ, alone and defenseless, and you killed him.
As you killed Yancsi. But you were not alone. We know
it, so why lie? We know everything. Why you murdered
him. Not for the reasons you claim. Yancsi bothered nobody. He was kindness personified, little Yancsi. Good and

innocent. You were jealous, that's why you killed him. To rob him of his blood and youth. As always. You need Christian blood to please your cruel and thirsty God. You think we don't know? We are well informed. You kill to live. You are cleansed by our blood. I know what you are hiding behind your Ark: the corpse of a Christian child. When you dance, it is around your poor victims that you dance . . ."

All the slanders, all the fables accumulated in the course of centuries seemed to be part of the sergeant's heritage. The Jews had nothing better to do than poison wells and souls, spread evil and pestilential disease, seduce Christian children and offer them in sacrifice to their Lord, who is none other than Satan. I must not listen, thought Moshe. I must not follow him. I must not absorb these senseless words. Escape. Change time and place. But not my name and not my self.

"I have no accomplice and my name is Moshe."

His broken voice was fading into the distance. Follow it? Across the courtyard, the street, the town, life. And then? Then an angel knocks at the grave and asks: Who are you? Moshe. My name is Moshe and I have no accomplice.

"Well, now he is calling us liars and imbeciles," said the sergeant without anger or sadness.

His thin, almost lipless mouth brushed against the crop before setting it gently on the table. He stood up and stretched, looked for something, didn't find it, and then, for lack of anything more suitable, grabbed a chair and brought it down on Moshe's head with such violence that Moshe collapsed, but did not let go of his ritual objects. For the sergeant this was only a prelude; he had just obtained confirmation that chairs had manifold uses and was somewhat annoyed with himself for not having guessed as much before. Very well, he would make up for lost time.

For Moshe too, sprawled on the floor, his body bleeding

and his mind on fire, this was no ordinary chair simply determined to dismember him—this was a throne, Satan's. And thousands and thousands of demons were kneeling before him. So this is it, thought Moshe. This is Satan's throne. Heavy. Crushing. My body lends it support, another dimension. Resist, I must resist. From then on he no longer felt pain. He had reached the limit, had gone beyond it. The sergeant could torture him till the day after doomsday, the pain could not increase. He had crossed the river, eluded the executioner. He had even succeeded in losing interest in him, in excluding him. Triumph of the imagination: Moshe beyond perception, free of his body, was running away in the rain and in the sun, all at once mute and singing, laughing and crying, alone and yet not alone, living in a time that was his very own. He relived certain dreams, certain encounters that had sustained him during his formative years. The lonely innkeeper whose drunkenness he shared so as to experience his downfalls and horrors. The unhappy vagabond he transformed into a preacher by teaching him three sermons suitable for every occasion. The young widow who one moonlit night appeared before him wrapped in a sheet, her eyes and lips silently, breathlessly yearning for him. He was afraid both to speak and not to speak, to look and not to look, afraid lest his voice betray him and become invitation rather than refusal. And the peasant woman who threatened to jump into the well if he, Moshe, would not promise her that she would be with child the following year. And Leah, so open and so secretive, so near yet so inaccessible in her outbursts of joy and pride.

The sergeant could trample him, lacerate him, tear him to pieces. Moshe was roaming far away, too far for the executioner to seize him. And here he is at the court of the famous Rebbe Zusia of Kolomey. A Hasid was singing and the still youthful Rebbe was saying that whosoever wished to rise, rise toward the higher spheres, had but to follow his song, a song older than the world, older than the word. "And once up there?" asked Moshe. "What happens to the song at the end of its journey?"—"It comes down again," said the Rebbe. "It sets out once more to find a voice that will give it a haven."—"And man?" asked Moshe. "What happens to man at the end of his journey?" —"He looks," said the Rebbe. "He looks below and helps others to come and join him."—"And that is enough? He does nothing but look? He does not go down himself?" At that point the Rebbe offered him something to drink and smiled. "I know what you are pursuing, I guess what is attracting you. My wish is that you may find it in fervor or in serenity and not in sorrow." Then the Hasid began to sing again and the Rebbe remarked: "Listen to him closely, for this song links us to another world; it deserves to be heard with all our being." And the sergeant was shouting in a loud, much too loud voice. The sergeant? Moshe wondered. What was a sergeant of the Royal Police doing at the home of the Rebbe of Kolomey?

"Fainted, gone, finished," grumbled Pavel, out of breath. "You see these Jews, my pet? Very disappointing, all of them. You touch them, and *pfft*, they come apart."

He opened the door and summoned an orderly, who appeared carrying a pail of water. He dunked Moshe's head into it, pulled it out, dunked it again, pulled it out. The sergeant and the Rebbe, Moshe thought. What do they have in common? Me, it's me they have in common.

"You see, my pet," the sergeant resumed with the same affectionate intonation, "they think they can escape us. Not so easy. We get them back. Always. A little water does the trick. They'll die when we are good and ready. Not before. Watch this one coming back. Slowly, slowly. We are waiting for you—come, we'll start all over again. Systematically. Methodically. Cautiously. To prevent you from slipping away. Death will not be your ally, but ours.

You will stay with us. And you will speak. We'll see to that. Then you may die. Not before."

Through swollen, puffy eyelids Moshe perceived the outline of a figure bending over him. It's Satan, he thought. That's fine. Let him stay close to me; he'll leave the others alone. As long as he is busy with me, mankind will be spared evil and pain. While he was playing with Job, Moses and his companions led their people out of Egypt toward freedom and the sun. Could suffering have a meaning, a justification? No, nothing justifies suffering. But then, how can one explain it? Except that nobody is required to explain it, only to fight it. Moshe tried to move. He could not. A frightening thought crossed his mind: If he breaks my arm, how am I going to lay tephillin tomorrow morning? Another thought superseded the first: Tomorrow? When is that? Could it be now?

"His accomplices will hand them over to us," said the sergeant. "You will see, my pet. In the end he will give them to us in such numbers that we will lack room in our prisons and fortresses. They will all end up here. Before us. Rich and poor, big and small, dead or alive, they will all fall into our hands, my pet, you'll see."

All the Jews? Moshe wondered. No, I alone. I alone in their name, in their stead. Like the Rizhiner Rebbe, I beseech the Master of the Universe: let my death be expiation. Not only for me but for the whole House of Israel.

"Well, your accomplices?"

"My name is Moshe . . . I, Moshe . . ."

He could but mumble his name. *Mo-she*. As long as I know who I am, while the sergeant does not, all is well, he thought. Let it be the opposite, and I am lost. The solution: to hold on. Hang on to the other Moshe; in spite of the blows landing on his head, his belly, his private parts. He is everywhere. Here he is at the court of Rebbe Zusia of Kolomey. He listens to the Hasid's song and to the Rebbe's exhortation to sing louder, and louder yet, and he

feels like laughing—he, Moshe, could roar with laughter.
Poor executioner, he doesn't know that his efforts are in
vain; he doesn't know that his blows are no longer effec-
tive. Moshe could laugh, laugh like a rewarded child, like
a robbed madman who has everything and nothing, who
gives everything and takes back only his laughter, a powerful, horrible laughter, a terrible and human, terribly
human laughter. Oh yes, Moshe could laugh now and tomorrow and until next year, and until death and even beyond, if only he were not afraid of offending the young
Rebbe listening and the Hasid singing tonelessly in a room
alternately somber and dazzling and somber again, and
cold, and stifling and somber . . .

He awoke much later, before nightfall and after the
rain had stopped, in an empty, dirty cell, shivering with
cold on a floor soiled with his blood.

That same night the chronicler noted in his Book:

> The Rebbe has dispatched emissaries to all the
> places of worship with mission to ascend the bimah in
> the middle of services and to proclaim a fast on be-
> half of the madman turned saint, or the saint gone
> mad.
> The situation is serious and getting worse. The de-
> mons have been awakened and are on the prowl. Will
> they be satisfied? At this moment, as I write these
> lines, Moshe is undergoing martyrdom. After him,
> whose turn will it be?
> Kolvillàg leaves history and reality to enter legend.
> Woe unto us, for that is the sign of upheaval.

The town: unrecognizable. The atmosphere: troubled,
uneasy. Jews and Christians no longer greeted one another. Strangers. Withdrawn, sullen. A town divided by an

invisible wall: mistrust. Both sides reopened wounds and grudges long forgotten, people hid behind unyielding masks. Mihai the Coachman denied his services to Yekel, the corner grocer. On his way to the slaughterhouse with his aged, scrawny cow, Stan said good morning to a Jewish cattle trader, who pretended to be deaf. A not quite awake schoolboy hurried to *heder*. A Jewish woman sent away the *Na-venadnik* knocking at her door; with his lambskin vest, his felt hat and muddy boots he did not look Jewish. Yet he was. "Oh, all right," said the woman, opening the door. "Come in, quickly. You should not be walking around by yourself." She offered him a bowl of hot milk, bread and a word of advice: "Go away, leave as soon as you can."—"But I only just arrived," he groaned. —"Too bad, too bad; you would have done better to by-pass this town . . ."

In the synagogues the worshipers abbreviated the services and went home. A traveling salesman, barely arrived, decided to take the first train out. Leave, escape. Too many rumors were making the rounds.

A visiting preacher asked the Rebbe for permission to preach the following Saturday. He was refused, for the first time in his career.

"Don't hold it against us," the Rebbe told him. "We will make it up to you. Leave by the next train. Don't wait for the end of the week. Who knows what can happen? A severe trial is beginning, how can we predict its outcome? You are here by chance, you are expected elsewhere. Go."

The threat was gathering momentum.

Curled up, his wrists and ankles bound, Moshe fought to remain awake. He tried to remember a certain melody, a liturgical piece: *I* was the one who learned that song. *I* was the one who memorized that prayer. It was I who delved deeply into this page of Midrash and that page of Zohar.

171

Thus I must maintain a keen consciousness and keep my inner self from dissipating. Prevent my body and my awareness of that body from merging. Stay on the alert. More than ever, for the stakes are higher than ever. Strain my will, triumph over my body. Listen and understand.

A faint noise on the other side of the door told him of a strange presence. Someone was watching him through the peephole; an intruding eye followed the tremors that were running through him. The eye of a fish? Of a prehistoric monster? Who was it? The sergeant with the riding crop? The orderly with the pail? The Angel of Death? Satan perhaps? Moshe, brightened by an outlandish thought, felt like sticking out his tongue. Only, that pasty tongue was filling his mouth. Impossible to move it. Besides, it's too late. Long ago, in my childhood, is when I should have stuck out my tongue. But I had no childhood.

I never played with boys my age, thought Moshe. I never shared their pastimes. The activities that thrilled them left me indifferent. Excursions, vacations, competitive sports—not for me. I lived too intensely, I grew old too fast. I don't remember having laughed one single time. Now I feel like laughing and I don't know how.

At the cost of an effort that made him dizzy, Moshe squirmed into a sitting position. His limbs were aching. He raised his hands to his eyes to open his eyelids, puffy and dirty like those of a drunkard. And now? he wondered as the door opened. In the semi-darkness he did not recognize the figure standing before him. From afar a new, amicable voice tried to make itself heard.

"I am the Prefect. I am sorry to see you in such a state. Believe me."

"I believe you," Moshe managed to say.

"I could not foresee. If somebody had told me . . ."

"I believe you."

". . . I would have made certain arrangements. Someone from the Council should have informed me."

Of course they should have. They didn't think of it. Perhaps they hadn't taken his plan seriously?

"No sense worrying about it," said the Prefect. "Too late to correct past mistakes. As for the rest, let me first of all reassure you. They will not beat you again, I promise you."

"You are kind," said Moshe. "I am not afraid of blows. Or of death either."

"What are you afraid of, Moshe?"

Moshe would have liked to answer: God, I am afraid of God—but chose not to.

"What are you afraid of, Moshe?"

"Myself, I am afraid of myself."

The Prefect opened the skylight to let in air; the glass shattered and he swore. "I am not, Moshe. I am not afraid of you. And . . . I find that amusing." He moved so as to face the prisoner, who could barely see but understood everything. "What has happened to your powers, Moshe?" he asked good-naturedly but with a trace of irritation. "It seems you had some, still do. Why don't you use them?"

Answer, how to answer? Moshe wavered. He would have liked to see the Prefect. Then he would know. But his swollen eyelids were too heavy. In his delirium he stood up, lunged and jumped: already he is far away, under different skies, his own features different; he is free, powerful and determined. Children smile at him knowingly: You say you have no accomplices—and we, what are we if not your accomplices? Old men pester him: Hurry, Moshe, we are running out of time, we are going to die. And the dead are whispering: We are waiting for you to disarm death; do you know that we go on dying? Moshe overtakes them, falls, gets up and flies away. A messenger takes him to the man in whom all men recognize themselves. Moshe shoves him with his elbow: Hurry, brother, let our time be yours. He talks to him in Hebrew and in Yiddish, his two mother tongues.

"I don't understand," said the Prefect.

"You are pretending," said Moshe. "Don't deny it. If you don't understand, we may as well tear our clothes and proclaim mourning. If you refuse to understand, it is our duty to announce the death of reason and the death of faith; in other words, the death of hope."

"I still don't understand," said the Prefect. "I should have taken along Davidov. As interpreter."

Now it was Moshe's turn not to understand. Davidov? In heaven? These two know one another? Since when? Davidov a Just Man! What a surprise!

"You are delirious," said the Prefect. "This brute of a Pavel does not do things halfway. I should like to help you. What do you need?"

"Nothing, nothing any more."

"Are you sure?"

"Yes. No. I am not sure of anything any more . . . except my powers."

He confessed: Yes, he has certain powers. Yes, he is capable of breaking all chains, of demolishing all jails, of punishing all jailers. With a single invocation he could overwhelm the sergeant. With a single formula the whip would scorch its master's fingers. One look would be enough to send the executioner to his knees. But Moshe will do nothing. One performs miracles for others. Not for oneself.

And with those words he held up his wrists, and the Prefect untied them.

"Thank you, thank you so much. I shall be able to put on my phylacteries first thing tomorrow morning. Is it tomorrow? What time is it? How long ago did the sun rise?"

"It is dark outside, Moshe."

"Since when?"

"A few hours."

"I haven't said my evening prayers. I must wash my

hands." Feverishly he bent over his hands without seeing them. Turning his head in all directions like a thirsty man searching for water, he babbled: "For the prayers . . . water . . . Not to drink . . . for the prayers."

Moshe could live without drinking. But not without praying.

"I shall see to it," said the Prefect.

"Thank you, with all my heart, thank you."

Thank you for the freedom, thank you for the promise. Thank you for cutting the bonds, thank you for the warmth, the help, the illusions, the images. Moshe feels a profound, an immeasurable gratitude toward the visitor and toward the entire world. Thank you, mankind. Thank you, hell. Thank you, Lord, for causing me to be born in this town, in the midst of this community, in this generation. Thank you for having made my path cross that of your living instruments. At the end of every experience, including suffering, there is gratitude. What is man? A cry of gratitude.

"You will eat and you will feel better," said the Prefect.

"Thank you, thank you."

Eat? He? Moshe is not hungry, he has never been hungry. Moshe could live without food. No, that's not a miracle. He could live without miracles. He could not live at all. The Talmud says that every birth is a mistake, and that it would have been better for man not to be a part of creation. But because . . . Yes, because. Because he does live, he sanctifies life. Because he does work, he justifies his own plan. Because he does sing, he corrects the divine outline. Yes, because. Because all this *is*, he says thank you. Because of it all, in spite of it all. Thank you, God. Thank you for having conferred these gifts, these faculties on me. Thus I can say: I, Moshe. Or else: You, God. You, man. You, world. You, Death. Ultimately the self increases its powers, it does not let them erode. Thus I can speak while laughing, laugh while keeping silent, keep silent while screaming, live while dying and see myself without seeing.

"Trust me," said the Prefect. "I shall take care of everything."

"Thank you, thank you."

Is there a prayer for prayers? If not, it should be invented. Leah told him one day: "I am grateful to you not only for what you do and what you are, but also for what I am. I am grateful to you for that very gratitude." And Moshe answered her: "I like what you just said but you must never say it again." And Leah understood. At the end of the word there is silence, at the end of silence there is the gaze.

A little water, Leah. For the prayers. Not to drink. Moshe was not thirsty. His throat was dry, his chest was ravaged, but he could do without drinking, and it did not even surprise him.

In the next world, that of unique truth, the soul steeps itself in the river of the red flames before it reaches the brook of the white flames. Thence, the angel Matatron leads it to the Celestial Tribunal, where it is asked: From what spring did you drink? With whom did you share your thirst and your water? And the soul answers: I am alone, I have no accomplice, I can do without drinking.

"Moshe," said the Prefect, "I'd like to ask you a question."

Questions, more questions. Is it the same in heaven? Evidently yes. Thus there will never be an end! No sooner is the grave sealed than an angel comes and knocks: You there, the deceased, tell me your name and that of your mother. If he remembers, he may enter the world of the dead. Three days later the interrogation resumes: Have you been honest in the performance of your trade? Have you lived in the expectation of the Messiah? What have you done with your life, with your solitude?

"I am alone, I have no accomplice," said Moshe, and his jaw was set. "Stop asking me questions, that's enough!"

Up above, facing the Tribunal, a soul may decide to challenge the questioner: You have questions? So do I. And mine are as good as yours. And then the angels, led by Matatron, cry sadly: Wretched soul, you are blaspheming, you are incurring eternal damnation. As for the Judge, He recommends clemency: Let them bring me The Book, let them consult The Law. Every situation is listed. Virtues and sins, punishments and rewards; everything is spelled out. The Law encompasses every human category: the just and the miscreants, the ascetics and the fools, the liars and the patrons, the misers and the poor who ridicule avariciousness.

But the madmen? What is the fate of madmen in heaven? Look well, the Judge commands, check it closely; I want a precise and thorough examination. The embarrassed scholars and specialists throw themselves into The Book and its commentaries, then into the commentaries on the commentaries. They are shamefaced, for the result is nil. The madman's fate has not been foreseen up above. Moses is summoned and so are the prophets and their disciples, and so are Rabbi Yohanan ben Zakkai, Rabbi Akiba, Rabbi Yishmael and Rabbi Yehuda. They question Rabbi Yitzhak, the Lion of Safed: And the madmen, didn't you think of them? Is it possible? Well, yes, so it seems. Nobody thought of the madmen. Meanwhile the mad soul, the rebellious soul awaits the long-delayed verdict. An angel—Matatron? he again?—dares to suggest a kind of solution, a compromise: all the Tribunal has to do is to solemnly proclaim that the madman is not mad. A wise solution that the court would be inclined to view as

equitable were it not rejected by the soul protesting vehe-
mently: During my earthly existence I claimed my madness as my own, I accepted it, I made it my home—what
right have you to deny it now?

Two members of the Court seize the opportunity to
shift the debate onto a strictly judicial plane, but the
Judge interrupts them and addresses Himself to the soul at
once responsible and irresponsible for the uproar: Your
argument is valid; true madmen are as worthy as true
saints. What counts is the weight of truth in man. Still,
considering the special aspects of your situation, for
which, as a result of a regrettable omission, no precedent
exists, I am forced to send you back into the world of the
living. Applause in the hall. Next case? No, not so fast. The
soul protests once more: You may send back only that
sinner who must expiate this violation or that transgression
of the Law; you have nothing to reproach me for; madmen
move inside a system all their own, where they alone can
pass judgment. The Judge deliberates at length and reiter-
ates the verdict: You must go back down, we have no
choice, neither you nor we. But this is unfair, cries the
soul, this is illegal! Indeed, says the Judge, but there is
no other solution . . . if you insist on maintaining
your status of madman. And then, the soul has an
idea: Very well, it says, I am going down again, but
on one condition—that I be granted permission, every
time I consider it appropriate, to remind you that injustice
reigns even in heaven!

"What is happening to you is unjust," said the Prefect.
"Martyrdom is always a result of injustice."

"What difference does it make?" Moshe was becoming
annoyed. "Even God is unable to solve this problem."

An unsatisfactory reply, he knows that: God has nothing to do with it. God is God and man is not human. The
strength of the one does not necessarily apply to the other.

God cannot help but be, but find, but win. Man cannot help but lose, but seek, but die, but live his death.

"Make an effort, Moshe," said the Prefect. "Try to listen to me well. Try to answer. Do you hear me?"

"I hear you."

He would have liked to see too. A curtain of flames separated him from the Prefect. At times he would catch a glimpse of a figure folding and unfolding its arms.

"You are sacrificing yourself," said the Prefect. "That is beautiful, even commendable. And foolish too. Are you certain it will serve its purpose? I confess that I am not. I respect you and admire you. And I feel sorry for you. You see, I no longer know whether this will stop the wolves from howling."

The pain. Here it came again. It struck his temples, his chest. Only now will I suffer, thought Moshe. Yet he must not allow himself to collapse. "Don't you remember?" he shouted. "They wanted a culprit, and now they have one!"

"Will it be enough? That is the question."

"What more can they want?"

"More culprits."

Only now am I really going to ache, Moshe thought. My head, my heart, only now are they going to burst. Hold fast? What for? Speak? Convince? "I am alone, I said that. I have no accomplice, I said that too. I am solely responsible, I said that. I have said nothing else. I have incriminated no one. What do you want of me—what else? Haven't I done enough?"

"More than enough. But events are overwhelming us. The wolves are howling and the prey seems slight to them. They are voracious, these wolves from around here, they want bigger game."

Moshe was listening, conscious of his failing strength. He did not even try to repress the sob forming in his chest. "This is unjust, terribly unjust. This was your idea, wasn't it? You gave it to Davidov, didn't you? Davidov informed

179

the Council . . . you needed a culprit—just one—and preferably a Jewish one, didn't you?"

"I don't deny it. The idea was mine, I thought it was good. It was meant to help me gain time. Unfortunately, I am like you in this affair: alone and without accomplices. And the mob across the street is growing by the hour. Once it starts to move, nothing will hold it back."

For the first time since his arrest—that morning? only that morning?—Moshe experienced total, all-encompassing pain, overflowing and reaching into his consciousness. Thinking was as painful as breathing, as moving, as speaking. "The mob, you, me. What do you mean? That the ordeal is useless? My sacrifice in vain? That I am of no use living or dead? I am sent back and forth from one world to the other, from one role to the other—and every time it's for nothing? Is that what you mean?"

There was such sorrow, such despair in his voice that the Prefect, moved more than ever, leaned over him. He touched his shoulder and said reassuringly: "Nothing is lost as yet, the game is not over . . ."

But Moshe stopped him. "The truth, I demand the truth, I deserve it! I don't want to be soothed or pitied. I want the truth, only the truth!"

The Prefect came closer, and at last Moshe could see him: his eyes, his chin, his high forehead. Anguish mingled with kindness. The Prefect meanwhile stood in the semi-darkness contemplating that bundle of flesh that wanted, that demanded. The truth. Which truth? The mob's or the prey's? The truth of the living or the truth of the dead? He smiled weakly.

"Very well, Moshe. I have too high a regard for you to lie to you or spare you. You want to know everything? All right. The situation is bad. The beast is baring its fangs. The mob is screaming about plots and ritual murder. I fear the worst—I fear a pogrom. When? No idea. In a day, a week. A little more, a little less. The capital has been alerted, but it turns a deaf ear. The militia will not obey me. How can I protect you? You can count on no one. Let us hope that God remains on your side. He seems to be your only hope."

"Hope?" said Moshe. "Don't speak to me of hope."

The pain crept over his skin, penetrated his flesh, his bones, touched the exposed nerves and transmitted a series of tremors of blinding force and violence to his brain. He had never guessed that he could feel such pain. Thus, at the end of pain, there waited greater, more intense, more naked pain.

The Prefect gone, Moshe cowered in a corner, as though to offer the enemy the smallest possible surface. Then he lay down on the ground, half rose, lay down again. It was no use. There was no shelter anywhere.

To restore circulation in his fingers, he tried to run them through his beard. Impossible. The blood had dried. His beard was as hard and cold as stone.

"Woe unto me, wretched mother that I am! They have murdered him, those degenerates, they have killed him, those enemies of Christ. I feel it, I know it, my body tells it to me, my heart repeats it, I swear it. I swear it on the head of our Saviour. My little boy, my lamb. So sweet, so gentle, so respectful. Always ready to help me in the fields, at the stable. Mothers of this town, grieve with me . . ."

The stableman's wife was lamenting from morning till night, mostly in public, acting out to perfection the role of mourning mother. She roamed the streets, the market-place, arousing wrath, indignation, the instincts for vengeance.

"Woe to the poor mother of this poor martyr. Yes, he is a martyr, my lamb. He died for Christ, my little one. Killed by their common enemy. Christ has taken him back to heaven, body and soul . . ."

181

So as better to be heard, she stood in front of the church, wrapped in her black shawl, and harangued the passers-by. Her husband, meanwhile, was at home drinking himself into a stupor.

"You who suffer for the Saviour's holy mother, weep for me . . ."

The priest, shrewd and extremely punctilious in matters relating to Christian history, thought it best to appease her: "Don't say that, my child."

"Why shouldn't I? I'm suffering!"

"I understand your sorrow, woman. But please leave Christ alone!"

"Leave him alone? Did they leave him alone? And my only son, my lamb, did they leave him alone?"

"Have you been drinking? Or have you taken leave of your senses? You dare pronounce Christ's name and that of your worthless offspring in the same breath?"

"If my son were not a Christian, they would not have killed him, right? So am I not entitled to shout that they murdered him because of Christ?"

The priest grabbed her by the shoulders and tried to take her home, but she wouldn't let him. Finally, seeing them holding on to one another, one was left with the impression that they were visiting the public places together and for the same purpose.

"We have sent out appeals," Davidov said calmly. "There has been no response. The various steps we've taken have been in vain. Friends cannot be reached, associates pretend disbelief."

In the course of the day the president had been admitted to see the Count. He had reminded him of the kindnesses and promises of his father, who had considered himself indebted to the Jews. Now that the latter lived in fear, they were requesting his hereditary protection. Any sign of friendship on his part would be helpful. A determined stand could result in a complete turnabout of the situation. Well? Would he follow in his father's footsteps? The question, which remained in suspense, marked the end of his plea.

The Count had listened patiently, courteously; they had drunk a toast. But in the end he had limited himself to advising the Jews of Kolvillàg against seeing the situation in too bleak a light. "I find your pessimism disconcerting," he had remarked good-naturedly. "You try so hard to prevent disaster, you end up provoking it. What an odd people you are."

"You reproach us for our pessimism, Your Excellency. Others find fault with our optimism. In fact, we are the most optimistic and the most pessimistic people in the world. A matter of perspective: we are long-range optimists, but pessimists for the immediate future. History has proved us right in both instances."

The castle, situated on Uncle George's Hill, dominated the villages of the valley. From the window overlooking the forest one could see the pointed steeple of Kolvillàg's church in the distance.

"Let us remain in the present," the Count had said, comfortably settled in an armchair covered with yellow and orange tapestry interwoven with blue. "A Jew admits to having killed a young Christian. If one were to believe you, you are about to be taken to the slaughterhouse, all of you, to the last man."

"Moshe is not guilty. He has killed nobody. Nobody has killed."

"Not guilty? But hasn't he confessed . . ."

"The poor man is mad. Raving mad. He aspires to martyrdom: to suffer and die in style, in holocaust."

"One does not exclude the other. Homicidal lunatics are not uncommon."

183

"Moshe is not mad like the others. If you knew him . . ."

"I wouldn't mind . . . But it's too late for that, or am I wrong? Perhaps after the tribunal has ruled on his case. You tell me he is innocent, and I would like to believe you. But then he has nothing to fear. And neither do you. He will be tried and acquitted. You see? You cannot keep yourself from painting too dark a picture."

Having made his point, he had accompanied the visitor to his coach waiting in the courtyard.

"I am petrified" was Leizerovitch's comment. "I know him and I can interpret his most insignificant statements. Now I understand why he has refused to see me. It all makes sense. He can't use rhetoric on me. I know him too well."

"Let's call a spade a spade," Yossel the representative of the Young Workers cried out. "The Count is lying. He is lying like a horse trader five minutes before closing time. He is in cahoots with the mob. Under the knightly mask hides the grimacing face of the assassin."

Davidov motioned to my father. "This comment of our friend Yossel will have to be softened somewhat."

"What?" My father was indignant. "Distort the truth? Falsify testimony?"

My conscientious father seemed outraged. I was watching him proudly from my corner.

"Suppose the Book falls into *their* hands?"

"They wouldn't understand a word."

"Proceed," said Davidov, resigned.

The Council had been in session since early afternoon. The threat of a pogrom seemed imminent.

It was Wednesday, market day. The town was swarming with peasants whose eyes gleamed as they stared at the

Jewish merchants and paid without haggling over prices. They stifled their sneers whenever a Jewish woman of proud bearing strolled by. There was something in the air, a kind of foreboding. The woodcutters with their axes, the farm hands with their pitchforks, the forest wardens with their rifles—one would have had to be blind not to catch their significance. Old peasant women crossed themselves at the sight of an old Hasid with the face of an ancient prophet. A bloodbath was in the making, a celebration of death.

"What do you think of it, friend Meltzer?" asked Davidov.

The man he thus addressed, a *shtadlan*, a middleman by profession, had arrived the night before from Raibaram, the town where he lived. He had a reputation for dealing with the most diverse authorities, and so Davidov had entrusted him with an eleventh-hour rescue mission.

"What I think of it?" he said, shrugging his shoulders. "Not much good. In fact, I have decided to go home. I feel that there is nothing I can do. A wall—I feel I am up against a wall. This is the first time this has ever happened to me. I contacted some of my most reliable people. Some owe me their fortune, others their career, others still consider me their intimate friend. Make them talk, I tried to make them talk. They all dodged my questions and reacted with nothing but surprise, skepticism and outrage. Nobody knew what I was talking about. Protestations of loyalty, of comradeship. Each assured me of his devotion. Comedians, the lot. I tried my luck with some of the underlings, I sneaked them a few bills; they gave them back. I insisted, I doubled the sums; nothing helped. And yet they certainly do need money, I am in a good position to know. Wasted effort. Mouths are clamped shut, palms are closed. Their way of being honest, of serving me notice,

185

warning? Their way of telling me that things are bad? That since they cannot be of service to me, they do not deserve a fee? How is one to know. I can only repeat: it looks bad, bad. I am going home with a heavy heart."

The chronicler stopped writing. His head was bent over the Book, his right hand was rubbing his temples; his migraine was giving him no respite. Outside, the wind was rasping in the trees, sweeping the windowpanes. Dumbfounded by Meltzer's report, the councillors were staring into space. The only sounds to be heard were the agitated, jerky breathing of old Gimpel on the verge of an asthma attack and the irritating tick-tock of the old clock.

"Thank you for your trouble, friend Meltzer," said Davidov. "In your opinion, what should be our next step?"

"To prepare yourselves, prepare yourselves for the worst."

He stood up and walked around the table, shaking hands.

"Go in peace, friend Meltzer," said Davidov. "Our wishes accompany you."

With Meltzer gone and Davidov seated again, the session resumed.

"Do any of you have contacts with the underworld?" Davidov asked with mock amusement. And more seriously: "It is sometimes easier to find an honest man among horse thieves, in taverns of ill-repute, among hardened criminals than in so-called respectable circles."

Somebody forced a laugh, and my father, without a word, scrupulously recorded it in his thick notebook. His heart was pounding hard, harder than during the *Kol Nidre* service. And strangely, he heard an obscure voice ordering him to record that too.

At the other end of town an eternally bereaved widow, Shifra the Mourner, opened the black gates of the ceme-

tery and headed straight for her husband's grave. In spite
of the strong wind, she succeeded in lighting a funeral
candle. She set it down on the ground, then burst into sobs.

"You there, up above, come to our rescue. Move the
heavens and those who dwell in them. Appeal to our ancestors, to the Just Men you have known and to the saints
you have served. Tell them in your own words that we
have been left to our fate. Tell them of our anguish. Let
them be our interpreters with God, blessed be He, so that
He may receive our prayers. Let them ask Him if He will
be proud, if He will be happy to learn that the Jewish
community of Kolvillàg—yours, theirs—no longer exists.
Let them ask Him if it is His will, His glory to reign over a
town without Jews, a world without Jews, a world peopled
with killers . . ."

Stretched out on the grave, the old woman was weeping
with even greater sorrow than at the funeral of her husband, the *dayan* who had had the good fortune, the saintly
man, of dying in his bed.

Within the walls of the House of Study, lit by a row of
candles, the faithful gathered behind Rebbe Levi-Yitzhak,
a nephew of Rebbe Zusia of Kolomey by marriage and a
great-grandson of the Great Maggid of Premishlan. The
Rebbe was concluding the *Minhah* service. It was still
early.

Ordinarily people met at dusk and in lesser numbers.
But this was a special occasion; the new scrolls of the
Law, whose transcription had been commissioned by Reb
Sholem, the richest Hasid at the Rebbe's court, were ar-
riving that very evening. Decided upon a long time ago,
the celebration had excited the congregation. This kind of
inaugural festivity was stimulating and rare. And yet, the
times being what they were, would it not be advisable to
announce a postponement of a few days?

187

After services Reb Sholem could be seen whispering, consulting the Rebbe, who, looking concerned but determined, was shaking his head no.

"The celebration will take place as planned," proclaimed Reb Sholem. "We may not offend the Torah. We shall keep the appointment but we will advance it by two hours."

When the Rebbe opened the door to return to his private quarters, the wind swept in and blew out all the candles but one.

For Shaike, leader of the militant youth, there was no question of preparing for a religious "wedding," but for a battle. He had gathered fifty or so members in the school hall that served as their meeting place. This is what he had to say: "Our leaders' policies are bankrupt and they admit it. The authorities no longer sell indulgences, they can no longer be bought, they no longer play at being benefactors. I say it's for the best. Gone the era of hypocrisy, gone the era of illusions. Now we know the score. And so does Davidov."

He was employed by the president, who loved to tease him about his revolutionary ideas. Gone, the time for teasing.

Shaike, a dynamic and muscular young man with fiery eyes, had gone through an apprenticeship in a vacation colony and had come back stuffed with ideology. A certain segment of the youth followed him. They liked the meetings, the singing, the dancing, the dreaming. They loved to recall the splendor of Galilee and of Jerusalem.

"We are going to fight," said Shaike, who was not adverse to grandiloquence. "The hour of truth has struck. The time for self-defense has come. It will be a difficult, heroic struggle. The chances of victory are slim, but history commands us to try, not to win."

"Pure suicide," someone in the last row was heard to mumble.

"Possibly," Shaike retorted. "No, probably. No, certainly. What are the alternatives? To let ourselves be slaughtered like sheep, or to die with weapons in our hands. Perish as martyrs, or fall as heroes. Two categories, two extreme points of view in which our history abounds. With nothing in between."

Sitting on benches, the boys and girls, the latter a minority, looked more like well-behaved, interested schoolchildren than like warriors. An algebra problem covered the blackboard. Through dirty, dusty windowpanes one could see three poplars, a tall one and two small ones, their stiff branches stretched over the empty playground as if to watch over it.

"Davidov and his colleagues consider us scatterbrains," said Shaike. "They had better keep quiet now; their methods have failed. Let's try ours. No more bargaining. No more servility. Gone, all ambiguity. Since the enemy is sharpening his sword, we shall forge our own. This pogrom will be unlike any other!"

Words—the impotence of words. Inadequate but indispensable to fight a battle. Shaike used them not so much to win as to win over. Many of the members present had once occupied these very same benches. This was where they had studied history, grammar, geography. Now they were listening to him talking of pogroms.

"But we are not armed," a voice objected. "This sword you mentioned—where will you find it?"

Many objections were raised: they lacked training, they were too few. If only we had more time, thought Shaike. We could learn to manufacture bombs in the manner of anarchists. But they lacked everything, including time. They had nothing but words:

"We have nothing? Never mind. We are not soldiers? Never mind. And what about Jewish honor? And Jewish history? And Jewish dignity? Do they count for nothing? We have no weapons? We shall fight without weapons. With planks and clubs, hatchets and iron bars, stones and bricks. We lack training? We shall acquire it in battle. We shall resist the attack, we shall not submit. We shall no longer be passive onlookers. If die we must, let us die standing, in the open air, not in cellars with the rats. With dignity, not resignation!"

Was it the speaker's enthusiasm or his listeners' naïveté? The atmosphere had changed. The ambivalence of words: helpless against the enemy, all-powerful for us. These boys and girls were transfigured; they saw themselves as disciples of the young General Bar-Kochba, occupying the Judean mountains, erupting into the legend of their people.

Then Shaike confronted them with this superb biblical challenge: "If among you there is one who is afraid, let him go home."

They were all afraid, but none dared to admit it. Their first victory was over fear. Tasting his first triumph, Shaike gave orders: pass the word, be on the ready, close the shutters, lock the doors, erect barricades, transform every dwelling into a fortress, make the assassins' task both difficult and costly.

"Now go. Give the alarm. Tell your friends and neighbors. We shall fight for them, for them too. Let them lend their support. Tell them what we expect from them. Let them open their eyes, let them stay awake. Let them be prepared. Go, tell your community that it is about to live an extraordinary moment—it has an appointment with history."

They all obeyed. They were afraid, but they obeyed. They dispersed, alone and in groups of two or three. Projected length of the operation: an hour, or two. Family, neighbors, friends to inform, to forewarn. These heralds of rebellion descended on the community, spreading dismay

—delivered their message and withdrew. People listened to them without understanding, without really hearing them. Some were petrified, speechless; others began to weep. A pogrom? In the twentieth century? Here? What exactly did that mean? A massacre? Like in the Middle Ages? Had nothing changed then since Chmelnitzki? But then what was the use of defending oneself?

Shaike was the last to go out into the courtyard. He went down the street toward his parents' house. After a few steps he stopped, turned back and went to the Kreiners', where his fiancée Piroshka was staying.

He had the odd sensation of walking in an unfamiliar street where all the footsteps were his own.

The cell was dark. Airless. A streak of blue light filtered through the bars in the skylight, glided over a large pail of water in the corner, played with the dust in the twilight shadows.

Moshe was sitting on the floor. He seemed feverish, his shoulders shaking with every breath he took.

"Peace be with you," said my father, placing a bowl of hot soup and a paper bag bulging with fruit on the wet ground.

The prisoner lifted his head in my direction. "So you thought it right to bring along my young companion? You did well."

"He insisted."

"He did well."

The man who stirred me more than anyone in the world was unrecognizable. His clothes were rags, his body seemed dislocated, patched, his arms and legs disconnected. His eyes and lips only by chance part of the same face, which itself was nothing but a mask shattered into a thousand fragments where nothing moved, nothing indicated life. A chilling thought crossed my mind: This was not Moshe,

191

this was an imposter! How could I be sure? Ask him for a sign? We would have to be alone.

My father cleared his throat and went about his duties as chronicler. "Aren't you afraid people will say that Jews are murderers?"

"Why do you want to know?"

"To understand you. And then to write it down."

"And what if you don't understand?"

"I'll write it, anyway. It is my duty to record everything, to transmit everything. Even that which lies beyond my understanding."

Moshe thought for a moment. I tried to intercept his gaze. In vain. Noises from the outside were distracting me: the sentry's steps marching back and forth, a horse neighing, a drunkard's cry. Life was continuing on the other side but not at the same rhythm. Was it the same life?

"No, people will not say that Jews are murderers. They will say that one Jew, mad to boot, turned murderer. They will blame the act on my insanity and you will all be cleared."

He had spoken with impressive calm. In my mind I had not yet resolved the problem of his identity. He could be anyone.

"What about me?" I asked. "What is my role in all this?"

He stiffened. The mask fell apart around his lips. He was about to answer, changed his mind. He opened his mouth several times, but said nothing. I felt the weight of his gaze.

"What about me, your disciple?" I continued. "Am I to follow you? To the end? Am I to succeed you? Or perhaps repudiate you? Forget you?"

Torn between discretion and his duties—as a father, as a chronicler—my father coughed into the palm of his hand, as he did whenever he was confused, undecided, embarrassed.

"In prison the Master is no longer free to teach by example. Therefore, he is no longer Master," said Moshe, his voice almost severe.

This is someone else, I thought, this is not his voice. This harshness, this certainty are not his.

"And Rabbi Akiba?" I asked with a touch of disrespect, if not anger.

Akiba, one of the martyrs in Roman times, taught till the end of his life. While he was in jail his students would wander back and forth outside, pretending to converse among themselves, and they would ask him questions on Talmudic law, thus outwitting the guards. And the Master would answer.

"No connection," said Moshe. "Besides . . ."

This is an imposter, I thought. Moshe had taught me that nothing in Jewish tradition was unconnected. In Jewish history everything is linked. The sacrifice of Isaac and the destruction of the Temple and the successive pogroms all over the Ukraine and Poland. Akiba was closer to Moshe or to me than I am to myself.

"Besides," continued Moshe, "I am not yet Rabbi Akiba."

He had said "not yet." My father could not repress a shiver. Rabbi Akiba: symbol of accepted, invoked, inspired suffering. His torture in the marketplace was the longest and the most cruel.

"Any regrets?" my father asked.

To that same question, asked by an adversary or an admirer, Rabbi Akiba had answered: No, on the contrary, this is the ordeal—and also the end—that I have wanted all my life.

"Why do you want to know?" asked Moshe.

"To record and to safeguard. For the sake of history. Aren't we the people of memory? Is oblivion not the worst of curses? A deed transmitted is a victory snatched from death. A witness who refuses to testify is a false witness. As for me, I do not refuse; on the contrary, I do nothing else, I yearn to do nothing else."

Moshe shook his head before he answered: "I don't mean to discourage you, but I don't believe in the written word; I never did. The words pronounced at Sinai are known. Perhaps even too well. They have been distorted, exploited. Not the silence, though it was communicated from atop that same mountain. As for me, I like that silence, transmitted only among the initiated like a secret tradition that eludes language. But even more, I believe in the other tradition, the one whose very existence is a secret. A secret that dies and relives each time it is received, each time it is invoked. Only the Messiah can speak of it without betrayal. Remains to be seen whether he will speak at all."

Was that the sign? Not recognizing his voice? Broken, hoarse, it did not carry the words but let itself be carried by them. It rose and fell and rose again but did not register inside me. Obstacle rather than link—could this be Moshe's voice? I compared it to the one still reverberating inside my memory. No, no resemblance.

"I imagine," said my father, "that by choosing total sacrifice you intend to lend greater meaning to your death than to your life. Am I mistaken?"

He was stubborn, my father, his obstinacy close to indiscretion. He sometimes hurt people's feelings with his compulsion to find out everything, consign everything to paper. Never mind if people were annoyed, antagonized or hurt. Professional conscience pushed to the extreme? A sublimated, outrageously magnified sense of duty? His zeal either angered people or made them smile. Recalling him now, his son also smiles and more than at that time. Poor historian! How could he have guessed that his labors would be in vain? He was the last of a line, yet his testimony would be forbidden, as would the mention of that interdiction. How could he have known that he was attributing to his mission a future it no longer possessed? That his project, at this very moment, contained its own negation? My poor chronicler of a father, how could he have imagined that, supreme irony, the idea of a *Herem* had only just taken root in Moshe's mind and that he himself was contributing to it to a considerable degree?

Telling of it now, his son is smiling, cannot help but smile. He was too tenacious, the chronicler.

"You ought to answer me, Moshe," he said gently but firmly. "Think of the future generations. Of the yet-to-be-born children. Don't you wish to take part in their destiny? Live through them? In them?"

The prisoner seemed to be irritated by these words. I could not be sure. Later, during his speech to the community gathered inside the synagogue, I knew I had been right.

"If you don't answer," continued my father, "I shall write down that you could not or would not answer. Even that is important."

And in spite of the prisoner's reticence, he kept insisting. Was Moshe aware of the prominent role of the witness in Jewish tradition? Even God needs him. The Bible tells us so and the Talmud confirms it: "If you shall be my witness, I shall be your God; if you shall refuse that role, I shall refuse mine." The anguish of the witness facing history; his obsession not to depart without having scarred a single consciousness or ripped a single veil. His reward: thanks to him, past and future generations are linked to one another; without him, they would remain alien.

"I feel sorry for you," said Moshe, bursting into laughter. "By wanting to know too much, you end up understanding nothing. There is a link between the witness and the object of his testimony. Between the one who writes and the dramas and triumphs he describes, there is a connection of truth if not of cause and effect. Are you aware of that? And do you persist in spite of it? The prophet who predicts an ordeal and the chronicler who depicts it are equally responsible. I feel sorry for you, my poor friend. Confer a meaning on death? Death has no meaning. It is useless. The first death in history was a murder. Senseless, absurd. Involuntary, unconscious. Cain killed for nothing. His brother died for nothing. Neither proved anything. No, my poor historian, to turn death into a philosophy is not Jewish. To turn it into a theology is anti-Jewish. Whoever praises death ends up either serving or totally ignoring it. A trait pagans and atheists have in common. We, on the other hand, consider death the primary defect and injustice inherent in creation. To die for God is to die against God. For us, man's ultimate confrontation is only with God."

He tried to stand, but failed; his legs would not support him. And so he motioned us to sit down beside him on the ground, which we did, Father on his right and myself at his left, like two disciples preparing to receive the teachings of their Master. And I was delighted to discover my father in a new role.

"You must know," Moshe continued, abruptly seizing my arm. "I have no fear of dying—nor of living. What frightens me is not to be able to distinguish between life and death. There are men who are dead and do not know it."

"Moshe . . ." said my father, beginning a question he would never complete.

"To be Jewish is to be able to distinguish," said Moshe, following his own train of thought. "In our tradition, danger is called mixture, the enemy is called chaos. To be Jewish is to live separate from others but not against others. His whole life long the Jew is committed to separating light from darkness, Shabbat from the rest of the week, the pure from the impure, the sacred from the profane, the return from the exile, life from death. 'And he stood

196

between the dead and the living; and the plague was stayed.' The emphasis is on the word *between*. Moses separated the first from the latter and thus succeeded in containing the scourge. To mingle categories is to destroy them. Just as one may not celebrate Shabbat during the week, one may not experience Shabbat without celebration. Israel may flourish in its kingdom and survive in exile but it may not transfer exile into its kingdom. *'And thou shalt choose life'* means you shall separate it."

"Moshe . . ." I said, not knowing what else I was going to say.

"In no way do I wish to go before my time," Moshe continued, unaware of my interruption. "The innocent man who allows himself to be killed voluntarily, whether he admits it or not, is taking sides with death. That is why I *wish* to be guilty. Since I shall be condemned, let me deserve it. The innocent man who has been punished constitutes a scandal as revolting as the criminal who has been rewarded. Yes, I refute my innocence. I shall assume my guilt by sheer will power. Sometimes I think I actually killed this Christian boy I have never seen; that it was important for me to commit this absurd act to achieve an end that is no less absurd. But I am afraid, I am afraid . . ."

The pressure of his hand became more insistent.

"If we are all innocent, then the mystery of evil, drawing its strength from our very innocence, will crush us in the end. For in order to realize himself, man must fuse all levels of being into one; every man is all men. Every man can and must carry creation on his shoulders; every unit is responsible for the whole. That frightens me. Where am I in all this? Created in the image of the One without image, man is so constituted that as he comes close to one extreme, he advances toward the other. It is frightening because, in the name of the absolute, he is called upon to do good and evil at the same time, relying on identical gestures and inventing identical forms. Chosen by God, Abraham came close to becoming a murderer on God's orders. I am afraid because that means that evil too leads to God, that death too—woe to us—leads to God. But then, where lies the solution? There is but one viable attitude: granted, everything leads to God; only indifference makes us stray. Whoever comes to God empty-handed cannot help but identify Him with emptiness. Better to live evil and death."

"Moshe," I said, surprised to hear him discourse at such length.

He caught me looking at him. He began to laugh again. "Thus, what is essential is to live to the limit. Let your words be shouts or silence but nothing else, nothing in between. Let your desire be absolute and your wait as well, for all yearning contains a yearning for God and every wait is a wait for God. Let your steps lead you toward yourself or me, no matter, for either way you will be taking the same path. Whoever walks in the night, moves against night."

He was no longer speaking to both of us but to me alone. As in the old days. My hesitation disappeared. I knew. He was raving and I accompanied him, I would have accompanied him to the end, with my father and even without him. But why was he laughing?

"Evil is Satan and Satan is more than evil, he is evil disguised as good, the link between the two. That frightens me. After all, his place is at God's right. An awesome concept, leading to horror. How is one to distinguish God in evil, Satan in good? Are we to understand that they maintain a dialogue, arguing over Job's heart, Abraham's faith, Isaac's reason? Who wins, who loses? God, Satan? No. Man wins and man loses—but he does not know it."

My father, notebook on his lap, was taking notes in the semi-darkness. Moshe did not take offense. He talked and talked, very fast, laughing, rocking to and fro, jumping from one subject to the next, from one image to the next as though he wanted to express it all in one single sentence, one single word. The notion of "Breaking the vessels" in Kabbala, the death of kings, the exile of divinity, the Great Return, the vast unification in the universe. Suddenly he came back to the messianic theme:

"The Grandfather of Shpole entreated God: Make haste, you must save the children of Israel, they cannot hold out any longer. If you do not save them as Jews, you will have to redeem them as pagans! And I, Moshe, I tell him: Hurry and send us the one we are expecting, otherwise he will come and no longer find us; and you yourself will no longer find him either."

And as though to prevent my father from interrupting his train of thought, he quickly went on, squeezing my arm with renewed strength:

"Let him come, let him come and all the commandments will be abolished. Thus states the Talmud. All the laws will merge into one, the one that opens not unto fear but unto joy—the joy of man facing his Creator, the joy of the Creator facing His reflection, the joy of mankind triumphing over fear and even over joy. When will he come? I wait for him, I call him, yet he is inside that call, he *is* that call, he *is* that wait. He comes and goes, he visits this dwelling and not that other, this man and not that other, not all together, not in the same way. His reign will come about when all men will be just or when all will be guilty. That too is stressed in the Talmud. In both instances the point is to carry out a resolution, not to deviate from the chosen path, to go to the end—and there, on the tightrope linking two peaks, lies the heady zone of sanctity. And I am afraid. For sanctity is not an end in itself. I am afraid . . ."

His voice choked. My father seized the bowl, dipped it into the pail and handed it to him filled with water. To grasp it, Moshe let go of my arm. I saw his gaping swollen lips and had to contain a scream. Yet I was still not certain, not quite, that it was he. Why was he laughing?

Moshe began to speak again, then paused in the middle of a sentence. We waited for him to finish it. For a long time he seemed absent. He was wandering among the rubble of his words, his thoughts reduced to shreds, unable to organize them. Then his eyes lit up and he emitted so raucous, so deep a groan that I too felt torn apart. Then, alternately crying and laughing, he uttered a sentence of which I can remember only the first part: "Since God exists, the meaning of punishment escapes me. On the other hand . . ."

That is all. I have forgotten many poignant and evocative words, many ideas received or acquired at the cost of sleepless nights and solitary dawns; I have forgotten what it was companions and friends did or said when parting with me at this or that crossing of the roads; I have forgotten what it was my dying mother made me swear on the eve of our separation and what I felt the next day. But this fragment of a cry, the germ of a doubt or of an understanding, has not left me. "On the other hand . . ."—on the other hand . . . what? What sort of evidence had Moshe stumbled upon in his delirium? That enigma haunts me—and I like it that way. It links me to Moshe, my mad, tormented friend, and takes me back into his dusty cell at once cold and stifling where, laughing and talking at the same time, he held forth incoherently on equally incoherent events.

Very well, I shall speak, says the old man. I shall speak of the joy, the madness, the fervor of the living. I shall also speak of the anger of the dead. For I have seen them. I have seen them emerging from pits and slaughter-houses and altars, in groups or alone, glowering and fierce. At first I was surprised, but later I found it natural. I understood that they had decided not to count on the living any longer but to accomplish the task of digging their own graves in heaven, unaided. And they had brought along an entire retinue of companions who had died before them, to cross the blazing town, the indifferent countryside. They had assumed the daring role of avengers determined to occupy the entire world so as to impose on it the awesome principle of equality at last.

I saw them at work, my boy, just as you see me now. I heard them just as you hear me. They were incensed, and with good reason. And if they were angry still, it would be with good reason. Incensed with you for wanting to join them empty-handed, and with me for having deserted them. By speaking to you I am repudiating my mad friend Moshe hiding deep inside my gaze and my remorse. Never mind. I am not afraid of malediction and even less of punishment. And even less of suffering. I am afraid of only one thing: indifference.

The beggars, the vagabonds, the simple-minded; the hungry homeless peddlers, the thirsty homeless drunkards crammed into the single dilapidated room of the shelter —the *hekdesh*—were chatting in whispers, their way of holding council.

After partaking of the meal offered the poor by Reb Sholem, they had left before the actual festivities. In the face of the approaching storm they chose to stay among themselves.

There was Leizer the Fat, with his misshapen, ill-proportioned body, his enormous head on a frail torso. People said of him that he could never see where he was going, only where he was coming from; his eyes and legs seemed to follow independent ways.

And Yiddel the Cripple with his heartbreaking smile; he never complained. Neither of cold nor of hunger. And yet he suffered both, a suffering he translated into a smile. He had a thousand different smiles; one for every occasion, for every sorrow.

And One-Eyed Simha, shrewd and eloquent. He dared you to point out his good eye. He confused you, made you lose. There were those who thought that, in fact, both his eyes were good.

And Kaizer the Mute, weeping as though he were drunk although he had not even emptied his glass. Quietly, silently he wept.

Seated on the floor with his back against the wall, Avrom the Wise, while meditating on the endlessness of his problems and worries, fingered his beard, putting it into his mouth whenever he felt that he had found a solution.

"I am not scared," claimed Yiddel, trembling with fear.

"And my name is not Leizer the Fat," sneered Leizer the Fat.

"And I am Sholem the Rich," trumpeted Simha. "And he is living off my benevolence."

"Amen," said a voice coming from the doorway.

Somebody stood up and went to place more logs on the hearth. Nobody objected. Ordinarily there would be a discussion. Some would appeal for economy in expectation of the heavy cold spells. Others would reply that the hearth was the responsibility of the community, let it worry about lumber, not us. Was it the threat of the pogrom? Or perhaps the bitter cold? But this time no quarrel ensued concerning the policies governing public heating.

"As for me, I am really not afraid," said Avrom the Wise, his beard in his mouth.

"And why would you not be afraid?" asked a voice coming from the farthest corner.

"Because unlike you I have a brain. And that brain is stuffed with problems—meaning thoughts. And among all these thoughts, which are beautiful and marvelous even if the problems are not, there is one more precious and rare than the others—it is called logic. Ever hear of it? No, and I am not surprised. It's not a piece of merchandise one buys or begs. One has it or, not. I have it, you don't. Wisdom is the most inequitably divided of gifts. That's the way it is and I can't help it. For your enlightenment I shall simply say that logic, then, is a superior thought, yes, su-pe-rior, for all others depend on it. And it never errs; it is always right. That's it."

"And it is logic that tells you not to be afraid?" sneered Leizer the Fat.

"Yes, indeed. It doesn't just say things in the air, unaccountably, foolishly. Logic explains things. And what's more, in order to listen to it, all the other thoughts in my head keep still."

"If only you could do as much!"

"You ungrateful idiots. You don't deserve what I am offering you!"

His listeners, some insulted, others amused, protested noisily, except for Simha, who raised his arm and demanded quiet: "Let's have some order, please! This is not the Community Council! A little decorum, gentlemen, otherwise I shal have to clear the hall!"

Even his detractors conceded that he possessed certain qualities. Nobody gave a better imitation of the president.

"All right, go on. We are hanging on your every word, our good and generous friend. Tell us what you know, let us hear the voice that commands all that respect."

Avrom indecisively rubbed his left thumb, then his right. He would have enjoyed being coaxed, if only for form's sake, but this was no time to play hard-to-get. "Since I am being asked so politely by this gathering, I shall condescend to throw some light on the subject before us. Firstly: our enemies—may the plague take them before lightning strikes them, amen—are jealous, that is why they are dying to see us die. Secondly: what are they

jealous of? Of us, here? Whatever for? Could they be
envious of our misery? But we are ready to let them have
it, and multiplied by two, if possible! Of our ailments? Our
worries? Our sorrows? Why don't they take them, and
today rather than tomorrow morning! Well then, I proceed.
Thirdly: they are supposed to be interested only in the
rich, the satiated merchants and the grocers stuffed with
money, the fat landowners and their jewel-bedecked
spouses. The rest of us, the deprived, the have-nots, the
disinherited, the last on every list including God's, have no
cause to fear—who would be stupid enough to covet our
fate? That is what my logic is telling me in a most solemn
voice. Consequently, I have the right to claim that I am in
no way frightened. And let whoever does not agree with
me speak up. I shall consider it a privilege to punch him in
the nose."

A vague murmur greeted his comments.

"Who am I to contradict you?" said Yiddel the Cripple.
"All this is very nice. But how can we be sure that our
enemies—may they burn like funeral candles—are
listening to the same voice as you?"

Taken aback—after all, he wasn't going to punch a
cripple—and unwilling to engage in polemics, Avrom
dismissed him contemptuously: "You are a bore."

"But a logical one," said a voice from the other end of
the room.

Avrom remembered that he had never liked that fool of
a Yiddel, an irritating clown whose place was in the circus,
if in fact there were a Jewish circus. "Ah, Yiddel, Yiddel,"
he said. "How lucky you are to be unlucky! Otherwise . . ."

"Hey, Yiddel," advised the same faraway voice, "why
don't you wish him your luck too!"

"Why should I be nasty?" said Yiddel. "I simply wonder
whether our enemies know what logic is. If you ask me,

they only know one thing: how to pillage and massacre. Without logic."

Avrom became annoyed, and the others, as always, split into two camps. There followed shouting, arguing, howling and ancient recollections of grudges long considered buried: You shoved me with your elbow at the house of Temerl the Widow. You pushed ahead of me at Yekel the Melon Vendor's. You played on Shlomowitz's pity by inventing a terminal illness for yourself. You didn't tell me about Shimshonski the Wine Merchant's only daughter's wedding. You stole old Nissel's money box. They were about to come to blows.

Once more One-Eyed Simha took it upon himself to restore order. "Aren't you ashamed?" he thundered. "At so serious a time you have the heart to fight? The fate of our community is at stake and you have nothing better to do than brawl like enemy dogs? If this became known, people would spit on us, and they would be right! Have a little dignity! We can handle this situation! We can show ourselves worthy of our poverty, worthy in spite of our poverty!"

He evidently convinced his cronies. Finished, the argument. Forgotten, the disagreement.

"He started it," grumbled Avrom the Wise.

"Me? I only asked a very simple question," said Yiddel.

"You see? He is starting again!" Avrom was indignant.

"Enough!" ordered One-Eyed Simha so as to forestall another flare-up. He waited, checked that the truce was not being violated behind his back and made a conciliatory summing-up: "Like you, Avrom, I respect logic. Like you, Yiddel, I believe that our foes couldn't care less. In other words, even if the entire world persuaded me that I am wrong to worry, I would still not be reassured. This is bigger than me. Moreover, let's not forget that this matter concerns us directly. Moshe is poor. He was what we are.

Consequently, if our enemies are contemplating vengeance, they will start with us, not with the rich!"

Not one voice spoke up against him. One could hear the wood crackling in the hearth and the wind shaking the roof. Odd-shaped shadows stretched over the damp walls and Yiddel made a concentrated effort not to see them in order not to smile at them. Avrom touched him on the shoulder as though to ask his forgiveness.

A gesture which did not fail to astonish One-Eyed Simha, who reacted by opening wide his eyes—both of them— himself no longer sure which was the good one. "It remains to be seen," he continued in the same tone of voice, "whether this is a matter of vengeance or not. Since we don't know, let us adhere to the following principle: the community is threatened, we have no right to dissociate ourselves from it. Whatever will happen to it, will happen to us; let us be equal in the face of the enemy. Since our brothers on the outside are frightened, let us be frightened too."

It will not be said that the beggars and the poor of Kolvillàg did not have a sense of honor and duty. They all applauded their inspired leader. Moreover, their freely accepted roles brought them closer to one another: forgotten the petty quarrels, the foolish grudges. Yiddel smiled at Avrom, who as a token of their reconciliation offered him a piece of cake recovered from the shadowy depths of his pocket. In the far corner they were indulging in shoulder-slapping, hearty laughter and self-parodies of fear. Everything seemed to be settling into harmony and order when suddenly a voice was heard, somber and prophetic: "Mercy! We are digging our own graves! Mercy!"

The gravedigger's hollow voice created its usual effect. They all withdrew into themselves, lumps in their throats, their hearts drained of all gaiety. Because of his profession Adam cast a pall on people. They avoided him, fled from his touch. They lowered their eyes when he passed so as not to carry away his gaze. They said: He'll see us in any case; he'll be the last to see us, we might as well be patient and not think about it. At the same time they took pains not to offend him; he was capable of taking his revenge— after. His very presence made them vaguely uneasy. Even Simha, mortal like the rest of us, notwithstanding his position as leader, was loath to cross him.

"Blind fools, that's what you are," scolded the grave-digger. "We bring on our own misfortune. You and I. If man did not fear death, he would not die. If a pogrom strikes us, this time it will be because we dread it and speak of it. Why can't you hold your tongues? Or discuss other things, why?"

"But what about the danger?" Simha asked timidly, to justify himself.

"Exactly! Because danger there is, let's not discuss it! Or even refer to it! In the beginning of evil and death there was the word. Read the Bible! It's all there! The word announces what it names, it provokes what it describes— didn't you know that? But what are you doing on Saturday mornings? What are you thinking of during the reading of the Torah? Unthinking fools, that's what you are!"

They could do nothing but nod their heads. Yes, he was telling the truth. Nobody listened to the biblical tales with enough attention. Yes, they should. Yes, they would. Nobody was going to get into an argument with the grave-digger over some story from the Bible. Yes, he was right all the way. They would keep silent. And thus save the holy community of Kolvillàg.

"Thank you, Adam," said Simha. "You are setting our responsibilities squarely before us. It is not enough to share our brethren's fear; we must save them. Let us be prudent, sparing of our words. Our fate depends on it. This community exists thanks to its beggars. Were it to disappear,

207

it would be because of them. Let us be proud of the mission entrusted to us—and may God have mercy on us!"

Did they believe these things he told them? Did he believe them himself? All we know is that these unfortunates, these orphans without memory, these dreamers without a future, withdrew into themselves, mute with fear, remorse and pity—above all, pity.

As for Leah, she was sleeping. Since her husband's departure, she had only one wish: to sleep. She alone was not afraid. But she suffered. And was ashamed of it.

Before he went to give himself up, Moshe had made her sit down facing him in the single room they occupied together. "I am going to have to hurt you," he had told her gently as he took her hand in his.

She had not answered. At the touch of his fingers she was afire. She ached and she liked her aching. Her body was at once abyss and sanctuary, sin and ecstasy.

"You have given me much joy and pride," he had told her with infinite gentleness. "Yes, much."

She shivered as at the birth of desire, as at a vision that modesty rendered imprecise, nebulous. "Don't say that," she said. "Don't say it or I shall cry."

"I should like this pride to remain. Will you help me?"

"I shall do whatever you wish," she said, her eyes blurred with tears. A new sadness had taken possession of her, endowing her face with ethereal beauty.

"Promise me not to suffer too much," said Moshe.

"I can't," she answered in a toneless voice. "I cannot promise, I would not be able to keep my promise. But I do promise you that I shall not cry."

And she was keeping her promise. Courageously, obstinately. And yet the temptation and opportunities were not lacking. For people were now kindly disposed toward the martyr's wife. And all that warmth, all that solicitude made her want to cry. She was no longer permitted to wash floors for the rich, do their laundry or take care of their chickens. People watched over her. They brought her the most succulent dishes, warm bread fresh from the oven and a new dress for Shabbat. They treated her like a princess. Though absent, her husband was still protecting her. She knew full well that it was to him they were paying homage through her. Every time she thought of him, her eyes filled with tears. She succeeded in holding them back only by remembering her promise. But how much longer would she be able to restrain herself? To make sure, she slept. Of course, there were times when she cried in her sleep, but that was permissible; Moshe had not forbidden it. Not explicitly. And so Leah liked to sleep in order to be free to cry.

Today she had been warned not to stay at home and been invited to come and spend the night at Davidov's home. She was marked, she was a target. If a pogrom broke out, she would become its first victim. She refused to understand that and nobody dared tell her openly. People said to her: "Leah, Leah, you must hide somewhere, anywhere."—"Why must I? Because my husband is in danger?"—"Yes, Leah. Because Moshe is in danger." She could see no connection. Had they let her, she would have gone to hide in prison. To be with her husband. And in her own way that was what she did. To be reunited with Moshe she took refuge in sleep. There, she and Moshe were safe. And since he was the only one to see her, Moshe could not become angry when she stupidly began to cry.

Notwithstanding the omens, there were optimists who trusted immanent justice more than forebodings and rumors. They did not exclude the possibility of a trial, but it would naturally be preceded by a bona-fide inquiry. The aroused mob would shatter a few windows, provoke incidents and riots, but surely they would stop short of a pogrom. A pogrom would take place only if, after deliberation of the court, Moshe were to be declared guilty. What they really needed was to build a case for the defense.

Though he was skeptical, Davidov discussed the suggestion with my father. "We must not neglect any possibility. I don't have much faith in it . . . But if you have a moment, glance through our reference books. You never can tell . . . it could turn out to be useful."

"I am not a lawyer."

"I know, I am not asking you to plead, nor to compose a legal document, only to draft an outline, a historical summary of the problem. As for the lawyer . . . I know where to find one."

And so my father immersed himself in martyrology. Names, dates, numbers. Sources, motives, consequences. Gloucester, 1168. Fulda, 1235. Lincoln, 1255. Pforzheim, 1267. Stupidity recognizes no borders; it transcends the centuries. The accounts followed and resembled one another. A Christian boy disappears and the Jews are massacred. Trente, 1475. Tyrnau, 1494. Bazin, 1529. With every approaching Easter, the Jews tremble. In Prague the Maharal creates a clay golem and entrusts him with the mission of outwitting the enemy. There are cases of fanatic Christians hiding corpses in Jewish homes and subsequently accusing them of ritual murder; the golem discovers the corpses and denounces the murderers.

Question: Why did the famous Maharal choose a golem rather than a man as his instrument? Answer: Israel's foes had fallen so low, had shown such intellectual baseness that they would have been unworthy adversaries for a man. Frankfort, 1712. Posen, 1736. Tasnad, 1791. Bucarest, 1801. Vitebsk, 1823. A long, bloody list. Damas, 1840. Saratov, 1857.

The world evolved, society was emancipated and

rejected obscurantism, but on this particular subject the myth lived on. Newly liberated nations moved toward enlightenment, trusting in reason, but the slander of ritual murder continued to spread from country to country, from town to town. Galatz, 1859. Kutaisi, 1877. Tisza-Eszlar, 1882. Accounts, reports, expert testimonies. The inanity of the accusations was demonstrated, sources quoted. The Bible was invoked, the Talmud, the Gaonim. Legend roused tempers, blinded reason, poisoned the heart. It was enough to make one despair, despair of mankind.

"Do you know what happened at Blois?" my father asked. "On Passover eve, in the year 1171, the Jews were accused of having killed a Christian child. Count Theobald condemned them to die at the stake. All except Pulcelina, a beautiful and well-bred woman whom he loved passionately. But Pulcelina rejected mercy and chose to share the fate of her people. The entire community died singing its faith in God."

He marked the passage, closed the book and added: "Pulcelina, beautiful Pulcelina, how I understand her. Better to die singing than to submit to stupidity."

Then, staring into emptiness, he went on: "I shall have to add to the list the name of Kolvillàg."

I should not have come, mused Davidov. I should have foreseen his reaction, his condescending advice to remain cool: "Christians are not barbarians, Mr. Davidov!" That was his set formula for use in conversations with Jews. Not that Stefan Braun, attorney, had many conversations with Jews.

The fact was that he himself was Jewish, albeit an ashamed, assimilated, perhaps even converted Jew. His help was solicited only in cases of extreme urgency. Indeed, this was the first time.

"You must help us," said Davidov, uncomfortable in

211

his too comfortable armchair. "Take on our defense. Do the necessary, the impossible. Use your connections . . ."

"And what for?" asked the lawyer.

"You know what for."

"At the risk of disappointing you . . ."

"Oh yes, you know. You cannot help but know. Every child knows. Don't pretend. You are neither deaf nor blind. *They* are concocting a nasty brew. A blood bath. A massacre. A pogrom."

"They? Who?"

"You know very well . . ."

"You mean the few boors who have no special affection for you? Who don't appreciate being robbed by Jewish merchants? And who happen to be Christian? But, my dear sir, we are no longer living in the Middle Ages. Really!" Braun's voice took on the inflection of an attorney addressing the court, his arms raised in a gesture of sincere indignation. "After all, my dear sir! Christians are not barbarians!"

I should not have come, thought Davidov. I was wrong. If our optimists were so interested, they should have come themselves to retain his services. His grandiloquence does not impress me. I have no use for it. If he has such a high regard for our enemies, let him keep them. The fool! As though he could truly be one of them! In their eyes, he is nothing but a dirty Jew like the rest of us.

"A question, Mr. Braun. May I?"

"Of course."

Davidov leaned forward and lowered his voice. "Between you and me . . . aren't you a little concerned? I mean, for yourself? Your family?"

"Mr. Davidov! I . . ."

"Don't go and get angry now! Your borrowed airs don't deceive me. Do you really think you can remain above the scuffle? There will be plundering, Jews will be killed—and you expect to be left unharmed? Do you really believe that? That our enemies are not your enemies too? That they will grant you immunity? Is that what's at the back of your mind?"

Braun was pale, as though he had just been slapped, and there was hatred in his voice when he spoke: "I forbid you, do you hear me? I forbid you to insinuate . . ."

"I admire your self-control!" said Davidov without raising his voice.

"Your insinuations, I know all about them! You people love to disturb others, upset their lives, implicate them in your affairs! No wonder you are not liked!"

"*You?* Did I hear you say *you?*"

"Precisely! You! All the members of the tribe! You are tactless, tasteless and without honor! You reward hospitality with insult! To courtesy you respond with insolence! And you expect to be liked?"

The poor lawyer was trembling. They were pursuing him into his very fortress, undermining his defenses. His round face was livid. His breathing came faster. He was like one possessed, in the grip of hate, the worst kind: self-hate.

"Why are you losing your temper?" said Davidov. "Did I offend you? I am here as a client. To solicit your services. One of us, a madman called Moshe, is in prison. We wish to provide him with legal counsel. We thought of you. Was that wrong of us? Are you not a good attorney? We pay cash."

Davidov's calm served only to exacerbate the lawyer's anger, accumulated over the years. Braun resented the fact that the Jews—whom he had repudiated—were repudiating him in turn.

"Stop it!" he shouted, pounding the desk. "I know your wiles! There's no point in lying! You didn't come to see the lawyer, but . . ."

"Yes?"

Stefan Braun chose not to finish his sentence.

Braun considered himself a full citizen. He saw himself on the other side, a stranger to our history, to our fate. His wife, a member of a Protestant upper-middle-class family, boasted of never having shaken a Jew's hand. They occupied a luxurious apartment near the municipal theatre. His neighbors were high officials, high-school teachers, assistant directors of various governmental agencies. They entertained only the elite. "The ghetto," Braun was said to have remarked, "is something I left behind. I have no intention of letting it follow me into my home." His father, like all pious fathers of renegade children, considered his son dead.

The lawyer had a son of his own—Toli—who was my age. The same teacher taught us to play the violin. Toli, who looked more Jewish than I, was at home nowhere, for wherever he went, he felt watched, observed, judged. He was precocious, but because of his extreme susceptibility he was even more melancholy and vulnerable than I.

As I remember him, Toli was a stranger to almost everyone; I suspect, even to his parents. He seemed out of place. His street was not really his street the way our street was ours; we played, rolled on the ground and did all the things children don't do in the presence of grown-ups. He lived on a lane, straight and bright as a path in a hospital garden. Carefully trimmed trees seemed to keep an eye on the sidewalks, which were so clean one hardly dared tread on them.

There was no neighborly calling from window to window, no chestnut fights among the boys, no housewives going to market in groups to exchange gossip on the way. This well-ordered and scrupulously observed serenity must have bored all the youngsters of the neighborhood, and Toli most of all. In the afternoon, on his way home from school, he would hurry toward the gates of his house. Frequently he caught himself on the verge of running, but that wasn't proper. He had been taught to exercise self-control, never to betray emotion, and think of what people would say. Viewing the world with disenchanted eyes, trapped by his father's lie, Toli would probably sooner or later have attempted suicide had he not caught sight of me one afternoon, chatting with a dignified and beautiful old Jew who looked like a legendary sage—his grandfather. Since then they had been meeting clandestinely and Toli at last was discovering what his parents had kept from him—the freedom of his childhood.

"Admit that it's the *Jew* Braun, not the lawyer, you're interested in!"

"I admit it. If you were not Jewish, I would not have taken this step. If there is any hope, it can come only from our own ranks. The others have sacrificed us in advance."

"I was right, then," sighed the lawyer. His voice was changed, weary. "You will never give up. And yet, I made every effort to escape you . . ."

"Escape *us?* But we are not your enemies, Mr. Braun!"

The lawyer stared at him for a moment, then rose and paced the floor thinking out loud: "I have cut all ties with my parents, broken my old father's heart, shamed my family, renounced my past and repudiated my people . . ."

He was enumerating his desertions and betrayals, counting them on his fingers. Suddenly he stood still, a gleam of curiosity in his eyes. "What do they say about me . . . back there?"

"Many bad things, sir, many bad things."

"Do they speak of me as a renegade?"

"Well . . . yes."

"But I never converted!"

This is news, thought Davidov. I would have sworn the opposite. One does not break with one's faith without embracing another. On Sundays did he not receive in his house the Protestant minister, along with the cream of gentile society?

"I did not convert! Do you want to know why? Because I loathe all religions! Judaism, Christianity, Buddhism. I am against every one of them, on principle. All religion is perversion; without it, men would be equal and brothers. And happy. Religions are the devil's invention; they are his most dazzling success. God himself could not have done better. Why in the world would I convert? I believe only in man—and even that . . ."

Davidov was moved by this last confession. He thought: Braun is more to be pitied than we are. He belongs nowhere, expects nothing from anybody. His condition confers on him nothing but burdens and none of the privileges. Having lived a lie, he now must watch it explode. Will he have the courage to retrace his steps?

He offered Braun an opening: "Will you help us? We need you. More than ever."

Braun, half amused, half chagrined, looked at him without hostility. "What if I told you that I should like— that I should like very much—to be of service to you. Would you believe me?"

"Certainly."

"And if I added that I am unable to do so—would you also believe me?"

Surprised, Davidov was about to answer, but the lawyer stopped him: "Don't answer. Don't say anything. Let the question remain question. Please." And, escorting him to the door: "I believe it is late, later than we think."

I did well to come after all, thought Davidov, stepping into the lane where everything seemed quiet and peaceful. I should come back one day. One day, one day . . . he repeated the words to himself while anguish was forming a lump in his throat as at the announcement of an irrevocable event, an event already present.

"And Grandfather?" asked Toli breathlessly.

The lawyer jumped. "Toli! You came in without knocking!"

His obedient and well-bred son certainly knew that he must not enter his father's study without permission . . .

"And Grandfather?" insisted Toli unhappily.

I should be getting angry, the lawyer thought. Scold him, call him back to order. What kind of manners were these? He is challenging me, provoking me, he knows very well that his grandfather . . .

"I have met him, you know," continued Toli.

Leaning against the door he had closed behind himself, he was expecting an outburst. His father was hardly one to encourage insubordination. He sometimes punished him, and on those occasions Toli prayed for death to strike him at his father's hands.

"I heard everything," said the boy, lowering his voice.

Nothing makes sense any more, thought the lawyer. My own son flouts me and I accept without a word. I should be rousing the entire house, I should be slapping him hard to bring him to reason, to discipline him, yet here I am, more astonished than angry; I am not even annoyed.

At the sight of his son—suddenly grown-up, different— he felt the urge to question him about his encounter with his grandfather: Where had it taken place? When? Under what circumstances? What had they said to one another the first time? But he did nothing of the kind. Ultimately it mattered little. What mattered was that it had taken place.

"So," he said, trying to appear stern, "now we are listening at doors?"

"Forgive me, I couldn't resist. When I saw the man enter your study, I was sure it concerned Grandfather."

Well, thought Stefan Braun, the circle is closed. The race is over. The game of hide-and-seek with myself is finished. I repudiated my father to save my son; and now my son wishes to save my father. Damn it, why am I not flying into a rage? I failed all the way, I have no allies, no support. I wasted my past and ruined my future—yet somehow I don't seem to mind. I don't recognize myself any more!

"I know where he lives," Toli was saying defiantly. "I have been there." And after a slight hesitation: "In fact, quite often."

Better and better, thought the father. He stared at Toli—so frail, so serious and obstinate—and was overwhelmed by an irresistible urge to laugh. Laugh about life and man, laugh about his people so foolishly determined to survive in a twisted, perversely evil world, and about himself most of all. But he must not. He must not make any noise; his wife was asleep. All right, he would laugh silently. Too bad Davidov had left. He would have invited him to laugh with him. Too bad his son could not guess how ludicrous the situation really was.

"Don't you think that we should . . ."

"Go and warn him?"

"Yes, Father. And perhaps . . . bring him here . . . Here he will be safe, whereas . . ."

Father here, thought the lawyer. Father with his beard, his caftan, his ritual shawl, his prayers, his songs, his prohibitions—here, in the house! He imagined the scene: his wife, tomorrow morning, enters the drawing room and—horrors—sees an old Jew—he must be old by now—wrapped in his tallith, rocking to and fro. What a sight! Mentally he burst out laughing. Unbeatable, that scene: my father and my wife.

"Let's not exaggerate, son."

"But I am telling you I heard everything! Grandfather is in danger, all the Jews are in danger, all the Jews are in danger—except us!" He blushed with shame. "Except us," he repeated.

"Tell me, are you that attracted by danger?"

"No, Father. Not by danger. Only by Grandfather."

"Don't worry. Jews like Davidov—that is the name of my visitor—tend to exaggerate, to dramatize. If one were to believe them, the whole world has but one thing in mind: to mistreat, persecute and annihilate the Jews. If the idea seems insane, so does believing it. You see, my son, in our day mankind and nations have rid themselves of many outdated rituals, hereditary taboos, savage and gratuitous hates. The era of crusades and pogroms is gone. Ours is dominated by humanism, liberalism. We no longer kill our fellow-man in the name of obsolete and absurd legends."

"That is not Grandfather's opinion," said Toli, bristling.

"How would he know? It has been a long time since he gave up living in this world; he lives in an unreal universe, in unreal times. He knows more about Abraham than about his Christian neighbors. His king is David, not the one ruling this country. His law is the Talmud and not the law of the land. Don't you think I'm right?"

He remembered the arguments he had used against his father, long ago, before their break. The arguments were the same, only the tone was different. And the old passion, the old fervor were gone.

"Grandfather says . . . Do you want to know what he says?"

"Of course," said the lawyer, swallowing hard.

"Grandfather says that when a Jew says he is suffering, one must believe him, and when he is afraid, one must assume his fear is justified. In neither case does one have the right to doubt his word. Even if one cannot help him, one must at least believe him."

"And what if I, a Jew like him, say that he is wrong? That they are all wrong?"

"You are not a Jew . . . not like him . . ." Toli stood

219

facing his father, stiff, vulnerable. He was looking at him, imploring him with his eyes. "Let's bring him here, right now! Father . . . This Davidov whom you saw . . . he spoke of a massacre, he mentioned the word pogrom. Have we the right to doubt his words?"

Stubborn little fellow, thought the lawyer. Besides, he is not so little any more. How he has changed! His shy manners hide a mature will.

"Davidov," said the lawyer. "The president of the community. The Jewish Prince of Kolvillàg. In his place I would be afraid too. Jews like him, people like him, have suffered so much, in so many places, for such a variety of reasons, that their distrust has become second nature for them, an instinctive defense. They see an enemy in every stranger, a killer in every passer-by. And yet, one day they shall have to free themselves, they shall have to adjust. I have told you over and over again, we are no longer living in barbaric times."

Even while he was talking he thought: If something terrible happens tonight, if their premonition comes true, I shall have lost both my father and my son. For Toli will not forgive me. What am I to do? Give in? Rush over there and bring back my old Jew of a father? Would he agree to come? After so many years, so many wars? Would he come alone? Without the tribe?

"I feel that even if Davidov's fears are unjustified, or only partly justified, Grandfather should be taken to a safe place," Toli insisted.

"You'll make an excellent lawyer. You have almost convinced me. Here is what I propose to you. Give me, give yourself one night to reflect. Tomorrow we shall see more clearly. If the rumors persist, I shall accept your arguments. Your mother will become hysterical, but between the two of us we'll calm her down. But all of this is academic, believe me. Christians are human beings like

220

you and me; all men are the same. There are fanatics among the victims as well as among the murderers; both are driven by intolerance. The enemy is in intolerance and fanaticism, not in man. You should bet on man, not against him."

"I'd like to," said Toli, a faint smile on his lips.

This conversation had done him good. Never before had he spoken to his father at such length. And surely not so freely. Did I persuade him? he wondered. We shall see. He took a step forward, said goodnight and opened the heavy padded door. With his hand on the latch, he turned. "You know, I . . . Grandfather . . . he is somebody."

Left alone, leaning against his desk, the lawyer felt a vague melancholy engulfing him. He would have been at a loss to say whether it linked him to the past or to the future. One or the other had just collapsed. For an hour he thought of nothing, letting himself sink into nothingness. Then he heard his son opening the door of his room, then the gate. He could have, he should have, run after him and brought him back; he did not. Perhaps, he told himself, it would be in vain.

And so, his head slightly raised, he listened to his son's vanishing footsteps, his son who left without informing him whether he planned to come home early or late, alone or accompanied, tomorrow or next year, as penitent or as avenger—or whether he planned to come home at all.

"Father, listen!" Azriel was shouting with amazement. "Am I going crazy or . . ."

Shmuel the Chronicler stood still and listened. "Or what?"

"Don't you hear?"

Strangely festive noises pierced the hush that enveloped the town.

"Have you forgotten?" my father explained. "The Rebbe has decided not to cancel the celebration."

"But the noise is not coming from the House of Study. Listen!"

It was coming from the direction of the asylum.

"Who is mad?" I asked. "They or I?"

"Let's go and see."

We were on our way home from one of our strolls. Rivka was waiting for us with dinner, she must be worrying—never mind, she would wait another hour. A celebration in the shelter was worth the trouble.

We had to use our elbows in order to get inside the overheated hall. Drenched with perspiration, breathless, the beggars were surrounding the Rebbe and his meager retinue, drinking to his health, encouraged by Adam the Gravedigger, who for the first time in his life seemed gay and exuberant.

Father inquired left and right, and finally found out what had happened.

The celebration could not take place in the House of Study simply because there had not been enough people. Shaike and his followers had carried out their mission well. Their warnings had brought results. In the face of a possible pogrom, the Hasidim, though filled with remorse, had felt compelled to stay home with their wives and children. And so, when the Rebbe, accompanied by a few disciples, among them Reb Sholem and the scribe Reb Hersh, arrived at the House of Study at the prescribed hour, they found the hall empty.

The Rebbe had staggered under the blow and had to be supported by Reb Sholem. "They didn't listen to me," the Rebbe whispered. "But I don't hold it against them. What right have I to judge?"

"What if we postponed the celebration?" Reb Sholem asked, "Until the situation calms down and people are more at ease."

222

"Yes, we have no choice. And yet . . . it's an insult to the Torah. We are depriving her of her celebration tonight."

"A private celebration just among ourselves would also be an insult," said Reb Sholem.

"Out of the question," decided the Rebbe.

A long silence followed. The Rebbe covered his eyes with his hands and, sighing, lost himself in meditation. After a while he said: "Since the people will not come to the celebration, we must take the celebration to them."

"What do you mean, Rebbe?"

"Is there a place where Jews live together? In numbers?"

"No, not really."

"Not one?"

"Not one, Rebbe. Except . . ."

". . . the shelter, the asylum."

The Rebbe shook himself. "Are those beggars not Jews like ourselves? Let us go there. What are we waiting for?"

There remained the task of convincing the beggars. To everyone's surprise, the gravedigger took it upon himself. One-Eyed Simha seconded him; Yiddel applauded. Motke the Porter and his colleagues were dispatched to bring a table from the House of Study, as well as chairs, wine and food. Reb Hersh the Scribe went with them to carry the holy scrolls on this memorable evening; he did not trust anyone else. Scarcely a half-hour later the celebration was in full swing.

Presiding at the table, the perspiring Rebbe, dressed in his Shabbat clothes, was mopping his forehead with a red handkerchief and singing with all his might. His head was constantly moving up and down, up and down, wavering between the need to forget and the need to remember.

"Perils and persecutions come and go," he cried out, "the Torah remains. Is that not reason enough to rejoice?"

"Let's make room for joy!" roared the gravedigger.

223

"Who needs sadness and fear! Let us sing! Show us, Rebbe, show us the true way to sing!"

"Through song," said the Rebbe, "man climbs to the highest palace. From that palace he can influence the universe and its prisons. Song is Jacob's ladder forgotten on earth by the angels. Sing and you shall defeat death, sing and you shall disarm the foe. Let us sing and we shall live, let us sing louder than ever before, with more fervor than ever before so that our very song may become our shield!"

He pounded the table, rattling the half-filled bottles and glasses. The gravedigger followed suit, and taking his task seriously, urged all those present to do the same.

And as the noise kept swelling, making the building sway, the Rebbe's face was lighting up more and more. At his right, Reb Sholem was clapping his hands wildly. His singing was out of tune but he was forgiven; his voice was drowned in the din. For once, the beggars had the Rebbe all to themselves, and they paid attention to nothing but the pure and savage passion he projected. Their most irrational, their most childish hopes were vested in him, and him alone. Successor and heir to a name dating back to the Maggid of Premishlan, he had the power to exorcise evil.

Legend has it that as long as he lived, the famous Maggid of Premishlan granted his protection to all those who came to bind their souls to his, then to all those who participated in his New Year services, then to all those who heard him welcome Shabbat on the threshold of his house, then to all those who offered him their gaze, and lastly to anyone who remembered a story about him.

And so, with such an ancestor, the Rebbe surely could countermand threats and decrees and impress his will on fate.

"Well then," bellowed the gravedigger, "that justifies our gaiety! Let us drink, let us sing!"

Leizer the Fat was roaring with laughter. Yiddel the Cripple was hopping up and down. At the approach of the storm, all these beggars seemed to want to celebrate one last time, to kiss the Torah and go away drunk with ecstasy, dazzled and singed by a Jewish celebration unlike any other.

The Rebbe paused to catch his breath, and the noise subsided abruptly. All leaned forward to get a better view. The Rebbe poured brandy into his silver cup and offered it to Reb Sholem, who took it but did not raise it to his lips. The two men gazed at one another, sharing the wait heavy with memories and nostalgia of another age.

"*Lehaim*," said Reb Sholem, moved. "To life."

"*Lehaim*," answered the Rebbe. "To survival."

Reb Sholem took a sip. Unable to empty the cup, he set it on the table. He was not a Hasid in the usual sense of the word. He did not even live in Kolvillàg. His attachment to the Rebbe transcended his own life. It had been his great-grandfather's custom to journey on foot to be with the Maggid of Premishlan every year on the particular Shabbat when the passage describing the exodus from Egypt is read. Once, at the Maggid's insistent request, he had stayed another week so as to hear him read the next passage, the one that describes the spectacular and majestic scene at Sinai.

"You understand, Sholem?" the Maggid of Premishlan had said. "Thanks to the Torah, the oppressed have acquired the dignity of princes. From this moment on, you must behave like a prince, do you hear me, Sholem?" Shortly thereafter the Hasid's fortunes rose like stars. As a token of his gratitude, he had a House of ~~~~ built in honor of the Maggid. Thus there we~~~~ ties between the two families. To express hi~~~~ and devotion, Reb Sholem commissio~~~~ from the most illustrious scribe, R~~~~ cuted on the most supple parchme~~~~

225

set into an especially built Ark in the Rebbe's study.

"All of us *lehaim!*" the gravedigger was yelling. "To life!"

"To life! In spite of our enemies!" Under his fur hat—his *shtreimel*—the Rebbe was soaking wet, but he was smiling. Great warmth, infinite kindness shone from his dark eyes.

"Let them rot!" shouted Leizer the Fat.

"Let us sing," ordered the gravedigger.

In the uproar, the Rebbe turned toward Reb Sholem. "My great-grandfather, the Maggid of Premishlan, liked to say: 'When Jews form a holy community under the sign of the Torah, they personify it; they become the Torah and the Creator beholds them with pride.'"

"Protect us from vanity," whispered Reb Hersh the Scribe, seated at the Rebbe's left. "As for me, I dare not identify with one letter, any letter of the Torah."

"That is not vanity," the Rebbe reprimanded him. "It is not vanity that moves us to pay tribute to the Torah."

"The most sincere intentions risk turning into vanity," mumbled the scribe.

"I am speaking of all of us collectively," said the Rebbe. "You speak of the individual. Of course temptation exists for the individual. To say that one is driving away vanity means one has succumbed. To believe that one is stronger than pride is to prove the opposite. Is there a way of circumventing the trap? As Rebbe Bunam used to say . . ."

Outside, a few steps away, a mob was prowling in the shadows, preparing to attack. And the Rebbe was still speaking of the struggle against pride, of the personal and timeless attachments that every man forms with the Torah while studying it, of the great Rebbe Bunam of Pshiskhe who . . .

"The great Rebbe Bunam liked to say that every man keep two scraps of paper in his pockets. One

reminding him that he is the crowning achievement of creation, and the second that he is but a handful of dust. The point, of course, is not to confuse the pockets."

"And what about the man with nothing in his pockets?" asked the scribe.

Reb Hersh's head was bowed; he seemed forever to be listening to a distant echo. Humble, diffident, frail, he spoke little and in a barely audible voice. His favorite expression: "Oh, me? I have nothing to say, since it has all been said before."

He considered the holy scrolls that were to be completed that evening—by calligraphing the last two verses of the Pentateuch—his masterwork. All his science, all his passion had gone into them. For every single letter of the tetragram, he had run to purify himself in the ritual baths. For every new chapter heading, he had invented an appropriately symbolic ornament. The *aleph* contained the troubling mystery of the beginning; the *yod,* the austerity of the cry. The *hey* suggested the heartbreak of revealed divinity. And yet at this moment when his glory was about to be sanctioned, he seemed more preoccupied than the Rebbe. Perhaps he regretted that his labors were coming to an end.

The Rebbe started to sing again and the assembly enthusiastically joined in; as long as the song continued they felt invulnerable. And it was then that an extraordinary incident took place. A heavy-set man wearing a black greatcoat and muddy boots cleared a passage for himself all the way to the table of honor. "I must speak to you!" he said.

The song died on every lip. People were shouting: "But it's . . . impossible . . . incredible. But it's . . . Kaizer . . . Kaizer! The mute!"

"Kaizer! You realize? Kaizer! And he speaks!"

"What's happening to him?"

Even the gravedigger, his mouth wide open, seemed

stunned. Simha was rubbing his eyes and Leizer his head. They stared at Kaizer, bewildered.

"I am a simple man," said Kaizer, addressing the Rebbe. "I attended no school, followed no Master. I barely know how to pray and love God. You, on the other hand, a descendant of the Maggid of Premishlan, can and must be obeyed down here and up above, You, one listens to in both worlds. Why don't you tell God to make His presence felt to other peoples as well? And to grant us some respite, some rest?"

His neighbors, who had recovered from their surprise in the meantime, began pushing him back toward the rear to question him. But the Rebbe gave orders to let him go on speaking.

"Time is short," said Kaizer tersely. "The sword is hanging over our heads. The blood will soon flow; it may already be flowing. Say something, grandson of the Maggid, say a word, just one, but let it be heard!"

Breathing heavily, the Rebbe savagely bit his lips as though determined to hurt himself.

"Well? You don't say anything?" shouted Kaizer, stamping his foot. "The grandson of the Premishlaner Maggid has nothing to say? They are readying themselves to slaughter his community and he remains silent? They are going to massacre innocent children and he remains silent, as I remained silent until now?"

Staring into space with almost demented intensity, the Rebbe clenched his teeth, clenched his fists with such passion that everyone expected an explosion to make the universe tremble. Finally he spoke up. "My great-grandfather possessed powers I was not granted," he said sadly. "One day he came to a village where the Jewish population feared a massacre. He was begged to repeal the sentence. He went to the synagogue, opened the Ark and pronounced the following words before God: 'Your Law commits You, Your commandments bind You. I could remind

You of *Thou shalt not kill.* I shall not do so. I shall remind You of something else. You entered into a covenant with Your people. We were to defend Your Torah, and You, in turn, would defend us. Are You going to honor the clauses of that contract or not? If You hand us over to the enemy, know that he will take possession of Your Torah as well.' And my great-grandfather won his case. I do not have his strength."

"Then I was wrong to break my vow, wrong to speak," said Kaizer. He made a movement as though to step back and leave. 'We counted on you!" he cried out, changing his mind. "I counted on you! I beg of you, in the name of your great-grandfather, put aside your doubts! Speak up! Shout! Awaken the heavens, shake those who dwell in them! Tell God that we deserve His mercy, we deserve it more than our assassins, don't we? Tell Him! For He doesn't believe me! Swear if need be, swear that we have not shed a drop of Christian blood, swear that every punishment would testify against Him! It is by keeping silent that you are perjuring yourself, Rebbe!"

Having spoken, Kaizer lowered his head. Drained of arguments, exhausted. Now there was nothing left to do but wait. And all those present waited with him. The Rebbe himself seemed to participate in the wait. His eyes burning with fever, he remained motionless. The silence became heavy, unbearable. Something had to happen, was going to happen—how could one doubt it? The Rebbe was going to change the course of events, impose grace . . . No. The wait had been in vain.

"Too many obstacles are obscuring our vision," said the Rebbe as if to excuse himself. "The accusation is too severe, the opposition too powerful. All the gates are closed. Our impulses fall back, inanimate. Our prayers are riveted to earth. Could God be turning His face away from His people? My great-grandfather found his way. Not I. I do not even know how to use my grief. The shadows are closing in. All that we have left is the Torah—may it intercede in our behalf."

My father had never seen him so resigned. Thousands and thousands of lives weighed on his eyelids, wept through his uncontrollable sobs. What did he see? His father, who resembled the Maggid of Premishlan? The Maggid himself? What grievances did he hear? Once more, as earlier in the House of Study, he hid his eyes. Was it to prevent those present from seeing the future, from beholding the gaping eye of the abyss?

"Let us begin!" he cried out abruptly. "It is getting late, let us begin the ceremony!"

At this signal, the crowd went into motion. Doors were opened. Outside in the courtyard a blue and purple velvet and satin canopy was erected, the ritual resembling that of a wedding. In the meantime the parchment was unrolled on the table, in front of the Rebbe and Reb Sholem. The scribe took his quill from the inkwell and carefully set it down. The Rebbe, Reb Sholem, the gravedigger, One-Eyed Simha and two beggars of lesser renown took turns: each wrote one word. The transcription completed, they wished one another good luck: *Mazal tov, mazal tov.* Then they wrapped the scrolls in their satin sheaths on which Reb Sholem's name could be seen in golden letters embroidered by his childless spouse. The Rebbe rose and the congregation stood aside to let him pass. He was followed by Reb Sholem and the scribe.

Under a sky whose stars seemed fixed in misty pallor, the canopy was barely visible. The wind played with its folds, slapping the damp faces. The first snows were not far away.

Carrying the Torah in his arms, the Rebbe recited the customary prayers, and the congregation, more subdued since the incident with Kaizer the Mute, repeated verse after verse. Then came Reb Sholem's turn to recite a chapter from the Psalms. He was followed by Reb Hersh, who after pronouncing one verse, burst into sobs and could not go on.

Pressing the scrolls to his heart, the Rebbe then started to dance with such frenzy and elation that one might have mistaken him for a bridegroom eloping with his young bride; he whispered words of love, and tears could be seen streaming down his face.

After the ceremony they filed back into the House of Study. The Rebbe replaced the scrolls in the Ark. In the great hall the tables were set.

"Sit down, let us sit down!"

At a signal from the gravedigger, Simha and Leizer intoned a Hasidic tune. But their hearts were not in it. Exhausted, the Rebbe fought against the ruthless invader, the one who in his black wings hides doubt and darkest gloom.

"I should like to understand," he said almost to himself. "I should like someone to explain it to me."

Those in the first row had heard him. The words was passed along. The beggars leaned forward in anticipation.

"They persecute us, they expel us, they nail us to the stake—why? They hand us to the torturer, to the hangman—why? They accuse us of all the sins, all the faults: we have too much money or not enough, too much influence or not enough. We are too educated or not enough, too devout or not enough, too Jewish or not enough. What do they want from us? Who is our adversary, who is the foe? I should like to have it explained to me. I never did understand it. But the question is not to understand but to believe, to study, to prepare by our deeds, by our intentions and by our suffering, the palace where the Redeemer is to reside.

"As a child, I remember questioning my father: I can perhaps understand the man who endures pain but not the one who inflicts it, I can understand the purpose but not the instrument. *Teku,* he answered, the Messiah will come and everything will be explained. Is *he* then the explanation? I asked, frightened. Whereupon, he quoted something the Maggid of Premishlan had said: 'When the Messiah will come, he too will demand an explanation and there will be nobody to provide it.' This reconciled me to him. I wanted to know why he was so late in coming, and I was told: 'Because of you.' This is what every Jew—adult or child—is told over and over again: 'If the Messiah is late, it is your fault; if he should appear, it will be thanks to you.' I remember protesting: 'Why make the Jews responsible for such events? And what if it were our enemies' fault? What if their persecution of us prevented the Redeemer from saving them?' "

And, after a pause, with a thin smile: "Well, in this solemn hour I say and I proclaim: If the Messiah is late in coming, it is not our doing; we decline all responsibility! If he is far away, it is not our fault but theirs!"

His face took on color again, his breathing came more easily. "Yet he will come, he is on the way, perhaps he is already among us. He will reveal himself, it is only a matter of hours, of days. He will appear, and then the people of hope and anguish, no longer a target for man's hate, will flourish in the love of heaven. He will come, he must come, he is our only hope."

Suddenly, as though he had reached a daring decision, the Rebbe seized his silver cup, filled it to the brim and cried out exultantly: "*Lehaim*, to life! To life, do you hear me? To life, for the Torah is life! It is to celebrate and worship it that Israel must stay alive. *Lehaim! Lehaim*, Israel! *Lehaim*, Torah! *Lehaim*, God of Israel!" He tossed his head back and emptied the cup.

The gravedigger was about to do the same when Kaizer the Mute stepped forward again. "Descendant of the Maggid," he said, "Listen to me. There is a flask in my pocket. It has been there for a long time, since the day a wandering Just Man imposed silence on me as a penance: I was to remain silent and become drunk without drinking. If I empty it with one gulp, like this, without cheating, will you drive away the Angel of Death? Will you tell the Messiah to hurry? Do it and I will get drunk—will I get drunk . . ."

He was already drunk. Otherwise he would not have dared use such language. He controlled neither his tongue nor his mind. The gravedigger was about to push him aside, muzzle him, keep him away from the table of honor, but instead of scolding the man, the Rebbe spoke to him warmly:

"Leave your flask where it is, brother Jew. The hour has not yet struck. He will come, the Messiah, don't worry. Will we be here to welcome him? I don't know. I only know that in the end he will not disappoint his waiting brothers."

"And that is enough for you?"

"No. But it must be."

"Then you will do nothing?" stammered Kaizer. "Nothing else? You will not protest, not in your name or ours? Then we shall all perish."

"Patience, brother Jew, patience. We must be worthy not only of the Messiah but also of the wait for the Messiah. Let us be thankful for the wait."

"Don't you understand?" roared Kaizer. "This is the end of the waiting, this is the end!"

He covered his mouth with his hand and turned away. Then this big man in the black greatcoat tried to make himself very small, and like a thief, looked for a place to hide. An indefinable murmur swelled through the audience. All eyes were glued to the Rebbe. My own eyes were following Kaizer the Mute, following him closely as he backed toward the exit, then into the courtyard and into the street. I wanted to cry. My heart was torn with pity. I had chosen sides with Kaizer, who had become a stranger once more. He looked like a beggar and moved like a drunkard. *He* had been right, not the Rebbe. I was sad. I was sixteen.

The night passed peacefully. No incidents, no trouble. There was nothing to report. So peaceful was it that at the first light of dawn the people left their underground shelters. A haggard Davidov went to bed fully dressed. Shaike sent away his watchmen and dispersed his fighters while still maintaining a state of alert. During a brief conversation after services, the Rebbe and Reb Sholem congraduated each other on the success of the celebration: "The Torah has protected us and will continue to protect us," said the Rebbe. The Prefect took off his vest, put away his gun and emptied one last glass before pulling the blanket over his head. There were shadows under his eyes, but Toli offered a smiling face to his father, whom he found sitting in the same place, in the same position he had left him the night before. Bent over the Book, the chronicler wrote:

> The Exterminating Angel has not yet entered the walls and I wonder to whom and to what we are beholden for it. Is it only a postponement? For the moment we are all survivors.

His duty done, my father stretched out on the sofa and fell asleep immediately. Two hours later he awoke in good spirits. We drank some coffee together. I teased Rivka: "No premonitions this morning?" She would not even dignify my question with a look. She seemed reassured. And that was the general impression: having survived the first night of anguish, Kolvillàg was breathing again.

But it was only a truce, and we knew it. Once aroused, the beast would not retreat to its lair without its prey. Living so close to the mountains, people here knew what to expect from wolves. Once kindled, their cruelty is satisfied only by blood. The respite was temporary, illusory. But just how short-lived would it be? A day? A week? Less? More? The other side could have informed us but it had chosen silence.

Not a single villager had come into town that morning. The shops were open, so were the taverns, but gentile customers avoided them. The stalls, the groceries, the hardware shops—all were deserted. Not one farm hand trying to borrow a few coins from the Jewish innkeeper, not one woodcutter demanding a large glass of whiskey on the cuff. Not one servant girl fingering a woolen or cotton shirt. Not one peasant exchanging whatever he had bought the week before. The market, the square: emptiness everywhere.

It was suspicious, disconcerting. It reminded one of Yom Kippur. One felt there had to be a connection with the situation, but the feeling was so vague, it defied formulation. A town living in slow motion. An idle town. An unreal town.

Awakened by his wife, Davidov washed his face, swallowed a cup of boiling coffee and ran to the Prefect's house.

The latter shared his fears. "Bad omen. If my men know something, they are keeping it from me. Naturally. They are in league with the mob."

"So are mine," said Davidov somberly.

His three employees, in his service for twelve years—since his father's death—had disappeared the night before, leaving their belongings behind. There had been smiliar disappearances from most other Jewish homes and establishments: clerks and stablemen, gardeners and servants, maids and nursemaids had all fled at the same time, as though obeying the same signal.

"A pity," grumbled Davidov. "I thought I could trust mine."

"Not I."

"There is no comparison. I treat my employees well. I am generous with them. And understanding. I have never offended their dignity."

"How naïve you are, Davidov. You think they hate you, the employer? You, the boss? It's the Jew they hate."

Davidov felt a wave of heat rising to his face. He unbuttoned the collar of his shirt. "Still," he said, "there is something in this I fail to understand. I was born here, this is where I grew up. As did my parents and theirs, my children and theirs. I know many people. Some hold me in esteem, others even have some affection for me. I share their joys as they share mine. Their fate touches me, their mourning affects me. An employee's wife becomes ill, I pay the doctor. Another employee is distraught, I send him away to rest. Up to his neck in debt, my neighbor comes to consult me, the Jew, and not his intimate friends. Matrimonial troubles? I am the confidant. I like to help, I like to seize an outstretched hand. I have never betrayed or abandoned anyone. I know that people count on me. They know that I expect nothing in return. And yet, not one of my acquaintances feels the need to come and speak to me. I ask for neither their help nor their support. Nor do I ask them to take a stand in the name of conscience or friendship. All I want is a token, a word, a gesture to forewarn me. Is that asking too much? Well, it's a beautiful world, your world . . ."

"Hey, wait a moment," the Prefect cried out in mock offense. "What about me? Aren't you forgetting that I exist?"

Davidov blushed, stammered excuses: "I expressed myself poorly. With you it's different."

"Thank you."

"You are different. You are a friend."

"Don't repeat it too loud, it may do me harm."

"I am not saying that you are every Jew's friend. Only that you and I are friends. That is enough for me."

"One compliment deserves another. For me, too, that is ample. Two friends like you, and I am ripe for retirement or the monastery."

There was a knock at the door. A constable appeared, bearing a message from headquarters: the prisoner was insisting on communicating with the Prefect immediately.

"Aware of the special interest the Prefect has shown the murderer, the captain decided to inform you of the request," the constable recited, standing at attention.

"May I go with you?" asked Davidov.

Moshe was pleased to see them arrive together. First, because he was afraid of not being able to express himself clearly in the native tongue. Second, because his plan concerned both.

"I should like to make a public address," said Moshe without preamble. "Help me."

The Prefect and Davidov looked at one another in amazement. Had they heard correctly? They looked him over more closely. Could he have gone mad, really mad? Could this be a delayed reaction to torture? Had Pavel subjected him to further brutalities? If so, Moshe did not show it. Seated with his back against the wall, he waited for their answer. Calmly.

"An address?" said Davidov. "You? When? Where? For what? Are you serious, Moshe? Come now . . ."

The Prefect came to the point: "You wished to see me, here I am. You wished to speak to me, I am listening. I admit I expected some unusual request, but not this one. Seriously, Moshe. A speech? At a time like this? People's minds are on many things, but not on speeches, don't you know that?"

Moshe was listening attentively, almost solemnly. "I know," he answered. "What I am asking is unusual. But important. Not for me. For the community. Not only for ours. For the entire community of Israel. I must speak. To explain the conclusion of an idea, the birth of a project. To publicly announce my last will."

"Already?" the Prefect teased. "Why such haste? At least wait until the trial!"

"One must refuse nothing to a comdemned man."

"You are not familiar with our judicial system. First we judge, then we condemn. The process is slower than you seem to think."

"Please, I know what I am saying. Neither one of us is in a jesting mood."

The two visitors looked at each other again, appalled. What did he have in mind? A plan to escape? To unmask the real criminal? Start an uprising?

Still, for whatever reason, whether because he looked so pitiful or because his voice appeared to be coming from far, far away, or because they felt that, anyway, all was lost, they gave their assent.

"This is Thursday," said Davidov. "Would next Saturday suit you?"

"Today."

"Today?" cried Davidov. For him, Moshe's madness was no longer in doubt.

"Today," Moshe repeated stubbornly.

"An ordinary Thursday? Who would come? How would you let the people know?"

"I'll speak at the synagogue."

"It will be empty! An ordinary Thursday! I like you, Moshe, and because I do, I beg of you to forget this whim! Give us time! Give us until Saturday!"

"Today," said Moshe. "I'll start at three o'clock."

He turned away from his visitors, as though to dismiss them. This affair has unsettled his reason, though Davidov. This was no longer a question of mystical madness, this was genuine insanity. A speech at the synagogue, that very day, at three o'clock. This sort of project could only germinate in an unbalanced mind. It was almost noon. All right, they must move quickly, start the race against the clock. There was not a second to lose.

"We'll see you later, Moshe."

He did not answer.

The two men left, shaking their heads, still bewildered.

"He had his way with us," said the Prefect. "I have the impression I am acting in a play he is directing. And he is casting the parts."

"Well, now you have another friend," said Davidov with a forced laugh.

They parted in front of the Town Hall. Davidov walked over to the community's office to make arrangements, give certain instructions. The scribe mobilized the beadles, who went to carry the news to the four corners of the town. Never before had an announcement spread with such speed. But would the public come? Before the church bell had finished striking two o'clock, the big synagogue was already filled. Davidov had underestimated both the popularity of the speaker and the curiosity of the congregants.

None other than Moshe—and at no other moment in his life—could have met this challenge: to gather the community on a simple Thursday afternoon. He had made the appeal and everyone had responded.

One easily understands why. He wore the crown of the martyr to whom nothing can be denied. Moreover, there was the mounting tension, the approaching storm. The prolonged, exasperating uncertainty. Collectivity offered the individual a shield against solitude. It reassured and inspired a sense of security, however false. Since they were all going to suffer together, the pain would be less intolerable.

A half-hour before Moshe was to speak, the courtyard was black with people spilling over into the street. The shopkeepers had closed their shops, the merchants had locked their counter tops, as they did for funeral proces-

sions. The four clothing goods stores had lowered their
shades, and so had the two watchmakers. At the Yeshiva
they interrupted the study of Talmud; at the *heder*, that of
the Pentateuch. Shaike and his comrades were in charge
of maintaining order. They did not know which way to
turn.

It was a spectacle without precedent in the annals of
Kolvillàg. Never had the ancient synagogue been jammed
with so many people from so many backgrounds. Not even
the Rebbe attracted such crowds for his semi-annual sermons. Even the visit of the famous Tzaddik of Ostrohov
—before his departure for Jerusalem—paled by comparison. With the exception of infants and the very old, every
Jew was present, waiting to see the prisoner, to listen to
him and if possible, reach out to him. Let him feel less
alone and everyone's solitude would be diminished.

At a quarter to three Moshe made his appearance
flanked by the Prefect and Davidov, followed by two
guards. For a moment the crowd wavered between curiosity
and reverence, between rushing toward the hero of the
day or moving back. Fortunately, it moved back. Moshe
and his retinue advanced between two silent rows.

At precisely three o'clock he ascended the bimah, kissed
the purple-satin curtain covering the Ark and turned to
face the hall.

A lectern had been set up for him. He ignored it. Standing straight, his head high, Moshe confronted his audience
as would an older, protective friend. He communicated his
silence, drawn from the source of his being, even before he
translated it into language. The entire assembly—the men
in the auditorium, the women in the balcony, the overflow
in the yard—froze. Such immobility, such silence must
have prevailed at Sinai. The town, the mountains, even the
fields and stones seemed electrified by the current emanat-
ing from this man and his fiery, hallucinated eyes, charged
with passion, terror and truth.

Assembled here were rabbis and assistants, judges and scribes, givers and takers. Hasidim and opponents of Hasidism. The dignitaries in the first rows, their eyes fixed on the madman turned leader, noticed neither his wounds nor the bloodstains on his tattered clothes. They were staring at his eyes, eyes that were reflecting their future of ashes dispersed by the whirling wind.

Leah was the only one who saw everything, understood everything. Seated in the place of honor in the balcony, at the right of the Rebbe's wife, she saw and suffered. But her mind was made up not to break her promise, not to disturb the mood created by her husband, not to embarrass him in public—she would not shout, she would not weep, not yet.

And so, when Moshe, still motionless, began to speak, people hardly noticed. He began in a very low voice, almost a sigh. It was like a wordless prayer, a monotonous litany.

"When I was a child I prefaced my words with those consecrating me to God. I begged Him to grant me permission to tell Him my prayers. I didn't know why, now I know. Man has no alternative, he is condemned to praise his Creator. Were he not to praise Him, he would curse himself. Better to speak to God than to man, better to listen to God than to His spokesman. Man has only one story to tell, though he tells it in a thousand different ways: tortures, persecutions, manhunts, ritual murders, mass terror. It has been going on for centuries, for centuries players on both sides have played the same roles—and rather than speak, God listens; rather than intervene and decide, He waits and judges only later. We do everything we can to attract His attention, to amuse or please Him. For centuries now we have given ourselves to Him by allowing ourselves to be led to the slaughterhouse. We think that we are pleasing Him by becoming the illustrations of our own tales of martyrdom. There is always one storyteller, one survivor, one witness to revive the murderous past if not the victims."

And like a Yeshiva teacher with his students, Moshe went on to quote texts and legends from the Babylonian persecutions in Judea to the butcheries throughout Central and Eastern Europe: Congregations that had disappeared, swallowed by the abyss; communities that had perished by the sword, by fire, by water. The enemy had ruled the elements and used them to decimate, annihilate the tribe of Israel. Yet one man had always remained behind, miraculously unscathed, one man who saw and recorded everything: the sorrow and the fury on one side, the indifference on the other. This Jewish memory not only robbed the executioner of his final victory, it haunted and punished him by reminding him of his crimes and citing them as examples and warnings for the benefit of mankind present and future. Since the executioner seemed to be immortal, the survivor-storyteller would be immortal too. Jews felt that to forget constituted a crime against memory as well as against justice: whoever forgets becomes the executioner's accomplice. The executioner kills twice, the second time when he tries to erase the traces of his crimes, the evidence of his cruelty. He must not be allowed to do it, he must not be allowed to do it, we have been saying and repeating throughout the generations. He must not be allowed to kill the dead before our very eyes. We must tell, awaken, alert and repeat over and over again without respite or pause, repeat to the very end those stories that have no end . . .

"Oh yes," called out Moshe, and he seemed to be smiling. I knew for whom he was smiling—for my father. "Oh yes, it has been going on for centuries. They kill us and we tell how; they plunder us and we describe how; they humiliate and oppress us, they expel us from society and history, and we say how. They forbid us a place in the sun, the right to laugh and sing or even cry, and we turn it into a story, a legend destined for men of good will, for spirits in search of faith and friendship, for men of heart. Yet the more they hate us, the more we shout our love of man; the more they mock us, the more we shout our attachment to history. The enemy can do with us as he pleases, but never will he silence us—that has been our motto. Words have been our weapon, our shield; the tale, our lifeboat. And we wanted those words strong, stronger than our foes, stronger than death. Since someone would be left to tell of the ordeal, it meant that we had won in advance. Since, in the end, someone would be left to describe our death, then death would be defeated; such was our deep, unshakable conviction. And yet . . ."

Moshe, sweat pouring down his face, paused before making his final point. His heavy, rasping breathing could be heard. For a moment he leaned against the lectern, but then he pushed it back so abruptly it almost toppled over.

". . . now the time has come to put an end to it," he continued angrily. "Put an end to it once and for all. We have been mankind's memory and heart too long. Too long have we been other nations' laughingstock. Our stories have either amused or annoyed them. Now we shall adopt a new way: silence."

Another pause to permit his words to sink in, take root inside us.

"We are going to start on an unexplored path, one which does not lead to the outside, to expression. We shall innovate, do what our ancestors and forebears could not or dared not do. We are going to impose the ultimate challenge, not by language but by absence of language, not by the word but by the abdication of the word. Brothers and companions, accept my plan. Let us take the only possible decision: we shall testify no more."

Moshe seemed rational yet like one possessed, free yet somehow directed. He explained: It was in prison, in his cell, while talking with the official chronicler of the com-

243

munity, that he had realized that the circle must be broken. Though his visitor, the chronicler, had spoken at great length of the grandeur and mission of the witness, he had pursued his own idea to its final conclusion. If suffering and the history of suffering were intrinsically linked, then the one could be abolished by attacking the other; by ceasing to refer to the events of the present, we would forestall ordeals in the future.

And here Moshe cried out in a burst of passion: "If you agree, if you give me your trust, we shall resolve the problem of Jewish suffering. We shall do it without the help of the Messiah; he is taking too long. We shall start right here. I have found the method, I have discovered the solution. Listen . . ."

His two hands were now gripping the lectern. He let his eyes wander over the assembly and raised his voice. "Whether or not our enemies scoff at us, trample us, mutilate us, we shall not speak of it. Whether the mob massacres or humiliates us, we shall tell neither God nor man. If we must die, then the story of our deaths will follow us into our graves, where we shall guard it jealously."

And he continued, prophetically: "Cursed be he who will uncover it, seven times cursed he who will let it be known! Thus the chain will be broken and our people will come out of the night. You see, it was important that I speak to you, that I share my discovery with you. Here is one solution we have not yet tried; that is its merit. It is the only one left that may work. I ask you to adopt it. No, I order you!"

Mad, Moshe. Mad, my friend. Madder than ever, madder than at the time of his first speech from this same podium. His eyes were jets of fire. His arms were blessing, threatening. He had at last found his true role, Moshe. He was sweeping us all away into his madness.

The Rebbe's face was pale; he was covering it with

his hands. Toli thought of his father, and felt choked. His grandfather, lost in deeper contemplation than usual, seemed to be dreaming his own death and that of his descendants. Adam the Gravedigger, in complete agreement with Moshe's proposition, made the greatest effort of his life not to applaud. Upstairs, a woman screamed; others were quick to join in. The chronicler was vibrating with every inflection of Moshe's voice; echoes of an ancient lament, confirming his failure. But I saw in Moshe's mysterious protest a paradox—it incited to joy, to fulfillment through joy, rather than to despair.

"Such is my wish, such is my will," Moshe solemnly declared.

Was it because of his past? Or of the guilt people felt toward him? Nobody challenged him. He had his way. He was triumphant, my friend. The crowd was ready to acclaim him, to crown him king and follow him to the end of his road, the very end, anywhere. At this point in time he personified for them the combined virtues of the sage, the prince and the visionary. He had but to command, they would obey. He knew it, for already he was commanding.

"Let us all take an oath so that those among us who will survive this present ordeal shall never reveal either in writing or by the word what we shall see, hear and endure before and during our torment! Let them tell nothing of us, nothing of what we are saying and dreading! May he who violates this oath be doomed to the throes of hell! May he who breaks this eternally sealed vow, he who defiles this oath be cursed! This vow, this oath, our community must sanctify on behalf of the entire people of Israel, placing it under the sign of the *Herem!*"

At the sound of this last word, the assembly shuddered. Old men bowed their heads. Terrified women covered their mouths. For it is a word charged with occult powers, weighed down with horror. It evokes ancestral maledictions and eternal damnation.

"In the name of this living community and of the divine presence it conceals, I pronounce anathema on the rebel and the renegade!"

The men were appalled; the women mute with fear. Instinctively, children clung to parents, their teeth chattering. Baleful angels and demons without name or master had flapped their wings at the invocation of the *Herem*. One must try not to flinch, not to see, not to be seen. Only Moshe's eyes remained deliberately open.

"My fellow Jews, brothers and sisters, impress this moment on your minds, for it marks a turnabout in the destiny and itinerary of our people. Meditate, withdraw into yourselves, pray to God to let you prove yourselves worthy of the courage within us. My Jewish brothers and sisters, repeat after me: I swear in the name of my allegiance to the covenant . . ."

And everyone, men and women, children and old people, I shall never, never forget it, moved by the same impulse, driven by the same force, jumped to their feet and together repeated word for word, verse for verse, the oath composed by the herald of a new era. The Perfect himself, fascinated, his heart pounding, heard himself recite without understanding:

"I swear . . .

—That if, with heaven's help, I should survive . . .

—I swear that if with heaven's help . . .

—Never . . . shall I reveal . . .

—Never . . .

—How I survived . . .

—Never . . .

—Nor how the dead perished.

—Never."

Were they conscious of all the implications of their

commitment? Did they understand its full significance? They seemed to have fallen under Moshe's spell.

"And if I break my word . . .

—Never . . .

—My soul will never find respite, never will it deserve divine mercy, never will it be redeemed.

—Never, never!"

Was this all? No, not yet. Determined to go all the way, Moshe restated the rules of the tradition. Excommunication takes place within certain well-defined formalities. The rabbis, the judges, the president, the cantor and other notables were ordered to wrap themselves in their ritual shawls. Another tremor, this one more tangible, ran through the assembly. So it was going to be a true *Herem!*

"May he who repudiates this pact be cursed," concluded Moshe, who, covered by his tallith, seemed taller than before. "By repudiating it, he will repudiate himself and us, the living and the dead, those of today and those of tomorrow. Never will he be forgiven, never will his sin be expiated. The judges will judge him, the victims will scorn him! Eternal will be his damnation, eternal his solitude!"

The black candles specifically reserved for the purpose were lit. The shofar was brought. Hushed and feverish, the crowd followed every move. And what if it were only a dream? Time stopped, turned back at lightning speed. And here they were, in another town, in a delirious, terror-stricken medieval ghetto. Who was present? Who was in jeopardy? The future travelers journeying to the Spain of the Inquisition? The disciples of the false Messiah Shabtai Zvi? How could I be sure that what was happening was happening to me? Only Moshe seemed sure of himself and of us, of his gestures and words as he pronounced slowly, accentuating every syllable, the ancient ritual formulas of anathema: the excommunicated renegade would forfeit all his rights and bonds, future merits and past attachments; he would not belong to any human family, to no world, neither that of the living nor that of the dead.

The shofar's plaintive, languid sound brought tears into the eyes of many. The ceremony concluded with the *Kaddish* recited by Moshe in an almost inaudible voice.

He turned to the assembly for the last time. "Better than our predecessors, better than our ancestors, shall we praise our God. We shall speak of Him so as not to speak of ourselves. What will remain of us? Something of our kinship, something of our silence."

His task accomplished, he was overcome by a profound lassitude. He came slowly down the steps, removed his tallith and went to join the president and the Prefect, followed by a thousand eyes that continued to observe him, to hold him back, as though to graft his being onto their own.

The congregation remained standing for a long time, transported, under the spell of the scene it had just witnessed. It was then that a cry rang out from the balcony, a harsh sob rending the air—poor Leah, she could restrain herself no longer.

PART THREE

The Madman
and the Book

Aᴎᴅ ᴛʜᴇɴ ᴄᴀᴍᴇ ꜰᴇᴀʀ. Dense, brutal. It swooped down and invested the town. As at the approach of a scourge, of an inexorable god, Kolvillàg crouched to let the Exterminating Angel pass. His breath could already be smelled.

Harassed men. Frightened women. Busy, excited children. Children love the unexpected, the unusual; to them nothing is more exciting than a catastrophe. Resigned old men. Some whispered Psalms, others feigned sleep.

Immediately after the ceremony, the crowd had dispersed. Night was falling from a misty sky. Why had the street lights not been lit? People advanced, groping their way; some tripped. Why wasn't anybody lighting the street lamps? People were in a hurry to reach home. The deserted streets announced, invited the invader, offered themselves to him from afar. In fact, Kolvillàg was already his.

Windows were closed, shutters locked in place, belongings put away. The cellar was turned into a shelter, the attic was inspected. Bags and carts were readied as though for a long journey. Barricades were erected as though to

251

withstand a siege. And then there were those who settled into passivity, perhaps to die at home.

The lamps and candles had been extinguished. Everywhere. Even in the *shtibels*, even in the mortuary chambers. Even the eternal light in the sanctuary had been snuffed out.

In most houses, the men, more restless than their wives, were at a loss. How were they to fill the hours of waiting? Nobody thought of fleeing the town; too many ties were holding them back—there were the old, the sick who could not be moved. And so, hiding in their pitiful fortresses, they waited for night to go away. Let dawn come; they had seen worse. The enemy would tire, depart. Everything passes. Pogroms flare up, bite into their prey and burn out. Everything goes on. Who shall live, who shall die? Dawn would tell. Meanwhile one could only be patient, force oneself not to move, not to betray one's presence. A night to live through—is that long? Never mind, they had seen worse. No night lasts indefinitely. Would the barricades hold? Morning would tell, death would confirm it. If at least one could resist, fight. Impossible. They lacked the experience, and also the will. Everybody cannot be a Shaike. All they had learned was the necessity and the art of waiting. If at least they could emulate the saints and martyrs of the faith, say no to the cross, shout their contempt for those who use it to kill. Impossible. Kolvillàg was neither Blois nor Mainz. Here the killers were hoping not to convert but to plunder and massacre. All one could do was hope in God, stay home and stare into space, into darkness, the wall, the ceiling or the door, above all, the door, the one that opens onto the courtyard or the street, a certain target for the first blow of the ax.

The Rebbe was pacing his study, from one end to the other, looking for a volume whose title eluded him. A

basic, vital book, conceived and composed for extreme
situations such as this. At the shelter, the beggars were
telling each other stories, memories. Strangely, Adam the
Gravedigger was the most talkative of all. Davidov
looked at his daughter, Tamar, sixteen and mischievous,
and regretted not having dispatched her to her Uncle
Peretz. He had wanted not to show panic; after all, he
had to set an example. And yet, and yet. On second
thought, if they had all sent their children out of town,
where would have been the harm? Too late. Stefan
Braun was watching his restless wife: Toli still had not
returned home. "Your Jews," she grumbled. "Always ready
to upset order." The lawyer did not answer, but he
thought: There was a time when I loved her. Toli was in
a narrow, lightless room, listening to his grandfather
commenting on the afternoon's ceremony: "Every community has the right to exclude anyone who by his actions undermines its very existence." And he went on to
quote Rebbe Nahman of Bratzlav: " 'A passenger on a
ship digs a hole under his seat, explaining to the other
passengers that what he is doing does not concern them,
since he is not digging holes under *their* seats—do the
passengers not have the right to render him harmless?' "
Leah was tossing on her bed, gnawed by remorse—she
had broken her promise, she had cried—and now she was
calling sleep, in vain. Moshe in his cell dreamed of an
appeased Moshe, confident and master of his pain, defeated
by God but stronger than death. The Prefect, a half-
empty bottle before him, was drinking.

My father was bent over the Book, writing in the semi-
darkness. Rivka served us coffee while admonishing me
to lie down. "You must save your strength," she said.
Another premonition? Had she some idea of what lay in
store for me? This night was to be our last together.
Father sensed it, for he sided with me. "You want him

253

to sleep? No. Let him stay awake. These hours we are about to live, you want him to sleep through them? No, son. Stay next to me." Rivka handed me a second cup of coffee. "You will be exhausted tomorrow." Tomorrow —how far away that seemed.

"Listen to what I am writing," said my father.

"Let it not be said that the Jews of Kolvillàg, in these dark hours, lacked solidarity. I say so with pride. Rabbi Yohanan, son of Zakkai, fled the siege of Jerusalem? We do not have his excuses though we shared his ambitions and every Jewish town belongs both to Yavneh and to Jerusalem. Here, not one flight has been recorded. I, Shmuel, son of Azriel, chronicler of Kolvillàg, say that which everybody repeats in his heart: whatever happens to the community I want to happen to myself as well."

Was he preparing me for what was to follow? Rather than concealing his fear, he opposed it to the one that penetrated the community. And he went on:

"A man who is afraid, how easy it is to speak of him: the child in him emerges, refuses to grow up, to choose, to die. But how can one describe a town that is afraid? Its fear is greater than the sum of individually felt anxieties; it is something else; it acquires divine attributes. It is time standing still, the object that survives you. Stricken with an obscure ailment, their eyes lifeless and their voices extinguished, people walk differently, express themselves differently, keep silent differently. With their hunched bodies, they look like birds of ill omen overwhelmed

254

by guilt. Children do not recognize their mothers, women turn away from husbands, men from their brothers and eventually from themselves; such is the nature of fear, such is a community in the grip of fear."

And the chronicler in my father tried to describe it:

"I shall remember it even in my sleep; I shall never be free of it, I know. Fear: a mute and blind raven bearing twilight on its wings. You dare not look into its eyes, you want to run; it follows you, precedes you. And so you remain riveted to the ground, barely breathing, watchful. You know it to be ferocious, fierce. You sense its proximity there—crouching, blending into the darkness—its fangs bared, ready to pounce at the slightest noise, ready to rob you of vision and life and of your very desire to go on living.

"Like a certain silence, fear has its own sound, its own weight. Heavy, impersonal, it hangs over the town: a leaden sky, a horizon of death. It permeates the trees, the walls, one's every movement. All-pervasive, it crawls from body to body, from house to house, from one creature to another. It restrains dying men from moaning and incites dogs to bark. It saps the blood out of your lips; it chokes you, fills your lungs until you feel them burst.

"A town that is afraid is a besieged, defenseless town. Heralding disaster, fear becomes disaster. The enemy's ally, fear becomes the enemy. Surreptitious, ubiquitous; both cause and effect.

"In a town that is afraid, yesterday's bonds turn into heartbreak. Fear is absorbed and communicated like poison or leprosy. Once contaminated by fear, you too become a carrier. And you transmit it the way primary experience is transmitted: involuntarily, unwittingly, almost clandestinely; from eye to eye, from mouth to mouth, to the unearthly sound uttered by a mouthless creature covered with eyes, a creature whose eyes signify death. It flaps its wings, and with its every flutter you slide closer to the precipice, where, finally, your fear, clinging to your breath, will founder. And at the bottom of that abyss there lies a town possessed by fear. But it is not a fear of God or even in God. There, fear *is* God."

Berish the Beadle, inconsolable widower, lifted his head toward his daughter Hannah. "I promised your mother on her deathbed that I would watch over you; and I did. I promised her that you would grow up into a good Jewish woman; you have. But I also promised her to make you a happy woman, and that part of my promise, daughter, I am afraid I cannot keep."

"Don't talk like that," said Hannah, a tall, bright-eyed girl. "Nothing is certain, you know. This night will pass; there will be others—happy ones, long nights of celebration."

Hannah did not believe her own words. She recited them absent-mindedly to calm her father. That he should be poor and weak, the laughingstock of the town—that she had accepted. But his quiet, contained despair was breaking her heart. He had of late become obsessed by a horrifying unmentionable vision of the rape of his daughter during a pogrom.

"You mother would never forgive me. And yet, it is not my fault. I have done everything to protect you, to offer you what a father like me can give a daughter like you. But your mother, of blessed memory, will choose not to understand, you know her. She will put all the blame on me. I didn't do this, I did that poorly. Everything will have been my fault, you'll see."

Hannah went up to her father and tenderly touched his elbow. "Stop, Father. Stop torturing yourself. If Mother is watching, she knows the truth, and even better than we do. She will not reproach you for anything; nobody will. Besides, nothing will happen, you'll see."

On the verge of tears, the beadle sighed: "I am afraid, Hannah. Not for myself, but for you. You don't know what they are capable of. You cannot know. An aroused mob respects nothing, pities nobody."

"Stop, Father. You are imagining things."

"You don't know what a pogrom is, you cannot know. Insanity unleashed, demons at liberty. The basest instincts, the most vile laughter. Hell's flames frighten me less; there is no blind cruelty in hell, no gratuitous savagery. There is no desecration in hell. No trampled innocence."

"Father, please. Stop. You exaggerate. As always. You love doing that. But now is not the time. Another time, all right? Tomorrow?" She took her father by the hand as if he were a sick man, and with infinite affection and tenderness, led him to his bed, helped him to lie down.

And then Hannah let herself fall into a chair, her hands clasped in her lap, painfully awake.

The Rebbe stared at the scribe and shook his head to indicate no. "We were wrong. Wrong to try, wrong to hope. Help cannot come from the other side. A Jew must not expect anything from Christians, man must not expect anything from man. Consolation can and must come only from God."

"Yes, we were wrong."

The Rebbe had sent the scribe to the other end of town with a note to the Bishop, requesting a meeting: "In the name of that which is holy to you and to us; in the name

of the esteem our predecessors manifested for one another, I beseech you to show your humaneness by receiv-
ing me at once."

Reb Hersh had returned empty-handed; he had rung
at the door of the Bishop's private apartments behind the
cloister, but the old servant had refused to open the door.
Though she accepted the letter, she pretended she would
be unable to hand it to her master before the next day,
the Bishop being away on a journey.

"She was lying," said the scribe in a rage, which was
unlike him. "The Bishop was at home. The servant was not
alone, I felt it. My eyes are sharp and so are my ears. I
heard noises, suspicious noises, dragging footsteps, whispers. Eyes other than hers were watching me. She was
play-acting, that servant. She was a good liar but a bad
actress."

"This new Bishop is not like the other one. He was a
fine man, our Bishop, open and good. Our people wept
when he died, or so I have been told. They were right.
Changes always work against us." He tossed his head back
and mused out loud: "I wonder what people will say
about me one day, and about you, Reb Hersh . . ."

Perhaps they will say nothing.

Now it was dark everywhere. In heaven and on earth.
The houses were dark. The streets were dark; the lamps
had still not been lit. So it *was* premeditated. Well, anyway, nobody was venturing into the street. Yet, it was
mild, as before the first snow.

A ghost town, the little town no longer cradled, no
longer protected by the surrounding mountains. Blind
houses, silent hovels—the very shadows were still, stifling
all noise at the source.

The Prefect had stopped drinking. Leah, resigned to
not sleeping this night, let her tears trickle into her mouth.

Her husband would not be pleased? She couldn't help that. These tears that were flowing, they were stronger than she. How could she hold them back? Davidov and his sons erected barricades, reinforcing them with beams. Tamar and her mother were already in the cellar. Berish the Beadle fought vainly against his nightmarish visions. Shaike and his comrades, assembled in their headquarters, awaited a signal from their strategically posted lookouts to move into action. The beggars listened to their new leader, Adam the Gravedigger, recalling his adventures in the cemetery. The Rebbe had given up on finding the book whose title he could not remember. He stood leaning against the bookcase, looking like someone trying to decipher a sign only he could see. Toli followed his grandfather into the kingdom of his childhood, but the old man was speaking so low that Toli missed three-quarters of what he said. Moshe in his cell was working on the speech he planned to deliver to the Celestial Tribunal.

Elsewhere and everywhere, there was a deceptive silence, a false peace. Behind bolted doors and windows people remained huddled in darkness—the darkness of fear, the darkness of death—resenting their hearts for pounding too hard and time for not running fast enough, nor far enough.

A grave-town, the little town the night watchmen no longer illuminated. Not a glimmer, not a sound. The river had ceased to flow, the mountain to tremble. It was as though even the wind had fled this uninhabited zone where silence and night had replaced nature and freedom.

"A town that is afraid is a banished town" noted my father in the Book.

In the windowless cellar where all three of us had taken refuge, he had lit a candle, not to write better—he wrote in the dark—but to be able to read, and make me read.

Excerpts from the Book of the holy community of Kolvillàg:

. . . On the morning of the fifth day of the month Tishri of the year 4973 (1193 C.E.) even while we were doing penitence, as one is wont to do between Rosh Hashana and Yom Kippur, the news was brought that the Crusaders were approaching, led by Petros, the warrior-bishop of sinster renown.

They had already crossed with their swords the holy communities of Srik, Ptur and Rulla, all of them felled during New Year services, their sanctuaries turned into cemeteries, the rare survivors into grave-diggers.

Without wasting a minute, the Rabbi of Virgirsk, the venerable Barukh ben Yehuda, ordered all the Jews to assemble immediately in his house. In less than one hour, all—men, women and children—had followed the call. The Rabbi ascertained the nobody was missing and then he addressed them thus: "It seems that the decree has been sealed and that it is without appeal. May His will be done, Amen. Let us pray, brothers and sisters, let us pray with all our strength. And thus may our departure take place in prayer and purity. Let us pray, brothers and sisters, since death is awaiting us and God is calling."

And all began to pray with fervor, so much fervor that they did not hear the killers break down the doors, nor did they hear their savage cries, or the sound of the sabers decapitating the first victims.

The fourteen survivors are unanimous in their deposition: all the Jews of Virgirsk perished without ever seeing their executioners.

. . . And this took place on the ninth day of the month Av of the year 5292 (1532 C.E.), a date commemorating countless afflictions. Never do we approach it without anguish and never do we know whether our lamentations bear on the distant past or on the present. This year it bore on the present.

We learned what happened from a certain Yona ben Shmuel, a butcher and poultry dealer by trade. Admittedly the trials he underwent have affected his reason. While unacceptable to a court, his testimony must nevertheless be acknowledged by history.

"It was funny," said Yona son of Shmuel. "There was this big fellow of a warrior, resplendent in his armor, irascible, authoritarian. If, by misfortune, there exists an angel or a god of war, he resembles him. Handsome, noble features, gentle bright eyes. I imagined his hands to be long, thin, nervous. I should have liked to see them and compare them to mine, which are ugly and rough—but he was wearing gloves.

"The soldiers, one after the other, showed him the victims before cutting them down. He did nothing but nod his head, as though to salute death.

"But when they presented Esther, the delicate and virtuous spouse of our benefactor Ephraim, he raised his arm. And the soldiers retreated as the woman moved forward.

"And she stood before him straight and proud, clasping the child to her breast. She looked at him wordlessly, steadily; she must have thought him capable of pity.

"It was funny because he held out both his hands and waited serenely. And Esther, whose face lit up with a mysterious smile, entrusted him with the child. And all those present who are still alive agree that her gesture had the grace of an offering.

"The child was not crying. Nor was the mother. It all took place in silence. Not one word was exchanged, not one cry was heard. Confident against all odds, the woman gazed at the god of death who did not wear a mask; and suddenly she understood that she had been betrayed. The god of death conceals from us his hands, his hands and not his face. A glint of terror tore through Esther's eyes. She wondered what to do with her discovery. She covered her mouth so as not to scream, and her eyes so as not to see, not to see her child splattering the muddy cobblestones and the god of death with its blood. The noble warrior seemed surprised, disappointed. And somewhat sad. And I, Yona, thought it funny."

A footnote by the chronicler Asher son of Jacob: We have stressed that Yona is no longer quite sane. But history accepts testimony even from those who have lost their sanity. Let us add, for the sake of truth, that Esther, spared, did not confirm the former butcher and poultry dealer's deposition. Nor did she deny it. Besides, it is said that she has lost the power of speech.

. . . And this is what a gentle and devout young girl did to save the life and honor of her community (1523? 1553? The date is blurred.).

Her name was Brakha—benediction. And that is what she was. For her parents and also for her friends. To see her was to smile, if only to receive her smile in return.

Widowed and of modest means, her father never complained. On the contrary, he never ceased to express his gratitude to God for having given him Brakha.

She was the dream of his dreams, the joy of his awakenings.

Came the ill-fated day when the oldest son of the squire, proprietor of seven hamlets and twelve estates, saw Brakha near the stream and desired her. So ardent was his desire that he offered her father a thousand ducats for one night with her. When he was refused, his passion became so violent that he declared himself ready to wed the young girl before God and the church. His distressed parents surrounded him with wealthy and coveted young girls, one more attractive than the next, but he rejected them all, rather rudely it must be said. He yearned only for Brakha, which was understandable, for she was truly beautiful and truly perfect. Eventually he foundered into the blackest of melancholies, refusing food and sleep; he had lost his taste for life. He grew thinner and thinner, and no longer left his rooms. And the healers summoned from far and wide confessed their inability to cure his ailment.

And then his father the squire followed advice tendered by sworn enemies of Israel. He resorted to a threat. If Brakha continued to refuse herself to his son, members of her family and friends and all the Jewish families would pay with their lives. That was the message he had delivered to the young girl and her prostrate father, allowing them twenty-four hours of deliberation.

Brakha asked to be taken to the dean of the rabbinical court, and this is what she told him: My beauty comes from God and from the people He places on my path; my life is mine but in some measure it is also theirs. That is why I wish to defer to the community; let it decide in my stead.

And the truth must be recorded even if it rends our hearts. To our great shame, as soon as the news

263

spread, there were those who thought of nothing but their own interests. It grieves me to admit it, but they resorted to the most transparent of arguments, to the most abject of means to persuade Brakha to follow the example of Queen Esther, long ago, and marry the lovesick young lord. But, and this too must be noted, there were also those, more numerous, who insisted on their inability to take a stand; the decision properly was the poor young girl's, and hers alone. And they made her understand that they would not judge her, that they would admire and love her even if her answer would result in the death of their children.

After a day and a night of solitary meditation, Brakha put the house in order, kissed her father, made him promise to take care of himself and also not to prolong mourning beyond the required period and went her way with a light and graceful step.

She went in the direction of the forest. There, with a knife she had concealed on her person, she mutilated her face and breasts. Her beauty chastised, she went to the castle but was refused admittance by the watchmen, for she was disfigured and her wounds were repulsive. "Tell the young lord that I came and left, and describe to him how I looked," she told the watchmen.

Her body was found the next day, at the bottom of a well. It is said that there were those who sighed with relief, but they were few and did so only in secret. The others, and they were the majority, tore their clothes as a token of mourning.

People still speak of Brakha's beauty, more even than of her death. That is strange and that is the reason why mention of it is made here.

. . . And this is how death came to a man both just and courageous, though misunderstood in his own day.

Zemakh fulfilled the duties of beadle at the Rabbinate of Klausberg. He cleaned the place, fed the hearth in winter, called the faithful to *Selihot* services, showed visitors to the rabbi's study, helped the clerk in charge of baths on Friday, carried messages, packages, never accepting payment. He was one of those persons who cannot say no.

As bad luck would have it, he was noticed by Lupu, nobody knows under what circumstances. It was a Tuesday, the twenty-first day of the month Tamuz, of the year 5563 (1803 C.E.). Never before had Lupu left his tower on Tuesday. It was morning and never before had Lupu ever gone out before noon. And when he appeared on horseback at the foot of the mountain, the Jews ran for shelter, so dreaded was he. Thus one fails to understand how Lupu and Zemakh could have met, nor why Zemakh considered it necessary, subsequently, to defy the most cruel of lords.

This Lupu was a monster, figuratively and literally. His body was twisted. His torso was that of a child. One eye, no forehead, crooked nose over a gaping mouth. He was so ugly that pregnant women exorcised him from their thoughts, and so bloodthirsty that his own brothers and sisters chose exile over him.

Why, O God of Abraham, Isaac and Jacob, why did he have to happen on poor Zemakh that morning? You who arrange encounters, why did You not prevent that one?

Zemakh had gone to run an errand for the rabbi. The place where he was noticed by Lupu was not

265

even on his way. Why did he make a detour? Why did he not take flight like everybody else? Did You bring the two men face to face? To bring sainthood to Zemakh and defeat to his murderer?

For that is what occurred. Before our eyes. In the marketplace, in full view of a large crowd. Yes, such had been Lupu's orders: a mustering of the population on the main square. Used to his whims and fearing his wrath, Jews and Christians obeyed.

Lupu waited for the square to fill before he dismounted. Planted on his ridiculously frail little legs, he was more frightening than in the saddle. One felt that demoniacal forces had chosen his body as symbol and instrument. People tried to look at him without seeing him. They feared, woe unto them, to be unable to resist laughter.

Meanwhile Lupu was tottering toward Zemakh, who, to everyone's amazement, did not step back.

The petrified crowd anticipated the worst.

Lupu halted in front of Zemakh. Midget and giant confronted one another for a moment in silence. Then Lupu grimaced, and screamed: "I should beat you, disfigure you, decapitate you, reduce you to my size, and I shall, unless your God helps you to persuade me of the uselessness of all this. I don't want to be changed; I only want your eyes to change. I want you to look at me and tell me that you see a man endowed with many talents, indescribable virtues, big and strong and handsome, the idol of maidens, the arch-foe of husbands, the envy of princes and the peer of sages. Go ahead, begin and you shall have your life."

And Zemakh, obstinate for the first time in his life, refused. "No," said he, "you are none of these things. You inspire fear and revulsion. You want my pity? I refuse it to you. Whoever feels compassion for a man without pity, will in the end be ruthless with a man of compassion, says the Talmud. I shall not lie to please you."

Lupu, prancing around Zemakh, bellowed like a small evil beast: "You will repeat what I have just said, you will sing my praises! To please me, yes! To please me!"

But Zemakh, not to be intimidated, persisted in his refusal. "To glorify the executioner is the basest of slaveries," said he. "To make him into a god, the worst of perversions."

Then Lupu ordered his servants to whip him. Zemakh suffered and said nothing. They set fire to his beard; he suffered and said nothing. They placed hot coals into his hands, they pulled out his fingernails, his eyelids; he suffered and said nothing.

To vary the torture, Lupu ordered a deep hole dug. Buried up to his neck, Zemakh drew the monster's sneers: "You see? You are the smaller of us two."

But Zemakh, though reduced to the state of object, did not weaken. Drunk with rage and humiliation, the monster finally implored his victim: "Very well, don't enumerate all my virtues, I shall be satisfied with three, with two! With one! Tell me that I am magnanimous, tell me that I am just! Tell me that people like me, find me handsome! Tell me and you shall have your life!"

But Zemakh, who since the day of his birth had never said no, rejected the bargain. He was heard moaning: "Life is a gift, and not a piece of merchandise."

Lupu forbade that he be disinterred before the next day. Too late to save him. He was mourned a long time as one of those Just Men whose hidden qualities are revealed only at the hour when body and soul no longer obey the same call.

The candle flickered, its flame wandering. Not enough air in the cellar. Better to put it out. Father closed the Book and sighed.

"And now—what will happen now?" I asked him. "Who will write what is to follow? This night. This fear. This uncertainty. Who will record them?"

"Not I."

"Who then?"

"I don't know. Who is right, Moshe or I? Who sees further? If I knew, I might find the courage to say: You, son. You continue my task and prove its validity. I don't have the courage. Could all these chroniclers and witnesses, my predecessors, have labored and lived in vain? We shall know that when we know the continuation and end of this story."

He laughed a small ironical laugh I had never heard from him before.

"But what good would it be, since we swore never to speak?"

Rivka lit a match, and when I saw the smile on my father's face, I understood how desperate he was. I always knew when he was fighting despair. What betrayed him was not his voice, not his eyes, not his hands, which at that moment were still, but his smile, which became strangely fine and peaceful.

We remained seated on the sofa that Rivka had moved from upstairs. We were intruders in our own home, strangers in our own lives.

Rivka was dozing near the door. Every few minutes she awakened with a start, and lighting a match, asked: "Has anybody heard anything yet?" And then she answered herself in a plaintive voice: *"I* can hear them."

I could hear nothing. And yet I was listening as I had never listened before. Sleep eluded me . . . well, I would sleep tomorrow. I would have time to sleep. After.

On the lookout. Silence. Night.

Father and his Book. Moshe and his vow. Rivka and her need for light, her need to see, to hear and ask the same question over and over.

All is premonition.

The past of Kolvillàg, the future of Kolvillàg. In a day, in an hour, there would be no more future, no more Kolvillàg.

Certainty at last? No more tomorrows?

On the threshold: the unknown. Imagination takes flight, alights not far from some inaccessible kingdom and leaves us behind, sacrificed, prisoners of night. Will it return? How are we to know? Will we be alive to summon it? How are we to know? Questions and doubts follow one another at the accelerated rhythm of our blood.

Such is a town besieged by fear.

Midnight: the hour of mystery, the mystery of time, of flight. Night within night, silence within silence. The Angel of Death chooses its prey and proclaims mourning.

Midnight: the exodus from Egypt, Pharaoh's defeat, conflagration in the Temple. Woman lamenting, man consoling her, both believing what they see and what they cannot see, what they say and do not say, and together they make their union into an invisible sanctuary.

It is at midnight that the prophet opens himself to the voice; the survivor to his ghosts. The king abdicating, the messenger recalled. All is vanity, the reign is crumbling, destiny is named suspense. It is at midnight that eternity is lit by the present and desire limited by our senses.

Midnight: the beginning of the beginning, the end of all ends. The day that was yesterday, the day that will be tomorrow: you are both link and conclusion. The rough sketch and the finished version: you are both judge and victim. You are conscience.

Open your eyes, don't say a word. Stay where you are, as you are, huddled in the dark. Don't move, don't run after images; you must make them yours without running, without calling.

Tensed to the point of pain, you will defeat pain. Listen and accept, that is all, listen and accept. Open your eyes and ears, open yourself to the night inside you, the night that is you, that is all. That is midnight, nothing else for no one else: all images contained in one, all words contained in a sigh. All faces illuminated by the same ray of light, outlined in the same way, all faces— the same face.

Midnight: in hiding, between two fires. Don't say a word. Listen. The enemy is coming, he is here; he is the sound of midnight.

Despite the fear, despite the unknown, do not deny

270

yourself, do not be denial. This is the hour when man draws closer to man, when absence acquires the weight of presence—and presence that of absence. Try to be present.

The enemy comes, he is here, he seeks his target, he seeks you. You are the target and you are no one's enemy.

Listen and wait. Listen and try to remember.

Midnight: the hour of separation, the hour that is a summons. Listen and receive. Open yourself to receive, and if it be a weapon you receive, then be the bow that is arched but not released. Just men have no power, victims have no answer. The man who hopes and the woman clinging to his hope no longer believe in sharing. Midnight: the end of hope. So be it! What matters is to survive.

Then came the attack.

Flashing, throbbing like the eye of a hurricane—shaking the earth.

Unleashed before dawn Friday, preceded by interminable howling of horses and humans turned wild by prolonged tension. It could be heard from one end of the world to the other. Swarming down the mountainside the avenging knights, defenders of the faith, happy and inexorable, galloped toward the Jewish quarter as though to surprise there a hostile army and annihilate it. Under their horses' hoofs and in their wake the earth was torn apart with an awesome roar. A rhythmic race of men drawn by primitive and absolute hate. Breathing in the night only to exhale it thick and murderous, they launched into their attack sure of liberating the demoniacal powers held in check by civilization and its laws. Toppling ramparts, crushing every breathing thing, horsemen and beasts announced the explosion and end of the world.

At the same moment, in the fields and valleys and hamlets, plunderers and graverobbers started on their own march. Armed with pitchforks, scythes, axes and hammers, they converged from all sides, forming a huge fan, circling the doomed quarter and cutting it from the outside world. To light their way, the ringleaders had prepared torches.

How many were they? I couldn't say. I was too young and too frightened to think of evaluating their number. Hundreds, thousands. Masses. Welded together. There was no seeing their end.

A sustained, piercing attack. They came from everywhere, in successive, unruly, constantly renewed and reinforced waves, breaking over us, crushing us.

Almost simultaneously, all of Shaike's lookouts sounded the alarm. Too late. The enemy had already struck.

Reeling under the impact of a series of deafening, violent blows, the quarter was disintegrating. No sooner were the first streets occupied than one could already see the caved-in hovels, the houses laid to waste. Ancient images of pogroms had reappeared: smashed doors, shattered windows, broken dishes. A crushed cat, a trampled rooster. Mingled with the aggressors' sneers were the sobs and death rattles of the tortured. Swords in the wind, whips in their fists, the howling and laughing invaders swept the barricades, sowing terror. Some killed and moved on, others took their time, amused themselves by whipping children in front of their parents, by violating the wife in front of the husband. Howling, laughing all the time.

A terrifying inhuman sound rose from the depths of the earth; something akin to the rumble, the roar of a mob of monsters, survivors of the flood, come to avenge and erase an ancient shame, a divine sin.

Moans of terror and pain, shouts of hate and triumph, screams of the wounded and sighs of the dying, the killers' clamor and the victims' whispers. Beings and objects, drained of real life, became one or clashed in the torrential, infernal din, whose volume increased and swelled, reaching from street to street, from hovel to hovel, from attic to attic, growing and multiplying every minute as though to submerge the whole world.

Armed with clubs, sledgehammers, kitchen knives and seven shotguns, the Jewish self-defense groups waited, waited for the propitious moment to intervene. Surprised by the speed and magnitude of the attack, Shaike had decided against immediate reprisal.

"You cannot fight lightning," he had told his comrades. Impossible to defend every structure, every yard. Better to stay together, form a single unit. Attack the enemy from the rear. When? Any time. Where? Anywhere. Whenever possible.

Wait, wait.

The enemy, combat, death.

"Don't lose patience," said Shaike. "For once our wait will have a meaning."

Stefan Braun and his wife, side by side in bed, heard the distant rumblings of the pogrom but pretended to be asleep. His father was lying in a puddle of blood and his son Toli, bleeding from a head wound, was wondering whether tradition allowed a grandson to say *Kaddish* for his grandfather.

Behind the barricaded door, Davidov and his sons lay in ambush for the first aggressor. They knocked him down. The second one too, and the third, before they succumbed to numbers. When the horde left, the women rushed from the cellar and threw themselves on the men to revive them. The dazed father regained consciousness. At his feet, his two sons—slain.

At the shelter, the crouching beggars had covered their ears. Some were thinking: This is our fault, it was wrong of us to be afraid. Others were saying: Let them come, we'll have a good laugh; let them try to steal our misery. Avrom the Wise was smiling to Yiddel, who was smiling to himself. Kaizer the Mute, mute once more, was quietly crying. Leizer the Fat was hungry but dared not admit it. The gravedigger thought of the work lying ahead of him.

Leah was no longer weeping. Before anyone else, before the lookouts, she had heard the enemy marching and had understood. A moment later, a shawl thrown over her cotton dress, she was running in the direction of the police station, colliding with the moving mass of the first horsemen. Did she see them come? Did she want to stop them? The time of a scream, of a warning—and Leah was nothing but a dismembered corpse: the triumphant enemy had won another victory.

The Rebbe was still in his study. Standing near the bookcases, he fingered an ancient volume, thinking: Well, I have found it at last. And then: I have found it too late; may the Law be fulfilled without me.

"Rivka," my father said. "You have been a mother to Azriel. Give him your blessing."

The son, holding back his tears, allowed himself to be blessed.

"Let us be ready," said the official chronicler of the holy community of Kolvillàg. "Let us be ready," he repeated without explanation.

Berish the Beadle jumped from his bed, rushed toward the cupboard. He opened a drawer and seized a knife. "If they come," he told his daughter. "Do you hear me, Hannah? If they come . . ."

Adam the Gravedigger turned to his friends. "I shall need help. You will help me."

"Who will write the ending?" I asked my father.

"The ending will not be written," he answered.

Seated in his armchair, the Rebbe took his head between his hands. "I, great-grandson of the great Maggid of Premishlan, I say and I declare that I do not understand, that I no longer understand."

275

The chronicler handed the Book to his son. "Will you remember?"

"Yes, Father."

"You will know what to say, what not to say."

"No, Father."

"Yes, you will."

Was it an order, a vow? Together we clasped the thick bound notebook; never had we been so close.

Rivka, on the verge of fainting, was softly moaning: "You are giving him the Book? Then this is the end?"

"A simple precaution," said Father to reassure her. "One never knows."

Wrong. He knew. My father knew that we would not see each other again. He knew that I was leaving for good, that he would not write in the Book any more. And I, did I know? Walls and words were about to separate us. I could do nothing but accompany him into the courtyard and obey. And look at him. At him and the others. From afar.

The mob had reached the house across the street and occupied Anshel the Shoemaker's place. The scribe lived directly behind us, alone. The sacred scrolls lay desecrated on the ground next to Reb Hersh, whose open eyes seemed halted at a certain word, and nobody would ever know which one.

And at the inn, an unknown Jew, the neck of a bottle in his mouth, hanging by his feet. Next to him, Sender the Innkeeper and his young wife. Nailed to the wall.

"Now, Hannah!" cried Berish the Beadle. "Now, daughter! Take the knife, take it, I promised your mother that . . ."

Three noble invaders seized the knife and used it to cut his beard. While they had their fun with him, two peasants took charge of Hannah. Father and daughter exchanged a glance and had the good fortune to lose consciousness at the same moment.

The Prefect, aware as never before, discovered a new anger within himself: an anger born of helplessness. At the first outbreak of the pogrom he rushed to headquarters. The guardroom—empty. The dormitories—empty. The office, the stables, the refectory hall, the sentry boxes—all empty. As foreseen, the constables were participating in the plunder, in the massacre, encouraged and led by Sergeant Pavel in person. Shoot them down, though the Prefect, I feel like shooting them down. Later. It could wait, they would get theirs. First he had to take care of more urgent tasks. Which ones? He tried to think calmly: Where would he be of greatest use? He thought of his friend Davidov. Then he remembered Moshe, the least protected. Chances were he would become the pogrom's first target. Was he still alive? the Prefect wondered as he went down to the cellar. A miracle, at last! Moshe! Alive! The seething, aroused horde had forgotten Moshe.

"Thank God," cried the Prefect. "I shall protect you."

"Too late," said Moshe.

"I'll save you," shouted the Prefect. "I'll save you in spite of them and in spite of yourself! And if someone tries to stop me, let him watch out!"

Moshe smiled at him, looked toward the skylight. "Too late," he said. His resonant voice was back. "The beasts have been unleashed—too late to restrain them. They will devour their prey and clamor for more. You were right, my friend. You know wild beasts better than I. Human wolves are insatiable; only death can appease them. You were right, not I."

"Thank you for the compliment, Moshe, but this is not the moment!"

"Yes it is. All we have is this moment. The night belongs to them. It is a night of punishment, of supreme ultimate stupidity; they kill themselves by killing, they dig their own graves by murdering us, they annihilate the world by

277

destroying our homes. Poor mankind is dying of stupidity."

Meanwhile the bloody orgy continued unabated. A woman on the verge of being raped tore out her eyes with her two hands; she was not spared. Her three young children saw the outrage without understanding. Nearby, a bearded old man of majestic bearing was nailed to a cross with daggers. Elsewhere a gang of hoodlums was having sport with the Rebbe, who resisted their efforts to make him kiss an icon. They cut off his head.

In less than one hour the Jewish quarter was laid bare. Corpses lay scattered on the ground, dying men called death. Gaping houses, more corpses intermingled. Stores, shops, apartments—the looters went berserk. Bolts of cloth and bags of flour, Shabbat jewels and caftans, chandeliers and china. They broke what they could not carry away. And the wine was flowing.

That was the moment, while the bandits pranced around with their loot, that Shaike and his men chose to carry out their first mission.

The location selected was the area near the still intact asylum. Just across the street, the invaders were ransacking the large grocery store belonging to the Poresh family. In their eagerness they had forgotten the asylum. Shaike and his friends immediately entrenched themselves there. The beggars watched in amazement as the young people prepared for combat.

Shaike posted three men near the store, an ideal place to ambush the pillagers, who, their arms loaded, were quickly overpowered, disarmed and taken inside the asylum—the first hostages. The operation was repeated, with the same result. Soon there were sixteen, then twenty-six hostages. But then, during the following raid, something went awry. Two hoodlums escaped and alerted the rabble: "Help, help! The Jews are fighting, the Jews are killing us!" The human wave immediately deviated from its course and rolled toward the grocery and the adjacent buildings.

Shaike did not waste a second. A few concise orders and a new plan went into effect. First he had the asylum evacuated, transferring the beggars to the Yeshiva, across the courtyard. Only the twenty-six hostages, their hands and legs bound, remained in the asylum, its doors bolted from the outside. Then the fighters gathered in the familiar school hall to prepare their next move.

Meanwhile the mob in front of the asylum stayed at a distance. Only Pavel, a torch in his hand, stepped forward and barked his threats: "Hey, Jews. Come out! Hands above your heads! Otherwise you'll burn alive!"

"Yes, yes! Alive!" echoed the crowd. "Let them burn alive!"

Thereupon one could hear the hostages protesting: "Don't do that! Not that!"

"They'll come out, you'll see, my pet," said Pavel to his beloved whip. "All Jews are cowards, they'll come out."

"Yes, yes!" shouted the mob.

"Alive, you'll burn alive," insisted Pavel, drawing a circle in the air with his torch.

"Well done," shouted the crowd, aroused by the prospect of the new and yet so ancient spectacle.

"Not yet!" yelled the hostages. "Don't do that to Christians! We are Christians like you! Your comrades, your brothers in Christ! Not Jews! There are no Jews here, not a single one."

The mob was not to be discouraged, not to be deprived of the promised entertainment. Protests flew from all sides:

"They're lying."

"They take us for fools!"

"Or choirboys!"

"Alive, burn them alive!"

"No, no," shouted the hostages in a panic. "We are Christians! Like you!"

Together and individually they swore, swore on the

heads of their mothers, living or deceased; of their spouses, beloved or loathed.

"Lies and profanations," Pavel declared. "This is a Jewish building. A shelter. An asylum. What would Christians be doing in an asylum? Don't tell me you thought you'd find some treasures there!"

The enthralled crowd was roaring with laughter. "Bravo, Pavel! What intelligence, Pavel! You shut them up! You'll be promoted, Pavel! You'll wind up captain! Bravo, Pavel!"

The people's hero: Pavel. Too bad he wasn't wearing his uniform. Next time, he promised his whip.

"Well?" he shouted. "You haven't answered yet! What were you looking for in the asylum?"

"Hostages. We are hostages."

"Shrewd, those Jews," said Pavel. "Never at a loss for answers."

"The truth, it's the truth! We swear it!"

"Hostages," inquired Pavel. "Whose hostages?"

"The Jews'—damn it!"

"But you said there were no more Jews in there. No good, find something else!"

There was a silence on the hostages' side. A moment went by before they renewed their pleas: "Our voices! Don't you recognize our voices?"

Pavel consulted his confederates; nobody knew them.

Then the hostages yelled their names: "Yonel, Yonel from Batiza . . . Simora, Simora Frescu . . . Laczani Pali . . . Ivan, Ivannn . . ."

Now the hostages really were panicky. They shouted and shouted:

"I live next to the woods . . ."

"The first house . . ."

"At the edge of the brook, that's where I . . . the edge . . . brook . . ."

"The yellow cabin . . . The cornfield . . ."

"Petrica, my wife! Help, my turtledove!"

280

The frenzied mob refused to believe, refused to listen. Its need to kill, to debase man, to offer him as fodder to the beast of night, was not yet assuaged. Drunk with power, with cruelty, it demanded more blood, more triumphs, more victims.

Now that most of the Jews were either dead, dying or entrenched in shelters whose discovery would require hours of searching the mob did not hesitate to set upon their own.

"They are Jews, Jews!"

"Let's get done with it!"

"Why are we wasting time!"

"One last warning," Pavel promised his whip. "And then . . ."

"Idiots!" yelled the hostages.

"For the last time," said Pavel, brandishing the torch. "Come out or you'll burn alive!"

"Imbeciles! Assassins! We can't come out!"

Finally a peasant recognized two of the voices. "Yonel and Ivan . . ."

"We don't believe a word of it . . ."

"Yes! We drink together . . . Christians, like you and me . . ."

Angered by the kill-joys, the townspeople called them drunkards, traitors. Jews. The discussions degenerated into disputes, quarrels. Ancestral grudges and hates between clans, tribes and families rose to the surface. It came to blows. In the heat of the fight somebody grabbed the torch Pavel was holding absentmindedly and hurled it onto the roof of the asylum, which burst into flames at once. Somebody else took revenge on the grocery store.

Suddenly a red blaze, spinning from the entrails of the earth and night, soared skyward, irresistibly sweeping space. Cases of matches, barrels of oil and kerosene and alcohol fed the furnace. The fire progressed with lightning speed. And the fighting continued as before, the rivals tussling while the stifling circle closed in around them. Down the next street the knell was ringing. Seven separate fires were spreading an unbearable heat. Sovereign, invincible, the fire invested the area, swallowed building after building, street after street, racing to light the sun and the horizon.

By its immensity, the fire assumed a divine role—gigantic, unpredictable, its very sight maddening. The town was toppling into illusion. Merchants and clerks, laborers and employers, girls and boys, all intermingled, young and old, killers and killed, murderers and victims, at once blinded and illuminated, fleeing in every direction, carried by the carrousel in flames. Expelled from time and nature, they seemed to float between sky and earth, between two burning walls. Some were roaring with laughter, others were embracing, still others abused one another, screaming in horror and also laughing in horror. A gentle-eyed woman tossed her infant into flames, while another, filled with compassion, sang a lullaby. Shifra the Mourner ran to the cemetery to join her beloved husband in the grave. There she met Adam the Gravedigger, who asked for her help. "All my friends are dead, who will bury them? And who will bury us? God perhaps? Will God be our gravedigger?" The stableman Dogor grabbed his wife and swept her into a frenzied, savage dance. The priest and the Bishop, under the icons' watchful eyes, in total disagreement on everything else, decided this was the time to debate orthodoxy and heresy. "It's your fault," shouted the lawyer. "Dirty Jew," retorted his wife.

"Go now," said the official chronicler of the holy community of Kolvillàg. "Go, my son, the moment has come." He did not explain, but I understood: it was now or never. The moment had come to leave, break out of the circle, slip outside; it was now or never. The moment had come to choose life. He gave me a strong push, and I had to obey. Clutching the thick notebook to my body, I left my

father, I left Rivka, who had been a mother to me, I backed
away from them so as to see them as long as possible. I
went on seeing them, and now as I speak to you, I see
them still.

Meanwhile, caught up in the frenzy, the killers were
killing each other, senselessly, with swords, hatchets and
clubs. Brothers and sisters striking one another, friends and
accomplices strangling one another. Few resisted, none
protested. An extraordinarily vigorous dancer leapt high
into the air, met the sword and fell to earth, decapitated.
A young girl combed her tresses; a stranger pierced her
chest.

While backing away I experienced a double sensation,
both odious and sublime. Flee, yes. Flee this setting fit
only for cruel and grotesque gods. Jump off this merry-go-
round before I find myself caught in the dizzying whirlwind; force myself, yes, force myself and save the Book.

Ultimately it saved me.

But nobody saved the Jews of Kolvillàg, or their assassins. When death reigns, no one is spared. When the
avenging gods are human wolves, there can be no hope
for man.

I backed away, my wide-open eyes recording the last
images of this town and this night. Moshe, in front of
the prison, shaking his head as though acquiescing: Too
late, too late. The Prefect crying: "But I want to save
you, I want to! In spite of yourself!" Nearby, the carnage
continues and so does the farce. And suddenly, in the
center of the turmoil, I think I see Yancsi, that thug of a
Yancsi whom fate has chosen as instrument. The sergeant
catches him and squeezes him in his arms: "You are
my whip, come let me hug you, my pet." Moshe's mask
crumbles and at last he bursts out laughing. Shifra the
Mourner has ceased to cry and so has Kaizer the Mute.
And all have ceased to live. Adam the Gravedigger recites
the *Kaddish* for the dead, the living—and himself. Be-

wildered, dazed, mad with fear, horses and dogs chase one
another in a race toward death, drowning out the sobs, the
sneers and the lamentations. The earth splits in a thousand
places and the houses tumble down. A reddish glow seen
in a shattered mirror. I back away, clasping the Book to
my heart; the farther back I am the more I remember,
and the more I know what it contains.

Ringed by the flames, the entire town was burning. The
hovels and the shops, the parchments and the dead schoolboys. "Is it over, Grandfather?" Toli asked. "I hope so,"
said the lawyer's father. "And Grandfather, who will say
Kaddish?" "*Yitgadal veyitkadash shme raba,*" recited Adam
the Gravedigger, digging his own grave. "I should have
sent her to her Uncle Peretz," said Davidov, carrying his
lifeless daughter on his shoulders, not knowing where to
go or why. "You shall live in spite of yourself," insisted
the Prefect. "You must be joking. It is all over," said Moshe. "All I want to do is cry, but I have forgotten how."

The town, in consuming itself, was telling a timeless
story for the last time, and there was nobody to listen.
Yiddel no longer smiles and Avrom no longer thinks.
Whom are we fighting now? Shaike was asked. But he
was already dead. The Book, said my father. The *Herem,*
said Moshe. It's my fault, but I was hungry, said Leizer the
Fat. Memory, insisted my father, everything is in memory. Silence, Moshe corrected him, everything is in silence.
I was stepping back and back, but the distance remained
unchanged. The prey of death, the price of life: Kolvillàg
was burning and I watched it burn. The House of Study, the
trees and the walls—whipped by fire and wind. The cobblestones—shattered. The Jewish quarter, the churches and
the schools, the stores and the warehouses: yellow and
red, orange and purple flames escaped from them, only to
return at once. The shelter and the orphanage, the tavern
and the synagogue joined by a bridge of fire. The cemetery
was burning, the police station was burning, the cribs were

burning, the library was burning. On that night man's work yielded to the power and judgment of the fire. And suddenly I understood with every fiber of my being why I was shuddering at this vision of horror: I had just glimpsed the future.

The Rebbe and his murderers, the sanctuary and its desecrators, the beggars and their stories, I trembled as I left them—left them, backing away. I saw them from afar, then I saw them no more. Only the fire still lived in what was once a town, mine. Charred dwellings. Charred corpses. Charred dreams and prayers and songs. Every story has an end, just as every end has a story. And yet, and yet. In the case of this city reduced to ashes, the two stories merge into one and remain a secret—such had been the will of my mad friend named Moshe, last prophet and first messiah of a mankind that is no more.

ELIE WIESEL

"Day is breaking, you must leave," said the old man.

I had to shake myself. I was returning from far away. The noises of the city were so many wounds. Walk, die, survive. The sky turning white. The vague pain I could not situate or name. The feeling of bereavement. I closed my eyes. Tomorrow, I thought. Tomorrow is named Azriel.

"Do you regret?" I asked him. "Do you regret having spoken?"

"No. And you?"

I smiled. "Why would I regret it?"

"Because now, having received this story, you no longer have the right to die."

I said nothing. A chilling thought came to my mind: if I no longer had the right to die, he no longer had to go on living!

Suddenly, I don't know why, I felt like asking him not to send me away. I dared not. I dreaded his refusal as much as his consent. Instead I formulated a question that had been on my lips for some time: "Who is Moshe?"

His eyes followed the night seeking refuge behind the horizon. For a moment I thought he was displeased and would not answer. But he surprised me.

"You. I." And he added half mockingly: "You when you open your eyes; I when I close mine."

With his hand he motioned me to go. I did not obey immediately. This sky lighting up. These streets filling with life. This town reawakening. Walk, die, survive. This new wound inside me—what had I gained in the exchange?

"You must," said Azriel.

"I must what? Leave? Die? Begin anew?" I rose. We parted without shaking hands.

Then the young man obediently returned home, and so did the old man. That undoubtedly explains why they never saw each other again: Azriel had returned to die in my stead, in Kolvillàg.

286

THE BIG BESTSELLERS
ARE AVON BOOKS!

World Without End, Amen
Jimmy Breslin   19042 $1.75

The Amazing World of Kreskin
Kreskin   19034 $1.50

The Oath
Elie Wiesel   19083 $1.75

A Different Woman
Jane Howard   19075 $1.95

The Alchemist
Les Whitten   19919 $1.75

Rule Britannia
Daphne du Maurier   19547 $1.50

A Play of Darkness
Irving A. Greenfield   19877 $1.50

Facing the Lions
Tom Wicker   19307 $1.75

High Empire
Clyde M. Brundy   18994 $1.75

The Kingdom
L. W. Henderson   18978 $1.75

The Last of the Southern Girls
Willie Morris   18614 $1.50

The Wolf and the Dove
Kathleen E. Woodiwiss   18457 $1.75

The Priest
Ralph McInerny   18192 $1.75

Sweet Savage Love
Rosemary Rogers   17988 $1.75

I'm OK—You're OK
Thomas A. Harris, M.D.   14662 $1.95

Jonathan Livingston Seagull
Richard Bach   14316 $1.50

Where better paperbacks are sold, or directly from the publisher. Include 15¢ per copy for mailing; allow three weeks for delivery.

Avon Books, Mail Order Dept., 250 West 55th Street,
New York, N.Y. 10019